D0804094

UNEXPECTED VISITORS

Three black sedans drew to a stop in the parking area. Twelve car doors opened at once and from each emerged a man dressed in a dark suit, white shirt, and dark tie, wearing the same completely blank expression.

Steve froze, wondering what on earth was about to happen. One of the men strode toward her.

"We're looking for someone named Carl," he said in moderately accented English.

"Nobody here by that name," Stevie said. "No Carls at all."

"Not Carl," the man said, ever so slightly annoyed. "Carl." He emphasized it as if saying it more loudly would make it clearer.

"There is no man here named Carl," Stevie told him firmly.

"Not a man. A girl," he said, the late-afternoon sun glinting off his reflective sunglasses.

"A girl? Carl?" And then it struck her. "Carole? You mean Carole Hanson?"

"That's what I said. Carl."

And then he held out his hand to show her something. It was paper. It had pictures of horses on it. And Stevie understood everything.

She signaled the man to follow her back to the schooling ring. As Stevie approached, Carole and Lisa stared intently at their friend, who was being followed by a very sinister-looking man in a black suit and shiny sunglasses.

"Oh, Carole!" Stevie sang out. "These guys have something to say to you!"

the SADDLE CLUB

HORSE SPY

BONNIE BRYANT

A SKYLARK BOOK
NEW YORK • TORONTO • LONDON • SYDNEY • AUCKLAND

Special thanks to Laura Roper of Sir "B" Farms

RL: 5, ages 009–012

HORSE SPY
A Bantam Skylark Book / September 2000

"The Saddle Club" is a registered trademark of Bonnie Bryant Hiller.
The Saddle Club design / logo, which consists of
a riding crop and a riding hat, is a
trademark of Bantam Books.

"USPC" and "Pony Club" are registered trademarks of The United States
Pony Clubs, Inc., at The Kentucky Horse Park, 4071 Iron Works Pike,
Lexington, KY 40511-8462.

All rights reserved
Text copyright © 2000 by Bonnie Bryant
Cover art copyright © 2000 by Alan Kaplan
No part of this book may be reproduced or transmitted
in any form or by any means, electronic or mechanical,
including photocopying, recording, or by any information
storage and retrieval system, without permission in
writing from the publisher.
For information address: Bantam Books.

If you purchased this book without a cover you should be aware that this
book is stolen property. It was reported as "unsold and destroyed" to the
publisher and neither the author nor the publisher has received any
payment for this "stripped book."

ISBN: 0-553-48698-5

Visit us on the Web! www.randomhouse.com/kids

Educators and librarians, for a variety of teaching tools, visit us at
www.randomhouse.com/teachers

Published simultaneously in the United States and Canada

Bantam Skylark is an imprint of Random House Children's Books. SKY-
LARK BOOK and colophon and BANTAM BOOKS and colophon are
registered trademarks of Random House, Inc., Bantam Books, 1540 Broadway, New York, New York 10036.

PRINTED IN THE UNITED STATES OF AMERICA
OPM   10 9 8 7 6 5 4 3 2

*I would like to express my thanks
to Special Agent Kingsley C. Chimene of the Secret Service,
Vice President Protective Detail, for his technical help.
Everything that is correct about protective services is due
to him. Any errors are all mine.*

"LOOK AT THIS GUY!" Carole Hanson held out the glossy magazine to her two best friends. "He's *so* good-looking!"

Lisa Atwood took the magazine. "Handsome!" she said. She passed the picture on to Stevie Lake.

"What a body!"

"What a face!"

"Have you ever seen such legs?" Carole asked.

"I bet he's a great jumper," Stevie agreed.

"He'd better be," Lisa said, looking at the caption. "His owner has him entered in every major show in the country."

"And I bet he wins them all—at least in jumping," said Carole. "Have you finished that article in *Modern Rider?*" she asked.

"Sure," Lisa said. "Swap you that for the new *Young Horsemen*, okay?"

"Deal," Carole said. "How are you doing, Stevie?"

Stevie looked up from her copy of *Rider and Trainer* with a big grin of contentment on her face. "I am so glad you know how to save your allowance and use it for magazine subscriptions," she said. "Otherwise I'd never have seen this article on longeing. It's going to do wonders for Belle's balance. Mine too, I think."

The three girls were sprawled on the furniture in Carole's room, combing through back issues of all her horse magazines and enjoying every minute of it. They were in the right environment to enjoy horse magazines, too, because Carole's room was simply filled with horses. Every inch of the wall was covered with horse posters—every inch, that was, except for the several square yards that were specifically devoted to photographs of horses—and some riders.

The girls often said that it would be hard to find three people who were less alike than they were, but they were firmly joined by their shared love of horses. In fact, they were all so horse-crazy that they'd formed their own club and called it The Saddle Club. It had only two rules. The first one was that all the members had to be horse-crazy. That was easy. The second rule wasn't always so easy. It was that the members had to be willing to help one another out, no matter what.

It often seemed that the one who needed help the most often was Stevie. She was an expert at getting into trouble, often brought on by schemes and practical jokes, two of her favorite things (right after horses). She was a fair student at school, and she claimed that she'd do much better if her teachers didn't always want to send her to the principal's office and make her miss class time. Her teachers and the principal didn't see eye to eye with Stevie on the root of that problem. One of Stevie's favorite targets for jokes and schemes was her brothers. She had three of them: one younger, one older, and one twin. She frequently felt a need to equalize her three-to-one disadvantage with jokes on her brothers. The results often got her in hot water at home as well as at school.

Lisa, on the other hand, was almost never in hot water. She was a straight-A student who had never been sent to the principal's office. She was always organized. Her homework assignments were handed in on time. Her clothes were always clean and ironed, which contrasted with Stevie, whose idea of clean when it came to clothes usually meant something rescued from the *top* of her laundry pile.

Lisa had a brother, Peter, who was much older and was living abroad. This meant that her life was similar to that of an only child. She got a lot of attention from both of her parents, but especially from her mother. Mrs. Atwood wanted to be absolutely certain that Lisa learned all the things a proper young lady should know. Lisa swore she'd taken lessons in everything that anyone could teach—from the obvious, like piano and ballet, to the more obscure, like embroidery and etiquette. Lisa went to all these lessons obediently, but the only ones she cared about were her riding lessons.

Clearheaded Lisa could often straighten out the tangled threads of Stevie's thinking and help solve the problems that their knots had caused. Lisa was the oldest of the threesome and also the newest to riding. In spite of the fact that her friends had years of experience beyond her own, she'd applied her cool thinking, her logic, and her determination to the subject of horses and before too long had become nearly their equal in skills.

Of the three horse-crazy girls, Carole was the horse-craziest. She'd been raised on Marine Corps bases where her father, now a colonel, had worked. They'd lived in many places, but the one thing all the bases had in common was that they all had stables. Carole often observed that the one true constant in her life was horses. She'd always had them, and she swore she always would. She knew she would work with horses when she grew up; she just hadn't decided what she'd do with them, whether she'd be a vet or a trainer or a breeder or a rider or a stable manager—or maybe all of those.

Carole's mother had died a few years earlier of cancer, leaving Carole and her father to live alone in the first house they'd ever owned. All through her mother's illness and Carole's grieving afterward, horses remained a source of comfort. Carole missed her mother every day, but she adored her father. In fact, she thought he was just about perfect. He didn't even mind that every surface in her room was totally covered with horses.

Carole flipped the pages of Modern Rider and got three sentences into the lead story when she realized she'd already read it. She tossed the magazine aside.

"So, what do you think about our new visitors?" she asked.

Her friends both knew what she was talking about. Pine Hollow, the stable where they rode together, was going to have two visiting champions.

"Polaris and what?" Stevie asked, forgetting the second horse's name.

4

"Jennie's Blue," Lisa supplied. "I think she's called just plain Blue, though."

"Right," Stevie said. "I didn't get why it is they're staying at Pine Hollow, though."

"It's because of Dorothy," Carole explained. Dorothy DeSoto was a former student of Max Regnery, who was The Saddle Club's riding instructor and the owner of Pine Hollow Stables. Dorothy herself had been a competition rider, probably headed for the international show circuit and the Olympics, when she'd been thrown in a bad accident that had hurt her back.

The good news was that she'd recovered. The bad news was that her doctor had explained that her back would always be vulnerable and she could never ride competitively again. One more injury and she might not be so lucky at all. Dorothy had taken the bad news in stride and made the decision to become a trainer. She had a farm on Long Island, New York, and two of her young students were fast becoming excellent riders. Those were the owners of Polaris and Jennie's Blue.

"Max said that Dorothy's back was acting up and she's confined to bed for a while," said Carole. "She asked Max to fine-tune the horses' training before the show in Washington in two weeks. Their owners can't do any work over the next two weeks—except for next weekend, maybe—so the horses will stay at Pine Hollow and get VIP treatment. Plus training."

"All the horses at Pine Hollow get VIP treatment," Lisa commented.

"Well, VIP-er," said Stevie.

"How could that be?" Lisa asked, applying her usual logic.

5

"I think what Stevie means is that we'll be responsible for some of the care they get, and what could be better than that?" Carole said.

"Well, do you suppose if we take the VIP-*est* care of them, Max will let us watch the training? It would be really good for all of us—and just plain fun," Stevie said with a grin.

"He might let us cool them down after a training session," Lisa said, imagining herself holding the lead of one of Pine Hollow's valuable visitors.

Carole was shuffling through the magazines again. "You know, I think I saw an article about young champions somewhere in here. I wonder if the writer mentions anything about these horses or their riders. What are their names?"

"Polaris and Jennie's Blue," Lisa said.

"I know the horses' names," Carole said. "I meant the riders'."

Stevie laughed. "Come on, Lisa, you know that Carole could forget where she left her own head, but she'd never forget a horse's name!"

"Silly me," Lisa teased, reaching once again for a magazine from the stack.

For a while there was only the sound of pages flipping.

"Not here," said Stevie.

"Nothing in here," Lisa said. "Except for a pretty interesting article about some president's daughter . . ."

"Oh, right. I started to read that one," Carole said. "Then I figured it couldn't be real."

"Sure it is," Lisa said. She held up the magazine and showed her friends the smiling picture of a girl their own age. "Karya Nazeem," she said. "Pretty name. Anyway, it says her father's just been elected president of this little country in the Middle East. It's called the ADR, the Arab Democratic Republic."

"I've heard about that place," Carole said. "Dad was talking about it. He said her father's a really good guy and he's trying to do all sorts of progressive things—"

"Not to hear Karya talk about it," said Lisa. She ran her finger along the column of type as she scanned the story. "She's complaining here about how nobody ever lets her do anything for herself anymore now that her father's the president. She says that being the president's daughter is mostly fine, but . . . Here it is: 'Sometimes I just wish they'd let me muck out my own horse's stall!' "

Stevie hooted with laughter. "I guess I should have picked my parents more carefully!" she said. "They, and everybody else, will always let me muck out anything!"

"Just the places that get really messy, like Belle's stall and your closet!" Lisa teased.

Stevie laughed, too. "Well," she started to protest, and then thought better of it. Her friends had seen her closet.

"Imagine never having to do any of the dirty work that has to do with horses," Stevie said.

"It would mean being just like Veronica!" said Lisa. Veronica diAngelo was a snooty rich girl who rode at Pine Hollow and always seemed to manage to get out of any kind of dirty work. In fact, she seemed to think that her only responsibility with regard to her horse was to ride him—when she felt like it.

That wasn't the Pine Hollow way—at all. Max believed that riding a horse was just one of the things that was important about horsemanship, and he insisted that all his riders look after the horses they rode as much as they could. The Saddle Club might have complained about mucking out stalls and cleaning tack from time to time, but they all agreed that these were important parts of horse care. Not only did they learn more about horses from the care they gave them, but their pitching in also meant that Pine Hollow could keep its costs down and make riding accessible to more people—including The Saddle Club.

"Well, we could invite the girl—what's her name?"

"Karya," Lisa said.

"Karya, right, and her horse is a chestnut Arabian with three white socks and a blaze on his face, right?" Carole asked.

Lisa laughed. "You're right, Stevie. Carole remembered every single detail about the horse, but not his owner's name!"

"Well, at least I know what's important!" Carole huffed, pretending to be annoyed. "Anyway, we should invite her to come ride at Pine Hollow. I'm sure Max will find a few stalls for her to muck out, and Mrs. Reg will no doubt have a saddle or two that she wants to be able to see her face in."

Lisa looked down at the magazine again. "We could, you know."

"We could what?" Stevie asked.

"Invite her to Pine Hollow," said Lisa.

"To muck out stalls?" Carole asked.

"Well, that, and I guess she could do some grooming, and I bet you could show her a few things about the fine art of picking hooves," Lisa said to Stevie.

8

"Wouldn't that be a dumb thing—to invite her here?" Carole asked.

"Not really," said Lisa. "Says here that she's looking forward to coming to Washington on a trip with her father. It doesn't say when, but I think it's pretty soon."

"Don't be silly," said Stevie.

"No, I mean it. Look at this," Lisa said, offering the magazine to Stevie.

"I'm sure you've read it right," Stevie said. "I just think it's silly to offer some president's daughter the honor of picking out Prancer's hooves."

"Let me see that," Carole said, reaching for the magazine. Lisa handed it to her. "Carole, you're not really considering inviting her to visit Pine Hollow, are you?"

"No way," said Carole. But she put the magazine down, walked over to her desk, and began shuffling through a pile of papers. After a few seconds she sat down at the desk, a pen in one hand and a sheet of her best stationery in front of her.

"Looks like you're writing a letter," said Stevie.

"I am," said Carole. "I'm writing to Karya Nazeem to invite her to come for a ride with us."

"Carole!" Stevie said. "She'll never do it."

"I know she won't. But she just might answer me. Or she might have one of her father's secretaries answer me, and then I'll have what I really want."

"Huh?"

"If they answer the letter, I'll get a stamp from the Arab Democratic Republic on the envelope, and that'll be a great present for Dad. He has a stamp collection, you know, and he

9

was talking about this country and this girl's father. He'd think that was cool."

"Great idea!" said Lisa.

"Isn't there someone else there you could write to?" Stevie asked.

"You think I should invite President Nazeem to pick Prancer's hooves?" Carole teased.

"No, I guess it's okay. You might just get an answer in time for your dad's birthday. It's what—four months?"

"Five," Carole said. "I think there's time."

She signed her name, addressed the envelope to Karya Nazeem at the president's residence, and pasted what seemed like plenty of postage on it. She'd mail it on her way to Pine Hollow in the morning. Five months would be plenty of time for an answer. She smiled, thinking how pleased her father would be with his new stamp.

STEVIE LEANED the pitchfork against the wall of the stall and rubbed the small of her back with both hands.

"I wish stall muck weren't so heavy," she remarked to Lisa.

"That isn't the only thing I wish about it," Lisa said, lifting the handles of the wheelbarrow to deliver their load to the manure pile behind the stable. "I wish it could self-destruct."

"Here are the fresh shavings for both stalls," Carole said, arriving with her own wheelbarrow. She dumped half the load in the stall where Stevie stood and took the remainder to the second visitor's stall. Stevie picked up the pitchfork with resignation and began spreading the sweet-smelling wood shavings around.

This wasn't her favorite part of working with horses, but she knew it was important, and she took a certain satisfaction in realizing that not much earlier the stall had been quite dirty and now it was almost ready for its newest tenant.

Lisa returned and began spreading the chips around the

other stall. "Too bad Karya Nazeem isn't here already," she remarked.

"Right. Welcome, Ms. First Daughter. Won't you have a pitchfork?" Stevie joked.

"No, thank you. I'd prefer a wheelbarrow full of horse manure," Lisa said back.

"We could go for a ride," Carole joined in.

"Not while there are saddles to soap and horses to groom!" said Lisa.

"Oh, she'd love this place!" said Stevie. "Too bad she'll never see it."

"No, I mean us," said Carole. "We could go for a ride."

"Oh, sure," said Lisa. "But I don't want to miss it when Polaris and Jennie's Blue arrive."

"We don't have to miss it," said Carole. "Max said they'd be here sometime this morning. We can just stay in the ring. There are a lot of things we can work on there. Max laid out some cavalletti for yesterday's class, and they're still there. It'll be good for all of our horses."

"As soon as we finish the stalls," Lisa said.

"Of course," Carole agreed.

They were almost done. They brushed out the feed boxes, rinsed out the water buckets, then stepped back to admire their handiwork. The stalls looked cozy and welcoming— just the kind of guest room a visiting horse would be glad to see.

"Okay, last one in the ring is a rotten egg," said Stevie.

It was a challenge her friends were happy to accept.

Ten minutes later, the girls had tacked up their own horses and met in the schooling ring for a practice session. At their last class, Max had had them working on the evenness of their horses' gaits, and now they used the poles laid out on the ground to help control the horses' steps.

The idea was that the placement of the poles would prompt the horses to adjust their strides, making movement smoother for the rider as well as the horse. It was difficult, exacting work, because there was a temptation for both the rider and the horse to speed up or slow down at will. Each girl and her horse took turns sitting out a couple of rounds, so that one rider could watch and comment on the others.

Stevie was the best at it, and both Carole and Lisa were grateful when she could help them out.

"Lisa, tighten up on your reins a little bit so Prancer will be sure to notice who's in charge."

Lisa took up some of the slack in her reins. Prancer's head perked up and her gait smoothed out.

"Carole, if you anticipate the turn too soon, Starlight's going to sense it and begin turning before you want him to."

Carole adjusted her posture, and Starlight immediately returned to a straightforward trot.

Both Lisa and Carole thought it was a bit ironic that the wild, scheming, joking Stevie was the one of the three of them who naturally understood the precision required in this kind of training. Carole was the best jumper of the three, Lisa the strongest pleasure rider, and Stevie always took prizes in dressage.

They were working on lengthening their horses' strides when the van pulled into Pine Hollow's driveway. There was no question about who was arriving. In the first place, it was a large luxury van, the kind that only wealthy people could afford to rent. In the second, and more important place, it had LONG ISLAND HORSE TRANSPORT painted on the side. Dorothy DeSoto's training farm was on Long Island, and that was where Polaris and Jennie's Blue were coming from.

"Let's give them a hand," Carole said. "Max is teaching a class in the indoor ring and may not even know they're here."

She didn't have to say it twice. The girls dismounted and secured their horses to the rail before heading toward the truck, from which two people were climbing down.

At first the girls assumed that the people getting out of the truck were grooms, but when they saw that both were middle-aged women and both were well dressed, they began to consider other possibilities.

"It's the mothers," Lisa concluded.

"A little odd," said Stevie.

"What's odd about it?" Carole asked. "Maybe they love horses as much as their daughters?"

"Cool," said Lisa, wishing her mother cared as much about her riding as these women must about their daughters'. She couldn't imagine her mother riding in a horse van for ten minutes, much less six hours! The smell alone would drive her out.

Setting that thought aside, Lisa stepped up with her two friends to greet the newcomers.

"Welcome to Pine Hollow," Carole said, offering her hand.

One of the mothers looked at her, smiled coolly, and nodded. The other was too busy waiting at the back of the van to even acknowledge the presence of the three girls.

The Saddle Club was not deterred. No doubt it had been a

long trip in the big van. The women were probably tired and eager to see to the horses.

"Where's that Mr. Regnery?" asked the woman at the back of the van.

"He's teaching a student right now," Stevie said. "We'll let him know you're here, but in the meantime, my friends and I can help get the hors—"

"We told him what time we'd be here," said the other woman sharply. "You think he'd have the courtesy to meet us so we can get this over with."

"He'll be right here," said Lisa. She was the closest to the stable door and only too glad to flee the mothers she'd so recently admired. Max would know how to deal with them.

Lisa found Max in the ring with a new rider having a first lesson. It was a woman named Frieda who seemed to be getting the hang of riding very quickly. Lisa admired the way she sat in the saddle and already seemed to have absorbed many of the basics of riding.

"Max, Polaris and Jennie's Blue have arrived," Lisa said when she could get his attention.

"Why don't you girls get them settled in? You know where they go, right? You did clean out the stalls, right?"

"Right on all counts," Lisa assured him. "But I think these women would like to see you. I think it would be a good idea."

"Well, I can't leave a new rider alone," Max said. "Tell them I'll be there in"—he glanced at his watch—"eight minutes."

"Okay," Lisa said. She returned to the driveway with the news, which was received with one grunt and one harrumph.

"We just cleaned out the stalls," Stevie said, trying to sound cheerful and welcoming. It hadn't worked before and wasn't working now.

"You?" one of the women said. "Does that mean there's no professional staff here for such duties?"

Stevie gulped, swallowing the words she really wanted to utter, and said instead, "At Pine Hollow, everybody pitches in, especially when it comes to pitching out—um, manure, I mean. I think you'll be pleased with the work we've done."

"Well, let's get this over with," said one of the women.

"Yes, ma'am," Lisa agreed. The sooner this pair was gone, the better.

"I'm Carole Hanson," Carole introduced herself, this time refraining from offering a hand to shake. "This is Stevie Lake, and this is Lisa Atwood." The girls nodded and smiled.

Finally the women relinquished their names. The woman by the cab of the truck was Mrs. Walker; her daughter, Ellen, rode Jennie's Blue. The other woman was Mrs. Hatfield; her daughter, whose name was Lucy, rode Polaris.

"We'll get Blue off this thing first," said Mrs. Walker, gesturing to the back of the truck.

"I think Polaris should get off first," said Mrs. Hatfield. "After all, he got on first and has been cooped up longer."

"Driver? Driver?" Mrs. Walker called.

"I've got paperwork to do, ma'am," the driver said from inside the cab. "And neither of those horses is getting off until I finish it."

At that moment it occurred to all three of The Saddle Club girls that the six-hour ride from Long Island must have seemed much longer than that to the driver—more like six weeks!

Stevie came to the rescue. She told the women they should take the few minutes to tour Pine Hollow and see where the horses would be housed.

That turned out not to be such a good idea. The freshly cleaned stalls for the horses were near each other but on opposite sides of the aisle. The girls had never particularly noticed this before, but it meant that one of them had a window that looked south and the other's window faced north. As was true with most stable windows, they were dusty and afforded little view, but the southern window did allow more sunlight through the grime.

"This will do for Jennie's Blue," said Mrs. Walker possessively, smiling at the stream of sunshine.

"Well, I'm not so sure about that," said Mrs. Hatfield. "I think Polaris would do better in the brighter stall."

The Saddle Club was relieved that the women seemed to have abandoned their concern about whether the three girls had done an adequate job of removing manure from the stalls, but shifting to an argument over which of the two stalls had a better exposure was bizarre.

"This one is right next to my horse," Carole said politely, pointing to the northern stall. "His name is Starlight. He's really wonderful. He seems to thrive on the northern exposure."

The two women looked at her briefly, and Carole knew her thoughts were irrelevant to their argument, which in any case bore little relation to reality.

"This one definitely is brighter," said Lisa, sensing that a resolution might lie in agreeing with the women. "And that's good, because it makes it seem almost as large as the other one." *That* shifted their attention.

Finally the women decided which horse would be in which stall, taking in such factors as the new latch on one stall versus the larger manger in the other. One had a little more headroom (though the headroom was more than adequate in both) and another was on the side of the aisle that generally got hay first in the mornings. When they chose, it was clear to the girls that each mother had been convinced that she had gotten the "better" stall for her daughter's horse.

The women walked back to the truck ahead of the girls. Stevie clapped Lisa on the back. "You have a great future as a diplomat," she whispered.

Carole agreed.

Lisa wasn't so sure. "That was the stupidest conversation I've ever had," she said.

"It wasn't the conversation that was stupid, it's those two women," said Carole.

"I don't think they like one another much," Lisa whispered, making her friends collapse into giggles at the understatement.

"And people say the way I act about Veronica is childish!" said Stevie.

Max was finished with his lesson and came out to greet the women, who seemed relieved to be with an adult. Max started to tell them how pleased he was to have both Polaris and Jennie's Blue in his charge, but as with all previous pleasantries, the women dismissed that.

"I certainly hope you'll have enough time to work with Polaris properly," said Mrs. Hatfield.

Max didn't skip a beat. "You bet," he said. "It's a pleasure and an honor to help out my former student just the way I did when I helped her train the first horse she ever worked with."

"Of course," said Mrs. Walker. "Well, let's get on with this."

It didn't take long before all the paperwork was completed, and the girls helped Max unload Jennie's Blue and Polaris and put them in their carefully selected stalls. Max and the mothers went over routines and regulations, checking through the paperwork while the girls filled the horses' water buckets and made them feel welcome.

"I bet you're glad to be away from that awful woman," Stevie whispered to Jennie's Blue. The horse whinnied a response that Stevie was sure meant she agreed totally.

Pretty soon the truck pulled out of the driveway, headed back for Long Island and carrying Mrs. Hatfield. It turned out that Mrs. Walker was staying over with a friend near Willow Creek and had to wait for the friend to pick her up. It didn't take long. A big dark-windowed SUV lumbered into the Pine Hollow driveway, where Mrs. Walker met it. She pulled open the heavy door and climbed in, greeting her friend with the words "Thank God you're here. I'm so relieved to have seen the last of that dreadful woman!" And then the door slammed.

That was exactly the way The Saddle Club felt. Times two.

"Are you going to stand there all day staring at that expensive car driving away, or are you going to come in here and give me a hand?" Max asked.

19

The followed him into his office.

"This is a big responsibility," he began.

"What's the big deal about looking after two more horses?" Stevie asked.

"It's more than looking after," Max said. "I have to continue the training so that this pair can be in top condition for the horse show. This is an important show by any standard and extremely important for the two riders. Ribbons here could make the difference in their futures. I have to have the horses totally ready."

"Can we watch?" Lisa asked, remembering the conversation she'd had with her friends the night before.

"Well, one of you can at a time," he said.

"Just one?" Stevie asked.

"The other two will be riding," said Max.

"We can watch and ride at the same time," Carole assured him. "And we'll keep our horses out of the way, too."

"That's not what I mean, Carole," Max said. "These horses are used to being ridden by young girls, not much older—or larger—than you three. I'm going to need riders, and their owners aren't here. Do you think you can give me some extra time between now and when Lucy and Ellen arrive? Can you ride, follow instructions, and help with the training?"

"Us?" Lisa asked.

Max pretended to look behind The Saddle Club. "No, not you, the girls standing behind you," he teased.

"Are you kidding?" Carole asked.

"I never kid about horses," said Max.

"Count us in," Stevie said.

"It's hard work," said Max.

"But it's horses," said Carole.

"It's a lot of time," said Max.

"It's going to be fun!" said Lisa.

"And I was afraid I was going to have trouble talking you into this," said Max. "Okay, look," he said, showing them the schedule. "It's going to mean being here before and after school almost every day."

"Can you talk to our parents?" Lisa asked him.

"Yes, I'll do that," Max promised. "I'm going to need their help and cooperation, too, getting you here and all that. I know they're going to ask each of you to promise that—"

"Don't worry, we'll keep up on our schoolwork," Lisa said, anticipating his concern.

"Thank you," he said.

"Can we start now?" Carole asked.

"No, these guys have had a long drive and they're tired. They get some time off. But tomorrow. At six-thirty—"

"That's dinnertime," Stevie started to say.

"A.M.," Max said.

Stevie grimaced. Morning wasn't her favorite time.

"Don't worry. She'll be here," Carole promised.

Max dismissed them then, asking them to give his new student, Frieda, a hand with untacking and grooming before they put their own horses away. They were practically walking on air as they left his office.

WEDNESDAY MORNING at six-thirty, Stevie stumbled into Pine Hollow—in the cheery, wide-awake manner she now reserved for that hour. The truth was, it wasn't very cheery or very wide-awake, but it was a manner she had perfected over the past couple of days. Secretly, she was almost getting used to the early hour, but she wouldn't admit that to anyone.

"Where am I?" she asked Lisa, who tended to be more genuinely wide awake and cheerier at early-morning hours.

"You're at Pine Hollow," Lisa told her. "Just where you're supposed to be, and where you've been the last two mornings. Now go put on a riding helmet so we can get to work."

Robotlike, Stevie followed Lisa's instructions, and a few minutes later, she was on board Polaris, remembering exactly where she was—Pine Hollow's schooling ring—and what she was doing—working hard.

Lisa was riding Blue, and Carole was leaning against the

fence, making notes on a clipboard for Max about all the exercises the horses were doing and the progress they were showing. Max was standing next to her.

"Polaris's stride is longer today," Carole told Max, stuffing the measuring tape back into her pocket.

Stevie was pleased. She'd been working on the length of the horse's stride, and it was nice to know that she was succeeding. It seemed such a small thing, but a horse with a longer stride could move more elegantly in dressage and achieve more variation when its rider asked for it.

"All right, let's trot these guys to stretch some more before we begin the balance exercises," said Max.

Stevie and Lisa began a rising trot, and Carole made more notes on the clipboard. Max was about to give them further instruction when the phone rang.

Carole sighed. Stevie and Lisa both grimaced. There weren't a lot of people who could be calling Pine Hollow at 6:45 in the morning. In fact, there were only two choices. It was going to be Mrs. Walker or Mrs. Hatfield. The smart money was on Mrs. Walker.

Max walked over to the barn door and picked up the phone.

"Yes, Mrs. Walker," he said after a few seconds. "Right, uh, Eloise, of course . . . Just fine, Eloise . . . We're working with her now . . . Right, both of them, of course . . . Yes, my young riders. The same ones as yesterday. We're about to begin the balance sequence," he said. He listened, sighing. Although Max was too much of a professional to let an important owner like Mrs. Walker know that he thought she was a nuisance, it was clear to The Saddle Club that that was exactly what was on his mind. And the fact was that she *was* a nuisance.

"Well, I've only got limited times when these riders are available to me, Mrs. Walker—Eloise—so I think I'd better get back to work. No, they're all good riders, Eloise, and they're taking turns so both the horses have experience with each of the girls. Blue is doing very well. Really . . . Um, Polaris is, too, of course. Right, well, they're both getting the same amount . . . Eloise, I've got to go now," he said firmly. "I'm sure you will. Until tomorrow, then," and he hung up the phone.

"She's going to call again tomorrow," he explained to the three girls.

Stevie snickered. Lisa's shoulders were shaking with laughter. Even Carole, the one most likely to sympathize with an overattentive owner, snorted.

"Something to look forward to," Lisa said.

Max ignored their joking and told them to begin a sitting trot with their feet out of the stirrups.

There was no doubt about it. Training for a show was hard work for the trainer, the rider, and especially the horse. That was why it was called a workout. Still, even though it was work, it was fun, too, and the girls were very glad they were doing it and not someone else. It was fun to be riding such wonderful horses and to do everything they could to help them get ready for the hardest work they would have to do— the horse show.

"Tell us again why it is we can't go to the show," Lisa said, knowing as she said it that she was nagging.

"Because the show is sold out," said Max. "This is the most

prestigious show in the state and it's been sold out for a month. Believe me, if I'd known when the ticket order form came six months ago that we'd be working with horses that would be vying for blues, I'd have gotten a half dozen seats for us. Now it's all I can do to get a seat for myself. Fortunately, Mrs. Hatfield has promised me one ticket for Saturday. But just one."

"Groan," said Stevie.

"Will you videotape it?" Lisa asked.

"No, but they usually broadcast some of the show. You can watch it on television," Max said. They all knew that the taped show was typically broadcast when a baseball game was rained out or, more likely, at three o'clock in the morning. As far as they were concerned, horse shows didn't get anywhere near enough attention on television.

"Now, are we going to talk, or are we going to work?" Max said.

"Work, of course!" Stevie said smartly. "Who would ever want to talk when she could be working?"

Max hid a smile, but they all got back to work.

When the phone rang the next time, Carole answered it because Max was concentrating on the exercise. It was Lucy Hatfield, a more welcome interruption.

"How's Polaris doing, Carole?" she asked.

"He's doing wonderfully," Carole assured her. "Stevie's riding him this morning, and he warmed up smoothly. Max is working on balance, and then next come the suppling exercises. I don't think we'll be able to do any more than that before we have to get to school, but this afternoon we're going to go through jump routines."

25

"Oh, I wish I could be there!" Lucy said.

"Sometimes I wish so, too," Carole told her. "Especially at five-thirty when I have to get up to get here by six-thirty! But now that it's practically the middle of the afternoon"— she glanced at her watch, which said 7:00—"I don't mind at all."

"Do you mind me calling?"

"Not a bit," said Carole. "If it were my horse, I'd be doing exactly the same thing."

"I can't wait to get there."

"And I promise you, you'll be pleased with all the progress Polaris is making."

"Just talking to you makes me feel better."

"No problem, but I've got to go now."

"Bye and, uh, thanks again," said Lucy, and she hung up.

It was the same almost every morning. They'd get a call from one or the other of the mothers, and then they'd hear from the girls. Each mother only seemed to want to be assured that her horse was getting better treatment than the other—as if the competition existed only between their daughters. As for Lucy and Ellen, they seemed to be friends as well as friendly competitors.

By 7:25, they had nearly completed their morning session and Max had the riders walking the horses to cool them down.

Max's newest student, Frieda, had showed up and was leaning against the fence. Carole was pleased to see her. She always liked it when a new rider took so enthusiastically to the sport. Frieda had signed up for daily lessons at eight o'clock during the week and had come early every time. Car-

ole waved to her, inviting her to come over to the fence
where Carole was now perched, finishing up her notes on the
morning workout.

"So, what are you all up to?" Frieda asked.

Carole showed her the chart. "It's a combination of
stretching and suppling," she explained. "Anything that will
help keep the horses in tip-top condition is what we're after."

"And there's no problem having them work together?"
Frieda asked.

"No, it works well," Carole said. "See, it's an easy way for
Max to be sure they both get the same amount of attention,
and we switch off riders at every session so they have different
experiences."

Frieda glanced at the chart, studying it for a few seconds,
and then shrugged. "It's all Greek to me," she told Carole.

"I can explain if you'd like," Carole told her. Carole liked
sharing her knowledge about horses with people, especially
when it was as interesting as the lesson plan chart for these
two championship horses.

"No, that's okay," Frieda answered. "Remember, you're
dealing here with someone who has just learned about
mounting a horse from the left side!"

"I saw you working with Max yesterday," Carole said. "I
think you're well beyond that!"

"Not much," Frieda said quickly. Carole thought she was
being a little hasty. For a beginner, she seemed to be a quick
learner.

Carole slid down off the fence, tucking the clipboard under
her arm. "Time to give those horses a little treat and then get
ready for school," she said. "See you tomorrow, I guess."

"Do you come after school, too?" Frieda asked.

"We do," Carole told her. "We get here about four. This afternoon I'm riding Blue, and Lisa will be on Polaris."

"I may stop by to watch that," Frieda told her.

"Great!" said Carole. As she walked back into the stable, she smiled, thinking about what a great rider Frieda was going to be—just because of her attitude. All riders should be as eager to learn as she was.

A few minutes later Frieda helped Lisa put the tack away, then carried a tick of hay back to Blue, who seemed relaxed and welcomed the quick grooming Lisa gave her.

"Do you ride her every morning?" Frieda asked.

"No, we switch off," Lisa said. "That way the horses get accustomed to having different riders. It gives us all equal chances to ride really wonderful horses, too. And then, this weekend, when their own riders get here, they won't think it's so strange to have another person on board. I think it works that way for the horses, but no matter what, it works for us."

"I can see you're having fun," said Frieda.

"We are," Lisa said. "Though I have to confess that sometimes I wish the fun didn't have to start so early in the day!"

She handed Frieda a brush and gave her a quick lesson in grooming, which helped Lisa finish the job so that she could get dressed and be off to school on schedule. That was part of the deal with her parents. As long as she was at school on time and got all her homework done, she and her friends were allowed to be at Pine Hollow for exercise sessions for an hour and a half twice a day. It was exhausting, but they all thought it totally worthwhile—for them as well as the horses.

Thursday was the same as Wednesday. When the girls arrived after school, Stevie settled herself on the top rail of the schooling ring fence. She nearly toppled from the rail when she dozed off. It had already been a long day, and this was their second trip to Pine Hollow. Carole, as usual, was all business around the horses and had Blue saddled and warming up in a few minutes. Lisa, ever precise and particular, took a little longer because she wanted to be sure the girth straps were even on both sides of Polaris's saddle. They were.

The girls were almost finished with the warm-up and ready to begin the afternoon sequence of exercises when they heard the first rumblings. Lisa noticed it because Polaris flinched. Carole was still totally focused on Blue's strides when Stevie put the clipboard up to her forehead to shade her eyes from the afternoon sun as she looked to the sky. Max just glanced up, looked puzzled, then turned his attention back to the horses.

The sound got louder. It was the insistent flapping of a helicopter. Stevie figured it must be some sort of traffic report helicopter, though she knew perfectly well that there were few traffic jams as far from downtown Washington, D.C., as Willow Creek, which was outside the Beltway.

The pounding noise grew louder.

"Some kind of accident or something?" Stevie asked Frieda, who stood next to her.

"Who knows?" Frieda answered.

"And who cares?" asked Carole. "I think Blue's ready for some trotting now. Lisa?"

"Ready over here," Lisa said. The girls signaled their horses for a trot.

Carole loved the gaits of these two horses. Blue's trot was smooth and fast. Any concern she'd had about the amount of work to be done or even the social studies test that she'd taken earlier that day left her mind and her heart. All she could hear was the beat of Blue's silky-smooth trot, and all she could feel was the suppleness of the animal that carried her and the fresh breeze that washed over her.

And all the while, the sound intensified overhead.

"What is going on?" Stevie demanded, realizing that she had to yell to be heard. She looked up again, as did everyone else. They saw that there were not one but two large helicopters overhead—directly overhead—and that they were descending. One clearly was going to land.

Polaris shied. Lisa tightened up on the reins. He calmed down again. Carole drew Blue back down to a walk. Her ears flicked back and forth, and Carole thought Polaris was probably almost as uncomfortable with the level of the noise as she was. She concentrated on keeping Blue's attention on the task at hand, which was trotting. Blue seemed to appreciate the instructions and gladly trotted on. Lisa and Polaris followed suit.

Stevie, on the other hand, gave up all pretense of watching her friends ride. There was no doubt about it. One of the helicopters was preparing to land in the field right in front of the stable, and the other was circling the surrounding fields and woods.

Max left the ring. There was no way he could allow a helicopter to land near a stable full of high-strung and valuable horses. He walked out into the area where one helicopter was hovering and began waving his arms and shaking his

30

head. The pilot apparently got the message and pulled up, nosing higher into the air and away from the stable. Within a few minutes, both helicopters rose over the copse of trees that bordered Pine Hollow's field and flew away.

Carole and Lisa returned their attention to their training exercises. Stevie, on the other hand, watched the road at the edge of the field. The helicopters might be leaving, but something else was arriving. She squinted. Three black sedans drove in a cluster along the two-lane road, heading for Pine Hollow.

She slid down off the fence and walked over to the driveway, arriving at the parking area just as all three cars did. Twelve car doors opened at once and from each emerged a man dressed in a dark suit, white shirt, and dark tie. Most of them wore sunglasses—mirrored sunglasses that hid their eyes completely. And they all wore the same completely blank expression.

Stevie froze, wondering what on earth was about to happen.

One of the men strode toward her while the others stood by the cars.

"We're looking for someone named Carl," he said in moderately accented English. The accent sounded vaguely Middle Eastern.

"Nobody here by that name," Stevie said. "No Carls at all."

"Not Carl," the man said, ever so slightly annoyed. "Carl." He emphasized it as if saying it more loudly would make it clearer.

"There is no man here named Carl," Stevie told him firmly.

"Not a man. A girl," he said, the late-afternoon sun glinting off his reflective sunglasses.

"A girl? Carl?" And then it struck her. "Carole? You mean Carole?"

"That's what I said. Carl."

"Hanson?" Stevie asked.

"As you wish," he said.

And then he held out his hand to show her something. It was paper. It had pictures of horses on it. And Stevie understood everything.

She signaled the man to follow her back to the schooling ring, where Carole and Lisa were now sitting on Blue and Polaris and staring at the cluster of sedans in the parking lot. As Stevie approached, Carole and Lisa stared even more intently at their friend, who was being followed by a very sinister-looking man in a black suit and shiny sunglasses.

"Oh, Carole!" Stevie sang out. "These guys have something to say to you!"

4

IT TOOK A MOMENT for Carole to absorb everything she saw before her. Until she'd seen Stevie coming toward her and Lisa, she'd been totally focused on the training exercise she and Blue had been doing. But now she found herself staring at four cars. Black. Sedans. And then all those men. Carole knew the look. It was very distinct and it was *very* official. The men were all wearing dark suits and white shirts. They were either funeral directors—which seemed unlikely because funeral directors didn't usually come in clusters—or government agents of some kind.

For a moment Carole thought the shiver she suddenly felt was coming from Blue, but then she realized that she was the one who was shivering. She was afraid. Her father worked for the government. If something had happened to him . . .

"Carl Hanzen?" one of the men asked. Maybe they had the wrong person.

"Carole Hanson," she said.

"That's what I said."

Carole dismounted and walked over to where the man was waiting to speak to her. If it was bad news, she wanted it right away. Before she reached the fence, though, she had a chance to look at Stevie, who was grinning like a cat with canary feathers sprouting from its mouth.

Then Carole, too, recognized the sheet of paper the man held in his hand. It was her letter to Karya Nazeem! Had she done something wrong? Broken some law? Offended some diplomat? If they were going to question her, shouldn't her father be there? Did she have the right to call a lawyer?

"We are here to, as you people say, RVPS," said the man, smiling.

"I think he means RSVP," Stevie suggested helpfully.

"As you say." He nodded briefly in Stevie's direction.

"It's French," Lisa piped up. "It stands for *Répondez, s'il vous plaît*, which means 'Please respond.' "

He smiled weakly at Lisa.

"Yes?" Carole said.

"Ms. Nazeem would like very much to ride here with you when she comes to this country next week," said the man.

Another man stepped forward. Carole hadn't noticed him before, perhaps because he was hidden among all the black suits.

"Let me introduce myself," he said, offering Carole a hand. "I am representing the Nazeem family and planning their schedules for their visit to the United States of America." He gave Carole a card with his name in Arabic script. On the other side was a translation into English. Carole tucked it in her pocket. "Is there someplace we can talk?" he asked.

By then Max and Lisa had given up all pretense of continuing their exercise program and were standing right behind Carole.

"We can go into my office," Max suggested, introducing himself.

"Satisfactory," said the secretary. "And while we talk, would you have any objection to the security team's looking around the stable? They will need to be sure everything is safest possible for Ms. Nazeem's visit."

"Everything here is very safe," Max assured him. "I always require that my riders follow my rigorous safety program."

"I am not talking about riding helmets," the secretary said. "I am talking about terrorism."

"That, too," Max said, nodding as if all of his riders were worried about terrorism. "Of course. This way, please."

There was no way Lisa and Stevie were going to miss a minute of this. They tied their horses to the fence in a shaded area of the schooling ring and tagged along after Max and Carole into his office.

As they walked, the man who had given Carole his card introduced himself as the Nazeems' secretary. Speaking very formally, he explained that the whole Nazeem family was coming to the United States, specifically Washington, D.C., and although Ms. Nazeem had many obligations of state, she had requested that she be allowed to ride while she was in America. Specifically, she had asked if she could ride with this girl who'd written her a letter and spend some time at Pine Hollow with Carole Hanson and her friends.

The secretary then looked at Lisa and Stevie. "These girls, I presume?"

"You bet!" Stevie answered. She didn't want anybody to make any mistakes about exactly who Carole's friends were. In fact, she didn't want to miss anything. She hurried to walk right next to Carole. Lisa walked beside Stevie.

The group entered Max's office and everybody took a seat. The secretary pulled a notepad out of his pocket to check something.

"Karya will be arriving in the United States next Tuesday," he said. "On Wednesday she will accompany her mother on a tour of the Beltway Mall."

Stevie stifled a giggle. The secretary glowered, looking at her over his reading glasses. "And what is so funny about that?" he asked.

"You don't tour a mall," Stevie explained. "You shop at one."

"Yes, well, they will observe things there, and that's a tour, right?"

"Yes, sir," she said, and then decided to keep her mouth shut, realizing that nice and efficient as this man might be, he'd been born without any sense of humor, so there wasn't much point in continuing a conversation with him.

"After that, there is a luncheon at the ADR embassy, and then there's something in the afternoon—a reading of essays about the produce of the fertile valleys of the ADR, followed by a dinner at the home of the agriculturist whose grandfather, also an agriculturist, developed the plan for the dam that provides waters for those fertile valleys. And the following morning, Mrs. Nazeem and Karya will meet with representatives of American labor unions who want to reward Mrs. Nazeem for her support of the labor movement in the ADR, followed by a visit to an exhibit at the International Commission on Hydroponic Farming at which Mrs. Nazeem will—"

Stevie could contain herself no longer: "Stop! Doesn't this girl ever get a break?" she asked.

"I was just getting to that," said the secretary. "She is completely free to do as she pleases from two-fourteen on Thursday afternoon until three-oh-four. Can she ride here then?"

Three young girls and a stable owner stared at the man.

"Forty-five minutes?" Max asked.

"That's not enough time to go on a good ride!" Carole said.

"And she won't have time to muck out a stall!" Stevie protested.

Lisa was calmer. "In order for Karya to enjoy herself, she's going to need to spend time at the stable, meet the horses, get used to the place, tack up, and go for a nice ride. We sort of got the impression—from the article we read—that she'd like to have that kind of time."

"How much time do you mean?" the man asked.

"Two to three hours," Lisa said without batting an eye.

The man looked at his notepad.

Max's phone rang and he picked it up. "Yes, this is he," said Max. "Yes, of course I know my own Social Security number." There was a pause. A puzzled look came over his face. "Well, you called me," he said. "Perhaps you'd like to tell me *your* Social Security number."

The secretary looked up from his pad. "That would be the State Department," he explained to Max and the girls.

"Is this someone from the State Department?" Max asked. A moment of silence. "Well, now we're getting somewhere.

Yes, Mr. Nazeem's security team is here. The secretary is in my office right now," Max said.

The conversation went on. It became clear to the listeners that someone from the U.S. State Department was asking Max to cooperate with the ADR security team.

"Of course I'll cooperate," Max said. "I always cooperate with armed men."

"Are you guys armed?" Stevie asked.

"I am not armed," the secretary said.

Stevie turned to her friends. "Well, that answers that. This man may not be carrying a gun, but all those other guys are."

"Of course they are," Carole said. "They're supposed to protect lives." Because her father was in the Marines, she was a little more attuned to such matters, although her father always kept whatever arms the Marines required him to have locked up in his office at work. She'd never even seen his weapons.

Max, in the meantime, kept listening to the State Department representative. "Yes, yes, of course. I understand. We'll certainly cooperate in any way we can. Definitely. Oh, yes, I understand, they'll need to check everything and everyone. Um-hmmm."

It went on like that for a while. Finally Max hung up the phone and turned to the secretary. "As you heard, sir, we're here to be as helpful as possible to you and the agents and we'll do everything we can to make sure Karya has a good time. Now, let's negotiate the hours, because Lisa was exactly right that two hours would be the mini—" The phone rang again. He picked it up.

This time it wasn't for him. It was for Carole. He handed

the phone to her. It wasn't the Secret Service, the State Department, or even MI-6. It was Karya Nazeem herself.

Carole could hardly believe it. She listened for a while and then began smiling. "Yes, everybody's here," she said. "There are a dozen men in black suits interviewing horses and looking in hay bales for spies!"

"Oh, they're like that," Karya said. "My father is always afraid for me because he has enemies and he worries that someone will try to get to him through me."

"You mean this stuff is for real?" Carole said. As soon as she said it, she was sorry. Nobody would send out a dozen agents just because it seemed like fun.

"I guess so. But I don't let it worry me. Now, what about Alek there?" Carole realized she was asking about the secretary, whose name she'd noticed when she glanced at the business card he had given her. "He proposed a forty-five-minute visit to the stable."

"Well, that's enough . . . ," Karya said.

Carole felt her disappointment growing until Karya continued.

". . . for me to have the complete tour you promised in your letter and for us to tack up our horses. That'll all take about forty-five minutes, right? And then we can spend about an hour or two on the trail, and then we can get back to the stable and groom our own horses, and then, if there's time, we can muck out some stalls. You did say something about being able to get special permission for me to use the pitchforks, right?"

Carole grinned. Already she liked this girl enormously.

"I think we can work something out on that. I'll get Max's

39

special permission for you to have access to one of the pitchforks. Now, would you like to talk to Alek and explain that forty-five minutes is inadequate and he's going to have to find a way to get you excused from the tour of the electrical plant that installed the gates on the dam . . . ?"

Now Karya giggled. "It's that bad, isn't it?"

"Sounded pretty awful to me," Carole confirmed.

"Let me talk to him."

Carole handed the phone to the secretary. He spoke to Karya in a totally unfamiliar language. Carole presumed it was Arabic and only then stopped to wonder how it was that this daughter of the president of a foreign land spoke such great English.

"We're going to like her a lot," Carole said to her friends and Max. It had only taken five minutes on the telephone for Carole to be sure of that, and her friends had heard enough of Carole's end of the conversation to know she knew what she was talking about.

Soon Karya was off the line and everything was all business again, but by then it was really just details. The girls had gotten what they most wanted, and that was a lengthy opportunity to visit with Karya, who would be at Pine Hollow the following Thursday, a week from today, arriving at the unlikely hour of 2:14 but being allowed to stay as long as she wanted. She'd convinced Alek that the diplomatic ribbon-cutting event could go on without her. He made large black X's in his notebook and everybody was happy.

Max then spent time with Alek, showing him and some of the agents, whom Stevie had immediately dubbed men in black (because most of them were, and looked as if they'd stepped off a movie set, down to their bug-eyed reflector sunglasses), all around Pine Hollow and giving them maps of the trails on the surrounding woods.

The Saddle Club worked with the remaining men in black, explaining who they were, giving them their names and addresses and their parents' names and occupations.

"And have they ever been arrested?" one of the agents asked Stevie. Once again, she couldn't keep herself from laughing.

"We have ways of finding out these things," he said sternly.

"Oh, I wish they had been," Stevie responded. "It would be so much easier for me!"

Her friends laughed then, too. In spite of himself, the agent cracked a smile.

"And you two? Your parents? Have they been arrested?"

"Not a chance," Lisa said.

"No way!" Carole assured him.

It went on like that for a while. The men questioned Red and Mrs. Reg. They made an appointment to talk with Max's wife, Deborah, and seemed concerned when they found out she was a reporter, but looked relieved when Max promised she wasn't planning to write an article about Karya Nazeem.

Finally they all left. That was when the girls remembered that Polaris and Blue were still tied out in the schooling ring. It hadn't done them any harm, but it didn't seem fair. The good news was that Max said there had been enough excitement for everybody for that day and the girls should just put the horses away, groom and water them, and head on home. He'd see them again first thing in the morning.

Carole's father was late getting home that evening. She'd

gotten dinner almost ready and was sitting on her bed reading her history assignment when the phone rang. It was Stevie.

"You know, Carole, those guys are doing pretty thorough checking. They already called my parents, and they've been in touch with the school. Do you suppose they might find out what I did to the polliwog in the bio lab?" Carole remembered Stevie's test with blue food coloring. "And you know it's *possible* that someone might get the impression that I am the person who telephoned the seventh-grade French teacher to tell him he had a burst pipe so he'd hurry home instead of giving his class a totally un-called-for pop quiz. Do you suppose the men in black can check phone records for that sort of thing?"

"Uh, Stevie, I don't think they really care about that sort of stuff," Carole began. "I think they're more concerned with matters of state—like have you been spying for any terrorist organizations or threatening to overthrow any duly elected governments recently."

"Well, sure, but people can jump to conclusions about the most innocent—"

There was a knock on Carole's door and her father came in. He had a seriously concerned look on his face.

"Hang on," she said, interrupting Stevie's next confession. "Hi, Dad," she said.

He acknowledged her greeting with a nod and then asked, "Carole, have you been doing any spying for a small Middle Eastern country known as ADR?"

Clearly, the men in black had been very busy.

"Gotta go," Carole told Stevie, and hung up the phone.

"Well, it's like this, Dad . . . ," she began.

FRIDAY MORNING brought good news. By the time the girls
had stumbled into the stable, tacked up Blue and Polaris, and
remembered who was riding and who was making notes, they
were ready for good news. It was their fifth very early morning
in a row and they were beginning to frazzle at the edges.

"The girls are coming!" Max announced.

"We're already here," Lisa told him, rubbing her still sleepy
eyes.

"No, I mean the owners," he said.

"Like, here?" Stevie asked.

"Yes, like here," Max said. "Ellen and Lucy will be here
this afternoon for the weekend. You're off the hook for exercising all weekend long."

"So we can sleep in tomorrow?" Carole asked.

"Only if you want to miss the best part of the day!" Max
declared. The girls groaned. They did not share Max's opinion about the best part of the day, since they each generally

43

thought the day should begin around nine o'clock, not six! But Max was teasing and they all knew it.

"What if they don't like the work we've done for them?" Carole asked.

"Of course they're going to like it," Stevie said. "They got to sleep late this week!"

"Don't worry, girls," Max said. "We were doing exactly what Dorothy wanted us to do, which is exactly what I would have recommended in the first place. Ellen and Lucy are going to be pleased, I'm sure. But before all this chitchat takes away the little time we have to work, let's pay attention to this morning's workout. What's up first, Lisa?"

Lisa checked the board. "Balance," she said. And the work began.

An hour later, while the girls were finishing up with the horses, giving them a grooming and some hay and water, they talked about what they were going to do with their sudden and unexpected free time besides sleep. They hadn't realized that Ellen and Lucy were going to be at Pine Hollow that weekend.

"Well, we're going to watch them train," Carole said.

"Some," Lisa said.

"And not at seven A.M.!" Stevie declared.

"Okay, so we can sleep a little later," Carole agreed.

"And that means we can have a sleepover," said Lisa.

"At my place," said Stevie.

They agreed.

"And that should give us enough time to plan for our visit with Karya next week," said Carole.

"That won't take much time to plan," Lisa said. "First we'll let her muck out a stall—one should be enough to remind her that she really doesn't much like to do that anyway—and then we'll ride to the creek and talk about everything in the world the way we usually do and then we'll come back here again. Easy as pie." Her friends laughed.

"Well, that's decided, so we'll have to talk about something else tonight," Stevie said.

"Horses?" Carole suggested.

"Works for me," Lisa agreed.

"Okay, then. Meet you here this afternoon so we can give these big guys a final grooming before Ellen and Lucy arrive."

They changed their clothes, grabbed their book bags, and accepted the lift that Deborah offered them to get to their schools.

Even though it was a Friday and even though that meant that Stevie had a French vocabulary test, Lisa had double-period chemistry lab, and Carole had to sit through Joe Novick's report on armor in the Middle Ages plus an assembly on fire drills, the day seemed to fly by. At four o'clock, the girls met on their way back to Pine Hollow.

" 'Dormitory!' " Stevie grumbled. "Who needs to know how to say 'dormitory' in French? I'm never going to live in one—at least not in France!"

"I take it the vocabulary test didn't go well?" Lisa asked.

"No, it went fine," Stevie said. "I just missed the one word."

"What is it?" Carole asked, though she wasn't sure why. She was taking Spanish.

"*Dortoir*," Stevie said.

"And you'll never forget it now, will you?" asked Lisa.

45

"No, but I'm going to have trouble working it into conversations, and I'm not sure how I feel about my best friend pointing out important life lessons like learning from my mistakes."

"That's what friends are for," Lisa said.

"Hey! They're here!" Carole said, interrupting the life lesson. Lisa and Stevie looked where Carole was pointing.

Max was in the schooling ring with two very familiar horses and two unfamiliar riders. They could only be Ellen Walker riding Blue and Lucy Hatfield on Polaris.

The girls paused where they were standing to watch. It was a pleasure. The girls and their mounts moved together in the wonderful liquid manner of the finest pairings of horse and rider, the animals responding to every slight signal from the girls, all the while looking as though it took no effort at all.

"Wow," said Stevie, unable to contain her admiration—or to express it any better than that, though that seemed to be enough for Lisa and Carole as well.

After a few minutes, the girls walked on toward the ring. They put down their books and climbed up onto the fence so they could watch.

Max was so focused on his work that he didn't even acknowledge their arrival until he completed the suppling exercise routine that was now so familiar to The Saddle Club—and was equally familiar to Ellen and Lucy.

And when it was completed, Stevie, Carole, and Lisa all applauded. "That was great!" Lisa said.

The riders noticed them for the first time then. "Girls, I'd like you to meet your stand-ins," Max said. The Saddle Club hopped down from the fence for the introductions. Of course, they already knew one another from the phone calls, but they'd never seen one another, so it took a few minutes to straighten out who was who.

"Polaris is wonderful to ride!" Lisa said to Lucy, patting the horse enthusiastically. Lucy agreed and thanked Lisa for her help.

Ellen and Stevie were chatting about Blue's flying changes, and Carole joined in on all the conversations. Not surprisingly, the girls found a lot of common ground.

"Ahem," said Max. "I think we have more work to do here. . . ."

While Max got back to work with Lucy and Ellen, The Saddle Club returned to their positions on the top rail of the schooling ring fence and resumed their silence except for an occasional whisper like "Oh, *that's* how that's supposed to be done!"

When the lesson was over, Stevie, Lisa, and Carole all jumped down off the fence again and picked up their conversations where Max had stopped them.

"Polaris always wants to turn left when we get to the fence at the far end of the ring," Lisa told Lucy.

"I know. He does that with me, too. I try to let him know I'm in charge of direction about four steps before he gets to make up his mind."

"That's just what I did!" said Lisa.

"It works, too."

"Most of the time," said Lisa. The girls laughed.

"And that's nothing compared to how Blue starts acting up when she thinks it's time for the lesson to be over!" said Stevie.

"Right," Ellen agreed. "Look at her now!" Ellen was seated in Blue's saddle and had the horse facing away from the stable. Except that the horse's head was turned almost completely around and she was gazing longingly at the stable door!

"I think she's trying to tell you something," said Carole.

"And her message is loud and clear," said Ellen as she dismounted. The girls all laughed together and then agreed that perhaps Blue had a good idea. It was time for a rest, and The Saddle Club could help.

Carole took Blue's bridle and led her toward the stable. Before she got in the door, two cars pulled into Pine Hollow's driveway. One was the big, shiny, dark-windowed SUV the girls had seen the day the horses arrived. It would be Mrs. Walker with her friend who lived nearby. The other was a rented sedan. Mrs. Hatfield stepped out of the driver's seat and glared impolitely at Mrs. Walker, who was climbing out of the passenger seat of the SUV.

"Ready to go, Lucy?" Mrs. Hatfield called out before Mrs. Walker had a chance to do the same.

"Let's leave!" said Mrs. Walker, cutting through the amenities.

"In a minute, Mom," Lucy answered.

"Have to look after Blue," said Ellen.

The girls hurried into the sanctuary of the stable with their horses.

"We can look after these guys," said Carole.

"No, it's okay. We can help."

And they did. It didn't take the five of them much time to look after the two horses. The odd thing, Carole thought, was how the whole mood had changed the minute the mothers had showed up.

"Is it always like that?" Stevie asked.

"They don't like each other," said Lucy.

"But you two like each other, don't you?" asked Lisa.

"Well, we've been competing against each other for a long time," Lucy said.

"And who usually wins?" Stevie asked.

"She does."

Both girls had answered at exactly the same time and pointed at each other. Stevie started to laugh because it was funny that each seemed to think the other was more successful, but then she realized maybe it wasn't funny. The girls clearly *did* like one another, but there was an edge, a part of each of them that recognized the friend as a competitor, or perhaps the competitor as a friend. Their competitiveness didn't have the same icy quality that was apparent between the mothers, but it seemed their friendship wasn't as close as each of them would like to believe.

"Come on, let's get these horses cleaned up and give them the rest they've so clearly earned," Carole said, breaking the moment of silence that Ellen and Lucy had produced.

Ten minutes later, the horses were groomed and fed and Ellen and Lucy had gone with their mothers. The women had sat in their separate cars in air-conditioned isolation, not saying a word to each other or to Max. Nobody had suggested to either of them that they do anything different.

When they'd gone, Lisa, Stevie, and Carole finished up the few chores that were left: They dusted off the saddles, straightening out the leathers so that there were no twists in

49

them as they hung, and they brought a fresh flake of hay to each horse.

"Well, that was interesting," Lisa said as the three of them sat in the locker area when they were finished.

"The girls really like one another," Stevie said. "I'm sure of it."

"They've got so much in common," said Carole.

"Right, they both own expensive horses and they train at the same stable, and they're serious riders, and they compete against each other . . . ," Lisa observed.

"And their mothers hate each other," Stevie added.

"And each other's daughter," said Lisa.

"And their horses!" Carole said. "How could anybody hate a *horse?*"

She was still shaking her head in incomprehension when they went to report to Mrs. Reg that everything had been done.

"Did you catch the mother act?" Stevie asked, referring to the bizarre behavior of the two adults while they were in the parking area.

"You know," said Mrs. Reg, without answering Stevie's question, "I remember a little boy from a long time ago."

The girls exchanged glances. Mrs. Reg had a way of launching into an old tale at the oddest time and in the oddest way. They never knew what the story was going to be, and often, when it was done, they never knew why it had been told. But they always knew that when Mrs. Reg had a story to tell, it was probably worth listening to. The girls perched on the chairs and benches in her office and listened.

"He had this pony he loved a lot. Sweet pony, he was. In fact, he was named Sweet William after the wildflower, but the boy called him Billy. Can't remember the boy's name. That pony had the sweetest, kindest disposition you ever knew—as long as that little boy was there. He'd do anything the boy asked. He never balked, never kicked, never bucked—as long as that little boy was there. But he was impossible when the boy wasn't there. He could barely be led on a line. He'd kick anyone who tried to clean out his hoof, and he'd bite anyone who tried to put a saddle on him. Impossible. That's what he was. But the boy never saw it. Can't blame him, really. The pony always knew whenever the little boy was around and behaved perfectly. It was only when he wasn't nearby so the little boy never witnessed, and never believed, what everybody else always told him—that Billy was a bad pony.

"Then, one day, the little boy got too big for Billy. He just grew too large to ride the pony, and though they were devoted to one another, the boy had to sell him. It wasn't easy for that little boy, but he did it. A nice family with a nice little girl, just the right size for Billy, came by. The little girl rode Billy and fell in love with Sweet William—she called him by his whole name. And sweet he was, until they got him home.

"That was when the new owners saw what the little boy never had seen. Billy kicked, bit, and bucked. He chewed on his stall door, kicked his manger off the stall wall, and even butted the family dog."

Mrs. Reg stopped talking. That was the way her stories usually seemed to end—right in the middle. That was one of the other strange things about Mrs. Reg's stories. Carole stood up, ready to leave and figure out exactly what Mrs. Reg thought she was saying. Lisa wasn't ready to give up, though.

"So what happened?" she asked.

Mrs. Reg looked puzzled, as if she didn't understand why anybody would be asking a question about what she'd said. She shrugged. "Well, the little girl wanted to retrain Billy, but her parents sued, of course," she said. "And they won."

She picked up her phone book, checked a number in it, and then lifted the phone from its cradle to make a call. The story was definitely over now. It was time to leave.

"ISN'T IT HEAVENLY to be able to sleep so late?" Stevie said, stretching and yawning.

"It's not late," said Carole. "It's seven-thirty."

"Yeah, but every day this week by this time, we've already been up for an hour and a half and at the stable for an hour," Lisa reminded her.

Carole stretched and yawned, too. "I feel soooooo lazy!" she declared.

"That's what Saturdays are for," said Stevie.

"Right—well, we'd better get moving or we'll be late for Horse Wise," Lisa said. Horse Wise was the name of their Pony Club, and it met every Saturday at Pine Hollow. Today was going to be an unmounted meeting; after that they usually had a riding class. Since Ellen and Lucy were at the stable that weekend, nobody was sure what was on the agenda, but the girls knew it would be something about horses, and that was good enough to get them up and out of bed.

Forty-five minutes later, they were walking over to Pine Hollow, each carrying a brown bag with a sandwich, some cookies, and some fruit for lunch. One of the wonderful things about Saturdays was that it meant being at the stable and around horses almost all day.

Today's meeting turned out to be mostly about competitive riding. Lucy and Ellen were there with Max to talk about their experiences. Lucy talked about the precision required to be successful in dressage competitions, and Ellen spoke about how much she and Blue loved to jump together.

"I know this sounds weird, but when we're really working right together," Ellen said, "it's hard for me to tell where I end and where my horse begins. People say that a horse and rider look like one when it's going well, but I can tell you that it doesn't just look that way, it feels that way, too."

Lucy nodded. "It may even be truer in dressage," she said.

"Maybe," said Ellen. "But maybe it's true for you in dressage and true for me in jumping."

"I guess," Lucy said.

Once again Stevie felt the ever so slight edge of competition between the girls and understood that perhaps it was one of the things that made each so good at her own specialty. And then Stevie's eyes moved over to the mothers. Mrs. Walker and Mrs. Hatfield were standing near each other at the side of the schooling ring. Mrs. Hatfield was staring intently at her own daughter, her lips in a stern, straight line. Mrs. Walker was glaring at Lucy, barely able to hide her contempt. It was a stark contrast to the relatively friendly manner between the girls.

It made Stevie, and everybody else who noticed, quite uncomfortable, and nobody was really disappointed when Max adjourned the meeting early. He also canceled their riding class, explaining that he had to work with Lucy and Ellen. Red would conduct a flat class for any beginner students who wanted to participate.

Lisa, Stevie, and Carole had another idea. They'd had a lot of lessons that week, and they were good and ready for a nice trail ride. They'd bring their sandwiches and have a horseback picnic—something they didn't have anywhere near enough opportunities to do. In fact, any one of them would have acknowledged that if they'd been able to do it every single day, it wouldn't have seemed like enough opportunities.

"Meet you by the good-luck horseshoe in ten minutes," Stevie said. She didn't have to explain.

Carole was tightening Starlight's girth when Frieda appeared. Carole was a little surprised to see her. She hadn't realized Frieda was around, and with both Max and Red busy with teaching duties, Frieda wouldn't be able to have a lesson.

"Are you taking the class?" Frieda asked.

"Uh, no," Carole said. "It's for beginners—not that I can't always use work on my basics, I mean. But Lisa, Stevie, and I are going on a trail ride."

"Trails? You mean not just in a circle?" Frieda asked, a smile coming across her face.

"In the woods," Carole said.

Frieda hesitated. "Um, it sounds so wonderful," she began. "Would it be okay if I came along? I mean, would Max and Mrs. Reg let me?"

It wasn't what Carole had in mind, but Frieda seemed so excited by the idea that she hated to disappoint her. Also, the woman had taken so many lessons over the last week or so that she was surely ready for a bit more fun.

"You can ask," Carole said. "We're taking sandwiches for a picnic, too."

"Great!" said Frieda. "I brought my lunch along. I even have extra brownies. Would you like some?"

"Let's go talk to Mrs. Reg," Carole said.

It didn't take long. Mrs. Reg said she was sure Frieda was ready for a trail ride and assured Frieda that the trio of girls would look after her.

"And teach me, too," said Frieda.

"Well, they'll teach you some things," said Mrs. Reg wryly. "But I'm not sure I want you to learn *everything* from them. . . ."

"We'll be good," Carole promised.

"Okay, then," Mrs. Reg agreed. "I think Frieda should ride Patch."

"Just what I was going to suggest," Carole said.

It took more than the ten minutes Stevie had challenged them too, but Carole was sure her friends would be as flattered by Mrs. Reg's confidence as she was and that they'd enjoy Frieda's company. Patch was as familiar with the trails as their own horses were. Nothing could go wrong.

It felt a little odd to all three of the girls to have an adult along on the ride—especially one who had so much to learn from them.

"Make sure you keep your heels down," Lisa said.

"And in," Stevie added.

"If your toes are pointed to the ground, it messes up your balance and control," Carole explained.

Frieda followed their instructions.

Carole also helped her adjust the reins so that they weren't flapping around.

"See, if you don't have them tighter, then when you go to give the horse a signal, you're going to end up yanking them back up to your shoulders. You should be able to give a signal by moving your fingers ever so slightly."

"Like this?"

Carole looked. Frieda had the reins so short that poor Patch's head was practically pinned to his neck.

"No, looser," Carole said. Frieda let the reins out until Carole told her to stop. "Good," Carole said, wondering quickly how someone could have forgotten as much as Frieda apparently had since her last lesson. She'd looked good in the ring on Thursday. Carole was beginning to doubt Mrs. Reg's judgment.

But then Frieda seemed to have gotten the idea and didn't need a lot more correcting. Pretty soon everybody relaxed and began talking. The girls told Frieda some of what they'd learned at the meeting that morning.

"You wouldn't believe all the equipment you have to take to a show!" Lisa said, and began enumerating.

"It's really a big deal," Stevie agreed.

"And all the beautiful tack!" said Carole.

"And all the beautiful clothes!" said Lisa.

"The field is open here—can we trot now?" asked Stevie.

"Definitely," Carole said. She signaled Starlight to trot and began posting to his smooth two-beated gait. Lisa and Stevie did the same. Frieda, Carole was pleased to see, followed right along. At least she remembered how to post!

"Very good," Carole said when they slowed down again.

"It's because you're such good instructors," said Frieda. Carole smiled.

Stevie led the group through the woods, up the curvy trail that cut along the side of the gently sloping hill through an open meadow. It was a well-known route—the girls' favorite. They knew where they were going, and Stevie found herself thinking about how nice it would be to share their favorite trail ride and picnic spot with Frieda. If Frieda was going to learn about trail riding from them, she might as well learn about the best kind of trail riding.

There it was, up ahead on the right. Stevie barely had to give Belle a signal. Belle knew where they were going, too. She turned into the clearing and stopped automatically in the spot where the girls always secured their horses when they visited the creek.

They all dismounted. Carole showed Frieda how to clip on a lead rope and secure Patch to a tree branch.

"Unless it's an emergency, you never use the reins to tie a horse," Carole explained. "It's bad for the leather and can make the bit very uncomfortable."

"She's a natural teacher," Frieda told Lisa and Stevie.

"Just try to stop her!" Stevie teased. "Now, where's the grub?"

Lisa handed her the backpack with their lunches in it.

The four of them headed for the rock the girls knew so well, shedding their boots and socks as they walked.

By the time all four of them had their feet dangling in the

water, Stevie had doled out the lunches, hefting Frieda's brownie-filled one expectantly.

"Are there a lot of paths around here?" Frieda asked.

"You bet," said Stevie. "They're all over the place. This is just our favorite."

"There's one through the piney woods," said Lisa. "It smells wonderful on a summer day."

"And there's the crooked trail," said Carole. "It goes on the other side of the hill—we could have taken it at the split by the big rock, but it twists so much that it's almost no fun."

"Are there others?"

"Lots," Stevie assured her. "Most of them eventually circle back to Pine Hollow."

"But not all, right?"

"No, there's the Rocky Trail. That ends up down by the highway. We never go on it, though, because you have to double back—and it's dangerous, anyway. People get lost on it."

"But doesn't everybody know the trails?"

"Not everybody rides them as much as we do," Carole explained.

"And the dummies who don't ride often sometimes forget to pick up a map."

"There are maps?"

"In Mrs. Reg's office," Carole said.

"Have you got a map?"

"Not with us, but don't worry," said Stevie. "You're with us and we know exactly where we are, how we got here, and how we're going back."

"I know that," said Frieda. "I was just curious."

"Well, ask Mrs. Reg for a map when we get back. She's got stacks of them."

"I will," said Frieda. "But I was thinking about that president's daughter. Like, what if you got lost when you were riding out here with her?"

"I don't think that's going to happen," said Carole. "We were talking about it last night, and none of us can think of a reason in the world to take anything but our favorite trail when we're riding with Karya."

"And besides, with all those men in black following our every move, I think it would be impossible for us to get lost even on our least favorite trail. There will probably be bloodhounds sniffing all over the place," Lisa joked.

"Sounds complicated," said Frieda.

"It is for them," Stevie agreed. "They have to plan all kinds of things to make sure we know where we are."

"And besides, they've checked everything out already," Lisa said. "In fact, I think they were doing background checks on all the horses."

"Like they're going to find out about Belle's criminal record?"

"Better hers than yours!" Lisa teased.

"I don't think they're worried about criminals," said Carole. "My dad was telling me that someone really has threatened to kidnap Karya."

"Don't politicians get that kind of threat sometimes?" Lisa asked.

"Definitely," said Stevie. "And the security guys have to take it seriously. See, Karya's father was elected, but there are

still people who wish he hadn't been. And I learned something else." She paused for effect. "I was doing some research
on the Internet and I found the reason Karya speaks such
wonderful English. Her mother is American. She was born in
Virginia, really near Willow Creek, and her parents still live
there. Karya's actually spent a lot of time here and learned
English when she was really little. Not everybody in the ADR
thinks that's a wonderful thing. It's not that it's bad, just that
it's . . . controversial."

"Oh," said Lisa. "That explains a lot."

"All the more reason for those men in black to be super-
careful."

"It's going to be wild around Pine Hollow on Thursday,
isn't it?" asked Frieda.

"In a way," Lisa said.

"What do you mean by that?" Frieda asked.

"Well, everything to do with Karya and us is going to be
wild. Metal detectors, lie detectors, spy detectors—you know,
the usual. But as for anything else, well, I expect that somebody would be able to walk off with the Regnery family silver
as long as they weren't armed and didn't have a criminal
record!"

"Well, I'll just have to look after the silver, then," Frieda
said.

"I'm sure Max will be grateful," Lisa teased.

"Uh-oh," Stevie said, looking upward. "Where did the
sun go?"

"What sun?" Lisa asked, looking up as well.

There, above them, a wide swath of dark clouds was suddenly gathering.

"I think our lovely day is coming to a wet end," Stevie said, standing up.

Everybody else took her cue. They pulled on their socks and boots, collected the remains of their lunches, and stowed them in Lisa's backpack.

"We'd better hurry," Carole said, urging Frieda to keep up with them.

"So, we get a little wet," Frieda said.

"More than that," said Carole. "I've seen some lightning in the distance. We want to be safely in the barn before there's any lightning. It's dangerous in the woods, as you know, and even more dangerous out in an open field, and we have to cross several fields before we get to the barn. There isn't any time to waste."

As if to punctuate her remark, a big gust of wind blew through the clearing, carrying the last of the picnic papers with it. Carole chased the paper down and then hurried to where Starlight was waiting patiently.

The riders mounted up and turned to the trail that had brought them.

"There's another way to go back," Lisa explained to Frieda. "But it's longer. We really have to get back to the stable as fast as possible."

Stevie led the way back as she had the way out, getting Belle to trot whenever the ground was clear enough for trotting to be safe. They could all hear the loud gong ringing at Pine Hollow. The gong was kept there to call riders back when the weather was turning bad. This was no time to dally.

The first streak of lightning startled Starlight. Carole tightened up on her reins to let the horse know that she was in

62

charge and everything was going to be fine. She glanced over at Frieda and was glad to see that the woman had learned her lesson earlier. Her reins had exactly the right tautness, and she held them in perfect form. In fact, Carole was pleased to see that she was using her fingers on the reins in the same way Carole just had.

And then came the thunder. What Frieda didn't know, and what the girls hadn't prepared her for, was that sudden loud noises sometimes frightened Patch. The boom of thunder that followed that first streak of lightning qualified as a sudden loud noise. Patch bolted

He left the trail, heading right down a hillside, around a rock, through some bushes, and out of sight before any of the other riders had a chance to react.

Lisa and Stevie were ahead of Carole and Frieda and didn't realize what had happened until Carole called them.

"We've got to help Frieda!" she cried.

Lisa and Stevie understood at once.

They all followed Carole. The good news was that they were not far from the field, and they soon realized that Patch had run for the freedom of the field. He'd taken off at a gallop and would keep going until he wasn't afraid anymore. That could be fifteen seconds or fifteen minutes, and if there was another boom of thunder—well, there was no telling. An experienced rider would know how to calm him down. Frieda, so recently riding with toes in, heels up, and reins flapping, hardly qualified as an experienced rider.

The girls rode their horses as fast as they could go to the edge of the woods until they spotted Frieda and Patch in the field and then galloped to catch up to them.

Carole was thinking about how they might circle around and cut Patch off. Stevie was wishing she had a lasso with her. Lisa was running through her first-aid basics, trying to anticipate the necessary steps to help someone who'd been thrown from a horse. None of that was necessary.

Frieda drew Patch to a stop and held him steady, using a tight rein and a firm grip with her legs around his belly. Patch's ears flicked nervously, but he obeyed and was completely still by the time the rescuers arrived.

"Wow!" Carole said, truly impressed that Frieda had been able to halt Patch so quickly.

"You might have told me what thunder does to this horse," Frieda said, but there was a small smile on her face. She was fine.

"We didn't want to have to," said Stevie. "We just wanted to get back."

"Well, then, let's get back," said Frieda. "And hope there's no more thunder on the way."

"If you see lightning, you just have to hold the reins extra tight—like you're doing—to calm him before the thunder," said Lisa.

"You were really great!" said Carole. "I would never believe you were just a beginner who didn't know what to do with her heels an hour ago!"

"Good instruction," Frieda said. "From you girls, it's the best."

"That must be it," Carole said proudly. Her friends felt good about their teaching, too.

And the better news was that there was no more thunder and lightning before they got back to the stable.

BY THURSDAY AFTERNOON, Lisa, Stevie, and Carole were all too excited about Karya's impending visit even to notice that they were still tired from their morning session with Polaris and Blue. Their fatigue was forgotten in the flurry of preparations for the visit from the First Daughter of the ADR.

The girls had no trouble getting excused from school early, though, true to Stevie's prediction, she was expected to write a four-page essay on some aspect of the ADR. She said she'd probably write about horseback riding in the republic.

Colonel Hanson picked up all three girls at their schools to bring them to Pine Hollow. He didn't intend to miss any of the excitement—and he wasn't the only one. Stevie wasn't in the least surprised to find that Veronica diAngelo really didn't have the orthodontist appointment she'd used as an excuse to cut school. What she had was a bad case of the envies. She was at Pine Hollow, waiting, when The Saddle Club arrived.

Veronica was not alone. There was no sign of Karya yet when the girls and Colonel Hanson piled out of the car, but there were plenty of signs that she was coming.

"The place is swarming with men in black," said Stevie.

"Only they're not in black anymore," Lisa observed. Stevie nodded; what Lisa had said was true. The security forces were making a noble, but futile, attempt to blend in with the regulars at Pine Hollow and had all donned varieties of riding outfits. One was dressed in high boots and old-fashioned britches, the cotton kind with the balloon thighs, and carried a riding crop. He looked more like a movie director from the 1940s than a contemporary rider. A few of them had decided to go Western, and one even had a fringed shirt that looked like something out of a Roy Rogers movie, with a neckerchief to match. A few were wearing riding helmets. The overall effect was that there was a costume party going on.

"Look at that," Carole said, pointing to one man who was wearing jeans and shiny black dress shoes. His chin was almost touching his collarbone, and he appeared to be talking to a black spot on his collar.

"Miniature walkie-talkies," Colonel Hanson commented. Even without their suits, they still had to be electronically connected.

Two of the men were pacing the driveway and grounds of Pine Hollow with metal detectors. Another pair had bloodhounds on leashes that were sniffing at every bush and around all the corners of the buildings—until they came across a couple of Pine Hollow's resident cats, which took exception to their sniffing. There was a hullabaloo of barking and cat yowling until the security guards pulled the bloodhounds away from the cats and Mrs. Reg shooed the cats back into the stable.

"This place will never be the same," Carole said, shaking her head sadly.

"It'll be back to normal tomorrow, just you wait," said Lisa. "Maybe even tonight when all these characters go back to the city."

"Well, it'll never *seem* the same, anyway," Carole said. Her friends agreed.

As they approached the stable, the secretary, Alek, stepped toward them from the doorway.

"Names?" he asked. The girls thought he should have recognized them, but they decided not to make a fuss. They told him their names. So did Colonel Hanson. Alek made a great show of checking the information against the sheet of paper on his clipboard, whispered a password to each of them—it was *Pegasus*—and then allowed them to enter the part of the stable blocked off, as he explained, for the exclusive use of Karya and other authorized personnel.

Veronica diAngelo was right behind them.

"Name?" Alek asked.

"Veronica diAngelo," she told him.

The Saddle Club paused to watch.

Alek scanned his clipboard.

"You are not on the list," he said.

"But I ride here. I keep my horse here," she said.

"Then you can go in the other door with the other riders," Alek told her.

"This is the door I always use," she said. Stevie could barely contain her smile. It wasn't often that she had the opportunity to see someone go toe to toe with Veronica di-Angelo—especially when she knew Veronica would lose!

"Not today, if you please," said Alek quite politely.

"I don't please," Veronica snapped back. "Let me in."

"You are not on the list," Alek repeated firmly. "I cannot let you in here."

Veronica took a deep breath, rose to her full height, and posed the ultimate question: "Do you know who I am?"

Alek shook his head. "No, I do not," he said. "And that is the point. You are not on the list. And that is the reason I have to ask you to use the other entrance."

Veronica had no other comeback. Utterly deflated, she headed for the horses' entrance to the stable and let herself in. She might have been effectively banned from meeting with Karya, but she was not going to let some foreigner with a clipboard know how deeply she'd been hurt. The Saddle Club ducked into the stable and watched, amazed, as Veronica collected her own tack, tacked Danny up by herself because Red was too busy grooming Barq for Karya, and rode out of the stable by herself. Pine Hollow had rules about buddy system riding, but nobody was stopping Veronica today.

"At least she's not taking the Regnery family silver," Stevie joked to her friends.

"At least she's not going to bother us anymore," said Lisa.

"Or get in the way of Karya's ride," Carole added.

The girls went on into the dressing area, which had been swept cleaner than they'd ever seen it. And the nicest part was that there were no security men in there because today it was a "girls only" zone. It took only a few minutes for the girls to change, after which they met up with Colonel Hanson and Max in the tack room.

There were others in there, too: a small cluster of security men using metal detectors, which were beeping like crazy.

"Of course they're beeping," Carole said. "The place is full of metal. These guys are nuts!" she declared.

"Well, perhaps looking for metal in a tack room is a little foolhardy," Colonel Hanson conceded. "But they've got a job to do. This young lady is the daughter of an important and controversial man, and there's no doubt that she is at risk wherever she is, even though we don't usually think of Pine Hollow as a hotbed of terrorism. You girls need to respect the fact that these fellows are just doing their jobs."

"Well, they're doing them pretty weirdly," Stevie said, glancing at one man who was scanning Starlight with a metal detector. Starlight's shoes set the machine to beeping. Carole went over to explain about horses' metal shoes and to calm the man down. He might know a lot about personal security, but he didn't know the first thing about horses. Stevie thought Carole was probably exactly the right person to straighten him out on that subject and suspected that before they were done, he'd have learned a *whole* lot about horses. Stevie almost felt sorry for the man as she heard Carole launching into a history of horseshoes.

While Carole finished up her lecture on horse hoof care, Lisa and Stevie went to check on Polaris and Blue, who were getting the afternoon off. It didn't surprise the girls to see that neither horse seemed the least bit flustered by the flurry of activity at the stable.

"They're used to being in the middle of madhouses, aren't they?" Lisa asked.

"I guess they are," Stevie said. "It can be pretty wild at a horse show. This pair is just taking it in stride."

"Well, they're doing better than anyone else here," Lisa said. "I can't believe what's going on."

"I wonder if it's always like this around Karya," Stevie said. "At first I envied the fact that she never had to muck out a stall, but if she's always got this many people looking after her, well, I think I might feel sorry for her."

"It must be calmer in her own home," Lisa reasoned. "I mean, like they've got a gate or something so the family can just be together, right?"

"Maybe, but I bet every time they look out the window, there are men in black to remind them of the dangers outside."

"Weird," said Lisa.

"Makes me think that living with my three brothers isn't the worst thing in the world," said Stevie.

"Well, let's go rescue that guy from Carole's forty-five-minute lecture on hooves and see if Red's finished with Barq and then wait for Karya," Lisa said.

The security man seemed relieved when Lisa and Stevie called Carole away from him, although she was annoyed to be interrupted in the middle of an explanation of egg-bar shoes. Red was, indeed, finished grooming Barq, whose chestnut coat gleamed from his attentions. However, the girls did find a security guard there as well, demanding an explanation as to why they had not been informed that this was the horse selected for Karya.

"We have no information on his background whatsoever!" the man declared explosively. "What if he is not satisfactory to Ms. Nazeem?"

Carole interrupted the tirade. "Let me assure you that she will be allowed to choose whatever horse she wants. We thought she'd like this one because he's a fine horse and an Arabian. It seemed like a good choice to us, but the ultimate choice is hers."

The man looked at Carole. Then he looked at Red, who nodded agreement. Then he left.

"Weird," Stevie said, echoing Lisa's earlier remark. "You'd think these men had never seen a horse before."

"They definitely haven't," Carole said. "That other guy—with the metal detector—didn't know the first thing about horseshoes!"

"He does now!" Lisa teased.

"You bet," Carole agreed.

"Come on. Let's go wait for our guest," Stevie said, looking at her watch. "It's almost two-fourteen."

The three girls trooped out to the parking area, delivering their password on the way out, though Alek told them they needed it only to get back in again, and settled onto the top rail of the paddock fence to await the diplomatic cavalcade they were sure would accompany Karya Nazeem to Pine Hollow.

Eight cars went by, but none of them had flags and none of them was escorted by motorcycles or police vehicles.

Someone rode by on a bicycle. Definitely not Karya.

A dented station wagon came along the road. It slowed down at the Pine Hollow entrance, passed it, stopped, and

71

then backed up. There was a woman behind the wheel, and a girl sat in the seat beside her. A man sat in the back. The station wagon had Virginia license plates.

"Must be some new rider," Lisa said, since none of them recognized the car or the girl.

"No, it's Karya," Stevie said unexpectedly. The way she knew was that suddenly all the men in black—no matter what colors they were actually wearing—began to swarm around the driveway, lining up to protect the passenger who would emerge from the car.

A girl about their own age, wearing jeans and a sweatshirt, climbed out. She reached back in for a bag that must contain riding clothes and boots.

"I'll see you later, Mom," she said.

"Call me at Grandma's when I should come pick you up," said the mother.

"I will—or someone else will," the girl said lightly, glancing at the phalanx of guardians around her. She closed the car door and then looked around while her mother backed the car out of the driveway. The girl's eyes lit on The Saddle Club, perched on the fence.

"Carole Hanson?" she called

Carole nodded.

"I'm Karya!" The girl waved.

8

As soon as the words were spoken, and before Carole even had a chance to wave back, the security men swarmed, enclosing The Saddle Club and Karya in a tight circle.

"This is weird," said Stevie. "Do I keep saying that?"

Lisa nodded. "It makes me feel really safe," joked Lisa, though she knew she and her friends all felt the same way. The presence of so many men trying to make them safe only served to make them feel endangered, totally aware of some new kind of vulnerability.

Within the circle, introductions were made quickly.

For all the fanfare that had attended her arrival, it seemed ironic that Karya so immediately put all three girls at total ease and made each one of them understand that they liked this girl who came with so many trappings.

"I'm so glad to be here!" Karya said, reaching out to hug her new friends. They were pleased to hug her back.

"You really want to muck out a stall?" Lisa asked her.

"Two!" Karya declared. "At home they never let me do anything!"

"We'll let you," Stevie promised. "In fact, we might even invite you back."

Karya laughed. "Let's get someplace a little quieter," she said. She looked around at the circle of men who enclosed them. None of the security men was making a sound, so the girls knew that Karya didn't mean quiet in the sense of noiseless. She just meant private.

"How about the dressing room?" Carole suggested.

"Much quieter," Karya agreed. The girls showed her the way.

They knew the guards were standing outside the dressing area, but inside, it was just the four of them. Karya took her riding clothes out of the bag and slipped into them quickly. There were no royal patches, presidential seals, or flags on her shirt. They were just riding clothes, very much like the ones The Saddle Club were wearing.

"Whew," Stevie said when Karya had changed. "I was a little worried you'd be dressed like the security guys."

Karya laughed. "Aren't they a hoot? All they know about riding they've learned from American cowboy movies. They blend right in here, don't they?"

"Yes, like a dozen sore thumbs," Lisa said, nodding. "Have you got them around all the time? I mean, they've been nice enough, but . . ."

Karya sat on one of the benches to explain. "Well, my father kind of insists on it," she said. "He got elected, and most of the people who voted for him really like him. Unfortunately, some of the people who didn't vote for him really hate him. They've threatened him and they've threatened me. They haven't threatened my mother, which is why she gets away with one guard—he was in the back seat. When I'm not with one of them, I need to have several. I think the collection they've assembled for our ride is more than usual, but my father wanted it."

"You mean they're just doing their jobs?" Carole asked.

"I guess that's a good way to put it," said Karya.

"They sort of give me the willies," said Lisa. "I was thinking about it when you got here. If it takes this many men to be sure you're safe, then you must be very unsafe."

"It's not really like that," said Karya. "And besides, after a while, you'll find you can ignore them."

"In those getups?" Stevie asked.

"It's not any easier when they're all wearing those subtle shiny black suits and bug-eyed sunglasses, is it?" Karya countered.

Stevie shrugged, laughing. "No, I guess not."

"And besides, they won't always be with us," said Karya.

"They'll let us ride alone?" Carole asked.

"Well, maybe not exactly *let* us . . . ," Karya said suggestively.

"I knew I was going to like you," Stevie said.

The curtain that hid the dressing area was pulled back, and Mrs. Reg came in. She introduced herself to Karya and then turned to The Saddle Club.

"I heard some talk about mucking out stalls," she began. "I think it's a fine idea, but I hardly see how any of that is going to get done as long as you all are sitting in here talking up a storm."

Karya stood up and saluted sharply. "Take me to the nearest pitchfork!"

Mrs. Reg smiled broadly and then glanced at Stevie, Lisa, and Carole. "You three could learn a thing or two from this nice girl," she teased.

"See what we have to put up with?" Carole asked.

"And you love every minute of it, don't you?" asked Karya.

"Yeah, but don't let Mrs. Reg know that," said Lisa in a stage whisper. Mrs. Reg ignored her.

The girls proceeded to the dirty stalls that had been saved for Karya.

There were three stalls to muck out, and then Nickel needed a grooming. It turned out that Karya was almost as good at picking out hooves as Stevie was, though Stevie was able to give her a couple of pointers.

"Some people think it's strength," Stevie said. "But it's not at all. It's the angle and leverage. It's really—"

"All in the wrist?" Karya said, imitating Stevie's motion.

"Yep," Stevie agreed, admiring the way the clods of dirt and the small clump of gravel flew out of Nickel's hoof under Karya's now expert wrist action.

Once Nickel's hooves were clean, Karya picked up a brush and began grooming the pony vigorously. He loved the attention, and it was clear Karya was enjoying herself.

A single guard—the one dressed in the fringed shirt—stood nearby. Stevie suspected that was just in case one of the horses pulled a gun on the girls. The guard had his back to the foursome. Stevie got an idea. Carole and Lisa knew it from the look on her face. Karya, too, knew a mischievous grin when she saw one.

Stevie put her finger to her lips. They all set down their grooming tools, tiptoed down the aisle, and sneaked into Penny's stall, two doors down. They crouched down so that they could see through the cracks in the board. They waited.

Eventually Stevie had to toss a small handful of feed pellets at Nickel so that he would make a sound that the guard would respond to. Nickel snorted. The guard turned.

Even through the cracks in Penny's stall wall, they could see the man's face turn pale. His charge had disappeared! Instantly he began running down the aisle, poking at a bale of hay, picking up a pile of leathers.

He paused, clearly frantic. Carole knew what was going through his mind. Either he had to find Karya himself or he had to admit to his colleagues that he'd let her get snatched out from under his nose. Then he stopped and looked again. There was no exit door behind him and there were only four stalls until the dead end of the hallway. He knew then that it was a joke and he called her name and spoke in a language The Saddle Club could not understand.

Karya stood up, a little sheepishly. Lisa, Carole, and Stevie joined her.

"It was just a joke," Stevie said.

"He knows that," said Karya. "Only he says it wasn't very funny and he promises we won't get away with it again."

"No, next time, we're going to have to be much cleverer," Stevie said. She noticed that Karya did not translate that for the agent. She just smiled.

The girls had completed their stable work, and it was time to finish the tour of the stable and then mount up for the best part of the afternoon.

"You've got to meet our championship visitors," Lisa said, leading the way around to the other side of the U-shaped stable.

"Blue and Polaris," Stevie added.

Carole explained why they were there; by the time they got to the stalls, Karya had the full story.

Frieda was standing by Polaris's stall when they got there. The girls were a little surprised to see her, though she often seemed to show up to watch them work with Polaris and Blue.

Carole introduced Karya to Frieda, who seemed surprised to see *them*.

"Aren't you going to be training this afternoon?" Frieda asked.

"No. This is the day we're going for a trail ride with Karya. Remember?"

"Oh, right. Is that why all those weird men are standing around?"

"Yes," Stevie told her. "But don't worry. As soon as we leave, they're all going to follow us so Max can give you a lesson in peace."

"No, I'm not having a lesson this afternoon. I just stopped by," Frieda said. "See you all later," she added. Then, before the girls could walk away, Frieda returned her attention to Polaris, rubbing his cheek and patting his neck.

"She's a little odd," said Karya.

"She just started riding," Carole said—as if that fact alone would explain anybody's odd behavior.

"She went for a trail ride with us last weekend," Lisa said.

"See?" Karya said, as if that proved something.

"What's so odd about that?" Stevie asked. "You're going for a trail ride with us today. We're good riders and good company and she really learned a lot from us. Lots of people want to ride with us—even some presidential daughters! Who knows who'll want to ride with us next week!"

"Let's stop all this talking and get to the important stuff," said Carole. Nobody asked what she meant.

Max and Red had tacked up all four horses while the girls had been doing the stable chores. Karya seemed a tiny bit disappointed that she hadn't been able to tack up her own horse, but Max promised her she could untack Barq when they got back. "And I suspect my mother will let you soap the saddle, too, if you want."

"It's a deal," Karya said, offering her hand.

The girls mounted their horses in the schooling ring and then walked them over to the doorway where the good-luck horseshoe was nailed. In turn, each girl touched the shoe.

"It's one of our oldest traditions here," said Stevie.

"See, nobody who has ever touched the horseshoe has been seriously hurt in a riding accident."

"Some people say it's because the shoe *is* good luck," Stevie told her.

"Personally, I think it's because it reminds us before every ride that riding can be dangerous and we have to ride safely," said Carole.

"Whatever," said Karya. "It sounds like it works."

Before they had a chance to leave, Alek came over to Karya with a few final words of instruction and, it seemed, a warning. He also handed her a walkie-talkie and waited patiently, his arms folded, until she clipped it to her belt. Then, and only then, were they finally allowed to be on their way.

They began walking their horses across the ring toward the gate to the paddock. Every ride began at a leisurely walk so that the horses had a chance to warm up. It also gave Stevie a chance to look around. As she and her friends moved toward the gate, the security agents spread out along the trail ahead. Stevie observed that one of them, standing in the middle of the field, held a pitchfork. In an effort to "blend in," the man had managed to stick out in the most bizarre manner. Well, she reminded herself, he was just doing his job.

Then she spotted a very large horse van rumbling along the road. "What's that?" she asked.

"Those are horses for the security men," Karya said.

"Max has horses they could use," said Carole.

"My father insisted," said Karya.

"So be it," said Lisa.

"Let's have some fun," said Stevie, her eyes once again twinkling in that manner that said trouble.

"No more hiding in stalls?" asked Karya.

"No, this time we're going to be much cleverer!" said Stevie.

"Let's do it!" Karya agreed.

THE GIRLS CONTINUED across the schooling ring at a sedate pace. Lisa dismounted, opened the gate to the paddock, and then, after everyone had passed through, closed it and latched it behind her before remounting and continuing toward the woods. As they walked and warmed their horses, they greeted the men who were stationed in the field along the path.

The men were very polite, nodding to each rider as she went by.

"Do you ride here often?" Karya asked, looking around at the field and the woods beyond.

"As often as possible," Carole told her. "We love our classes, flat and jumping; we always have a good time at our Pony Club meetings, mounted or unmounted. We love competing in shows, too. But there's nothing we like better than a good trail ride."

"And, as far as we're concerned, any trail ride is a good trail ride," said Lisa.

"Are there a lot of trails?"

"Dozens," Stevie said. "We usually go about the same route because we have a favorite place to go to."

"Are we going there?" asked Karya.

"Absolutely," said Carole. "That is—if you want to."

"I want to do it all," said Karya.

Stevie, in the lead, looked back to see if everyone was ready to pick up a trot. She could see that they were, but she could also see something else. "Look at them," she said, pointing back at the stable. The girls paused and looked back. What they saw was four tacked-up horses in the schooling ring and four riders trying to mount them.

The agents had obviously unloaded the horses and were getting ready to ride them, though the quickest glance revealed that two of them really didn't know what they were doing. One was even trying to get on from the wrong side.

Stevie smiled. This was going to be a piece of cake!

"Ready to trot?" she asked. They trotted.

It was easy to see how much Karya was enjoying herself. There was a big grin on her face and she moved perfectly on Barq, rising and sitting with his trot as if she'd been riding him all her life.

"An Arab, just for me?" she called forward to Stevie.

"Yes, we thought you'd like that," Stevie answered. "Plus, he's a really good horse."

"He sure is!" Karya agreed. Then she and the other girls all turned their attention to their goal—the woodlands that lay invitingly across the field.

The shade of the walk along the wooded pathway was as welcome when it came as the sunshine had been in the field.

"This is what I've been hoping for!" Karya said.

"And that's the way we feel about it every single week," Lisa confirmed. "There's an open area up ahead where we can canter, too."

"I'm ready!"

The girls rode on, chatting easily. It came as a pleasant surprise to each of them how naturally they seemed to get along—the three American girls and the Middle Eastern president's daughter—and it served to remind each of them how strong a bond horseback riding could form between people.

"We joke sometimes that we couldn't be more different," Lisa said, briefly describing the differences among the members of The Saddle Club to Karya. "But horses bring us together every time."

The walkie-talkie at Karya's hip buzzed. She rolled her eyes up to the sky. "They can't see me, and they worry," she said. Slightly annoyed, she unclipped the device and pushed a button. She talked into it. There was a response. She and Alek spoke back and forth a few times.

She clipped the walkie-talkie back on her belt. "He doesn't want us to canter," she said. "He tells me that they have trouble tracking me when we go that fast."

"We can trot," Carole said.

"We can canter," said Karya. Then she very carefully and very decisively turned off the walkie-talkie. And they cantered.

Before too long, Stevie was leading them off the main path and into the small clearing by the creek.

"This is beautiful!" said Karya.

"We knew you'd like it," Carole said, dismounting. She secured Starlight to a bush and then held Barq's bridle while Karya dismounted as well.

The girls led their guest over to the spot where they always took off their boots for the refreshing toe dunk. While they were removing their boots, they could hear horses going by on the main path. The riders spoke with one another, and there was no doubt that they were the agents, since they were speaking a language none of The Saddle Club recognized. The girls remained quiet, allowing the security men to pass.

"One . . . two . . . three . . ." There was a long pause. "Four," Carole said.

"All clear, then," said Karya.

The girls relaxed.

And then they heard another horse.

"Must be a really bad rider to be so far behind the bunch," Lisa observed.

"Who knows?" said Stevie.

"Who cares?" asked Karya. "We're here, and that's enough for me."

The girls settled in, feeling totally relaxed and alone for the first time.

"So what's it like being the daughter of a president?" Stevie asked.

"Sometimes it's a lot of fun," said Karya. "Everybody is really nice to me. I go to school in the capital, and I know my teachers give me better grades now that my father is president than they did when he was merely a member of the congress."

"That works for me!" Stevie said.

"I like that part, too, but then there are the times when I'm just not allowed to be myself—times I have to be places for show."

"The list of stuff Alek read to us sure sounded boring," said Carole

"And then there are times when I wish my teacher would tell me that I'm not doing a good job. It's a little hard when you can't trust people to be honest with you just because of who your father is."

"I never would have thought of that," said Carole. "I just felt sorry when you said you didn't get to take care of your own horse."

"And you were right to feel sorry. Most people laughed at me when they read that. I knew you really understood when I got your letter, and that's how I knew I just had to be here. And I was right! This is perfect!"

"Wait until we show you the rest of the woods!" Stevie said.

"Do you really think we ought to do this, Stevie?" Carole asked, unsure exactly how her father would feel if he ever found out about their trying to elude the security agents.

"Definitely," Stevie said.

"Absolutely," agreed Karya.

"Okay," said Lisa.

Carole sighed. "All right," she agreed.

"What did you have in mind?" Lisa asked Stevie.

"Well, I thought we'd take the Rocky Trail up to where it meets the Pine Trail and then back down into the valley across that big open stretch—where we can really canter—

and then back into the maple stand to where it comes out next to the highway. We could cross there, but I think we're better off doubling back across the creek before we get back to the pasture."

"But the Rocky Trail can be dangerous," Carole said.

"Not that part of it, and the mountain view is so beautiful from the top!" said Stevie. "And as long as we ride carefully and get back safely, there's no harm, is there? What's the worst that can happen—that Karya misses out on a ribbon-cutting ceremony at a hydroelectric plant model?"

"That's about it," said Karya, her eyes sparkling with delight.

"Then let's go."

The four girls pulled their boots back on and went back to their horses. The animals were ready for their drink at the creek; after their thirst had been satisfied, the riders remounted and took off across the creek in the opposite direction from the trail plan the girls had left with Max.

It didn't take long for the security agents to become concerned. They'd expected the riders to reappear along the path they'd left for the visit to the creek.

Pretty soon the girls could hear the men calling out to one another. Then they could hear the *buzz-click* of walkie-talkies flicking on and off all around them. And they could also hear some of the agents calling to Karya.

Karya had a big grin on her face. It was infectious, and the girls had to share her excitement at the game they were playing with the security agents. For a moment she clicked on her own walkie-talkie and listened to the furious buzz back and forth among the riders and the men on foot. She giggled at their chatter. Then she turned the walkie-talkie off again.

"Oh, this is wonderful!" she said. "Now show me this view of yours!"

"This way!" Stevie announced, waving them all forward.

ONCE AGAIN, Stevie was in the lead. She could feel the excitement of the chase welling in her chest. Around her, not more than several hundred yards away, agents of the ADR were searching for them, and she knew, deep in her heart, that they were not anywhere near as clever as she was. She could outfox the best of them. They were well equipped with electronic devices, but they didn't know the woods, and from what she'd seen, they didn't know much about horses or riding, either. This was going to be fun.

"Ms. Nazeem!" one man called out.

Stevie put her finger to her lips to remind them not to answer, but it wasn't necessary. Nobody had any intention of responding.

"Karya!" came another cry.

"This way!" Stevie whispered, pointing upward.

The girls followed.

The Rocky Trail was as treacherous in parts as any trail the girls had ever ridden. It was hilly and had twists, curves, and switchbacks. It also lived up to its name, which meant that it could be slippery for a horse's hooves.

It wasn't used often, and Max never bothered much about keeping it open. That meant that branches hung down low along the trail, and storms during the previous winter had laid a couple of trees across it. The girls proceeded slowly.

"You're going to love this," Stevie assured Karya.

"I already do," Karya said, ducking a big maple branch. "We have no woods like this at home. It's beautiful."

"Karya!" came another cry from deep in the forest. The man's voice yelled something else, too.

"What was that he said?" Lisa asked.

"He said I should, um, stop this nonsense right now. See, they're not worried, just annoyed with me."

"Are you going to get in trouble?" Lisa asked her.

"Only if they tell. And the only reason they'd tell is if we make a mistake."

"And we won't do that," said Stevie. "We know exactly what we're doing. Come on, there's a clearing up ahead where we can make some time at a canter."

Stevie focused her attention on the path, which she knew would become narrower and steeper before the clearing. The dappled sunlight laid patches of bright and dark on the forest floor, and all around, birds were chirping. The sounds intermingled with the cries of the agents and the occasional staticky crackle of a walkie-talkie. It was interesting how clearly sound carried through the forest.

And then she realized there was another sound. It wasn't

behind them or below them. It was up ahead and it was unmistakable. It was a horse.

"Someone else is on the trail," Stevie said to the riders behind her. Carole frowned. She hated the idea that one of the agents, who were so clearly inexperienced riders, might get onto this trail. The girls would end up rescuing him instead of the other way around.

"Nobody passed us, did they?" Lisa asked.

"No, and the only other way onto this trail is across the creek beyond the clearing," said Stevie.

"Five horses," Carole said, suddenly remembering and not liking what she recalled.

"What?" asked Karya.

"There were five horses," said Carole.

"No, the agents only had four horses," Karya said. "I'm sure of that. That's all the van holds."

"There were five horses on the trail," said Carole. "First four went by, and then, a few seconds later, another. There's someone else in the woods."

"On this trail?" Stevie asked.

"Obviously," said Lisa.

"But who?" Carole asked. "And why?"

"There's only one way to find out," said Stevie, giving Belle a little nudge that made her pick up her pace. The other horses followed obediently. As soon as the path leveled, Stevie began trotting. So did the other riders.

A fresh scattering of manure confirmed to Stevie that they were right—someone *was* ahead of them. Every ounce of logic she had (and while her friends often said she was totally lacking in it, Stevie knew better when it came to horses) told her it didn't make any sense. If one of the agents was trying to find them, why would he go along this obscure trail? And how could he not be aware that the girls were behind him? There was something very odd going on, and Stevie had every intention of getting to the bottom of it right away.

The woods opened up into a high meadow. It was time to canter. Stevie signaled Belle for the fast gait and the mare responded, eager for a chance to stretch her muscles in the open field. As they flew across the grassy expanse, Stevie pointed to the vista to their right.

"Beautiful! But let's hurry!" Karya responded. She was as much into the spirit of the chase as Stevie and her friends were.

"We really shouldn't go there," Carole said, looking at the trail before them where it entered the forest. "It's a dangerous trail. We can go back now. . . ."

"But who's riding ahead of us?" Stevie asked. "We need to find out."

"One of the security men could be in trouble," Lisa reasoned.

"It's an adventure!" said Karya. "Come on, girls!"

Carole sighed. Maybe her father would never find out. She nudged Starlight forward and followed Stevie, Karya, and Lisa into the woods, wondering what lay ahead.

As they entered the woods, it suddenly grew much darker. The dense greenery overhead nearly blocked out the sun. The horses were forced to slow to a walk, as the horse they were following had done.

And the trail rose again, too, twisting into a series of hairpin turns as it ascended the steep hillside. This was the steepest and most dangerous part of the whole Rocky Trail. And it was where they finally spotted their quarry.

"Hey! Who's there?" Stevie cried, gazing at the rider hurrying up the hill high above them.

The only answer the rider gave was to strike the horse with a riding crop. The willing horse flinched but responded, clambering up the treacherous hillside even faster.

"You're going too fast!" Carole cried. "You'll hurt the horse!"

Once again the rider struck the horse with the crop.

"That guy's nuts!" Stevie said.

"That guy's a girl," Karya said. "Or a woman, really."

"Who would do something like that?" Lisa asked.

"Someone who's nuts," Stevie said.

"That makes sense," Lisa agreed.

"No, it doesn't," said Carole. "It's dangerous."

"So who is it and why?" Stevie said.

"I don't know, but I know we'll find out," Carole said. All worries about herself and her friends fled from Carole's mind. There was no way she would allow any rider to put any horse in that much peril. "Stevie, isn't there another—"

"Yep! Come on, Karya—we're going to cut them off at the pass!"

At that moment they came to a Y in the path. The main fork of the path continued up the hill, following more switchbacks to the crest, where the wild rider had gone. The other, straighter segment of the trail actually went around the hill. It was a longer route but an easier way to get to the top, something an inexperienced rider unfamiliar with the trails and the terrain would not know.

"Karya and I will go this way. Lisa, you and Carole keep after her!" Stevie said.

The riders split up. Carole looked ahead anxiously, still wondering who on earth would ride the way that woman was riding. And then the horse came into an open area where the sunshine streamed into the woods, almost like a spotlight. It was impossible not to recognize the horse when it was highlighted that way.

"Polaris!" Carole said in a loud whisper.

"Frieda?" said Lisa.

It was. They recognized Frieda, the beginning rider who hadn't known to keep her heels down and toes in as recently as a week before. Now there was no doubt about it: The woman was riding like a champion. The only thing wrong with what she was doing was that the way she was riding, she was just about guaranteed to hurt the horse.

Carole called out to her as loudly as she could. "Frieda! It's us! It's me, Carole!" she yelled. "You can't go that fast. It's dangerous!"

In response, Frieda once again took the riding crop to Polaris's flank, and this time she whacked him viciously.

And then Carole knew one other thing: Frieda didn't care.

"We've got to stop her!" Carole said to Lisa. She didn't have to say it twice.

Without saying a word to each other, Carole and Lisa urged their horses up the hill.

"WHAT'S GOING ON?" Karya asked.

"I don't know," said Stevie as the two of them rode as fast

93

as they safely could along the trail. "But whatever it is, it isn't good."

"So, tell me what you do know."

"Well, I just realized who that horse and rider are—Polaris and Frieda."

"That's the woman we met, and she's riding one of the champion horses, right?" Karya asked.

"Right," said Stevie.

"So, what's wrong with that?"

"For one thing, it's not her horse. For another, the last we knew, she was a beginning rider, and she's got that valuable horse riding on a dangerous trail at a pace that is sure to get at least one of them, probably the horse, hurt really badly."

"Why would she do that?"

And that was the question to which Stevie needed an answer. She shook her head. Nothing was making any sense. All she knew was that there wasn't any time to waste.

"We could really use some help here!" she said, thinking out loud.

"I think I can do something about that!" said Karya, reaching for her belt.

Stevie hit herself on the forehead. Why hadn't she thought of that? They could bring the full force of the security agents of the ADR to their aid instantly!

Still moving uphill at a rapid clip, Karya switched on her walkie-talkie. She was instantly inundated with a barrage of clicks, buzzes, and whistles, followed by several angry and insistent voices.

She spoke into the machine. Someone answered her. She

issued rapid-fire instructions in a language that meant nothing to Stevie, and then she looked puzzled as she held the
device to her ear. "Huh?" she said.

She spoke again, nodded, then hooked the transmitter
back onto her belt so that she could listen for progress while
keeping both hands on Barq's reins.

"They tell me they've already got the helicopters de-
ployed," she said after a moment.

"Won't do much good in these thick woods," said Stevie.

"Well, it might scare that woman, Frieda."

"Maybe," said Stevie. "But I wish I knew what was going
on."

"Well, why would she ride that other girl's horse?"

"I have no idea—unless she was trying to steal it . . . Oh,
my," Stevie said, a light breaking over her.

"What?"

Before Stevie could answer, Karya's walkie-talkie buzzed.
Karya took it off her belt and responded into the mouthpiece.

While Karya spoke with the agent on the other end,
Stevie's mind raced. She wished both that she'd been smarter
to begin with and that she'd studied Arabic.

"What's going on?" she asked when Karya stopped talking.

"He said they are after the person who is chasing us."

"Nobody's chasing us. We're chasing someone!" said
Stevie.

"That's what I told him," Karya said. "And he said the
helicopters are getting closer."

"Not to us, they aren't," Stevie said, vaguely aware of the
distant sound of helicopters—still way too far in the distance

to be menacing anyone. "Come on, we'd better get a move on!" Stevie nudged Belle, who once again obediently responded and picked up her pace.

"Hurry, Belle, hurry!"

On the other side of the hill, Carole and Lisa were beginning to gain a bit on Polaris and Frieda. The horse was a dressage specialist, which meant that he could ride elegantly, but that didn't guarantee the kind of stamina needed for a mountain chase.

"Frieda, stop now!" Carole called fruitlessly.

"What's going on?" Lisa asked, utterly confused by the very strange turn of events.

"She's a spy," Carole said. "We thought she was just a student, but she's a spy!"

"How can she be spying on Karya when she's running ahead of us?" Lisa asked, following Carole as well as she could.

"Not Karya," said Carole.

"Who's she spying on, then?" Lisa asked.

"Polaris!" said Carole.

"What's Polaris got to do with spying?" asked Lisa.

"Later—I'll explain later," said Carole, carefully guiding Starlight along the final rocky ascent.

Lisa sighed. She'd figure it out later. For now, she just had to follow, and it wasn't easy. Prancer wasn't made for riding on this kind of terrain any more than Polaris was. She could get badly hurt, and Lisa didn't want to risk that.

Badly hurt. The phrase stuck in her mind. *Badly hurt.* That could happen to Polaris. There was only one person who would want Polaris badly hurt. There was only one person who hated Polaris and who would see it as a good thing if Polaris was put out of commission, either temporarily or permanently. It could only be Mrs. Walker.

Mrs. Walker hated Lucy Hatfield, hated Mrs. Hatfield, and hated Polaris, the only real competition her daughter had. The girls didn't hate each other, but the mothers did.

"She's spying for Mrs. Walker!" Lisa blurted out.

"That's what I said!" Carole retorted. "Now, pay attention. There's another patch of rocks ahead!"

Lisa paid attention.

"Where are you?" Karya spit into the walkie-talkie in Arabic. Even though she couldn't understand the language, Stevie knew exactly what Karya was saying, because she was also looking up at the sky, hoping to see a helicopter coming to their aid.

"No!" Karya called out. Annoyed, she stuck the walkie-talkie on her belt again.

"They keep telling me they're closing in and have the kidnapper in their sights, but there's no sign of them. I don't know what's going on and neither do they."

"Then we're just going to have to do this ourselves," said Stevie. She gave Belle one final kick and the horse sprang up the last ridge of the hillside, coming to a stop where the trail opened out into a small hilltop meadow.

Everyone was there.

Frieda was on Polaris, standing in the middle of the field. Carole and Lisa appeared out of the woods on the far side.

"You're a spy!" Lisa called out.

"I wouldn't put it that way," said Frieda. "Just helping a friend even the playing field for her daughter."

"By endangering a helpless animal?" Carole said.

"I wouldn't put it that way, either," said Frieda.

"Well, you were galloping along a rocky trail," Stevie said. "That's dangerous. You could have killed Polaris."

"I never intended to kill him," Frieda said. "I just wanted to borrow him for a few days. And I want to thank you three for all the help you gave me."

"Not like you needed our riding lessons," Carole said.

"Hardly," Frieda agreed. "Do you have any idea how hard it is to pretend to be a bad rider when you're not?"

"You nearly had us fooled," said Lisa.

"I had you *completely* fooled," Frieda responded.

She was right about that.

"Well, we've got *you* fooled now," said Stevie. "You can't get away from us. And we'll protect Polaris."

"I've already won," said Frieda. "Polaris picked up a stone way down at the bottom of the hill. He's good and lame by now. I don't have to borrow him. He'll never be able to perform in the show, and that's all we ever really wanted. And there's nothing you can do about it. If you tell someone, I just say I took Polaris out for a ride. So what? Okay, I didn't have the authority to do it, but they can't throw me in jail. What's Max going to do? Ban me from the stable? I don't plan on coming back anyway. And even if you do say anything, I'll be long gone by the time you get back to Pine Hollow. So thanks for all your help—I'd never have been able to do it without you. Good-bye."

With that, before anybody could stop her, Frieda slid down

out of Polaris's saddle and walked straight into the thick underbrush that surrounded the hilly meadow. The girls couldn't follow her on horseback and didn't want to. They wanted to look after Polaris.

Carole slid out of Starlight's saddle and walked over to where Polaris stood, favoring his right forefoot, confirming Frieda's assertion that he'd been lamed.

Stevie looked at the woods where Frieda had disappeared and explained to Karya what was going on.

"The highway's right down there, maybe a half a mile. I'm sure she's got a trailer and a truck waiting. She'll get away all right, but she won't get away with this."

"She won't get away, either," Karya corrected Stevie.

Once again she clicked on her walkie-talkie and spoke into it. She looked puzzled, glancing expectantly up at the sky.

When she was done talking, she told the girls that her agents swore they had the kidnapper surrounded.

"Kidnapper?" Lisa asked. "Frieda's a horsenapper."

"Well, they don't know that," said Karya. "But anyway, they assure me that nobody is escaping their—what's the word?—dragnet?"

"That's the word," said Stevie.

11

FRIEDA WAS GONE, but Polaris was safe. Their dash up the treacherous hill had paid off, as had Stevie's good memory of the paths, which had enabled them to surround Polaris and Frieda. Maybe Frieda had gotten away—just for now, if Karya's agents were doing their job—but the girls had Polaris.

Carole patted Polaris's neck reassuringly. The other girls joined her.

Polaris stood nearly motionless except for his chest, which heaved while he caught his breath from the exhausting chase up the mountain.

Carole picked up his reins and held him near the bit while she patted him. "It's okay, boy. We're here and we're going to look after you."

"We won't let anything else happen to you," said Stevie.

"We shouldn't have let this happen, either," said Lisa.

"We didn't *let* it happen," said Stevie.

"Of course we did," Lisa said. "In fact, we practically gave Frieda instructions on how to do it!"

"What do you mean?" Stevie asked.

"Don't you remember what she said? How she couldn't have done it without us? Well, we told her all about the trails, especially this one that leads out to the highway."

"I guess I did that," said Stevie.

"And then I told her she'd be able to steal the Regnery family silver today because everybody was going to be so busy looking after Karya."

"How were you to know that a nice lady like that was going to try to do something so evil?" Karya asked.

Carole looked over at her friends and provided the answer none of them had really wanted to think about. "Maybe just because a grown woman wanted to spend so much time with three girls? Shouldn't that have tipped us off instead of making us feel like we were these super teachers?"

"Maybe," Karya conceded.

Carole shook her head, annoyed at herself as much as her friends. But they weren't the ones who mattered now. The important thing was to see what needed to be done for Polaris.

Carole ran her hand down the horse's left foreleg. She'd learned long ago that when she expected trouble on one leg, she should check the other one first so that she'd have something to compare with. Polaris seemed to know what was coming. He didn't move. He didn't flinch.

Carole began again, this time sliding her hand down his right foreleg. Again the well-trained horse didn't move. Carole closed her eyes, imagining the left leg as she felt the right one. She sighed with relief. They felt exactly the same. There was no sign of swelling or heat. The only thing she noticed was that both of Polaris's legs were sweaty, as were the girls' own horses.

She picked up his right hoof and took a look.

"There it is," she said. The four heads clustered over the hoof. A stone was tightly lodged between the metal shoe and the frog of Polaris's foot.

"No wonder he's favoring it," Stevie said. "That's got to hurt."

"Not for long," said Lisa.

She reached into her back pocket and pulled out a hoof pick.

"You're always prepared for something like this?" Karya asked, surprised.

"Only when I'm traveling in the woods with the daughter of the president of a country I'd never heard of until two weeks ago!" Lisa said, laughing.

She handed the hoof pick over to Stevie, the acknowledged champion at dislodging stones.

Stevie looked at Karya. "Would you like to try?"

"No, you're much better at it than I am—plus, nobody ever gives me a chance to do it myself," Karya reminded them.

"Okay, here goes," said Stevie.

She held Polaris's foot securely between her knees and began working around the stone.

"It's always a good idea to get all the soft stuff out first," she said, as if this were a routine Pony Club demonstration. "That way you can be sure of what's easy and what's not."

102

Once the dirt was out, Stevie handed the hoof pick back to Lisa, then prodded very gently under the shoe with her finger to be sure she knew just where and how the stone was stuck. That way she could tell how much leverage she'd need and what angle would work to loosen it. It wasn't science; it was instinct, and it was something she really couldn't explain any better than that to anyone else.

When she was certain she knew what to do, she took the hoof pick in her hand again, thanked Polaris for being such a cooperative patient, and gave one swift and sure twist of the tool that brought a large round stone flying out of the horse's hoof.

"Ta-da!" Lisa announced, grinning.

Stevie didn't smile yet. She checked to make sure she'd gotten the whole stone and that there wasn't another one in there. Then she lowered the horse's hoof to the ground, never taking her eye off his leg. She stepped back and watched.

The girls held their breath. They needn't have bothered. As soon as he had all four feet on the ground, Polaris lowered his head, took three smooth steps forward, and began sniffing at the grass in the meadow. He took a small mouthful, ripped it off, and began munching. A few seconds later he looked curiously at the cluster of young riders who seemed to be staring at him, then took three more steps and another mouthful.

"I think he's okay!" Carole said.

Stevie picked up the stone she'd dislodged. It was smooth and round, and that was nothing but good news. A pointy stone could cause no end of trouble. A round stone might cause a bruise but was much less likely than a pointed one to damage the soft flesh.

Stevie gave Polaris another well-deserved pat and then took his bridle to lead him forward so that Carole could observe his walk with her keen eyes. No trouble. Stevie began jogging. Polaris trotted obediently. No problem.

"He's okay!" Carole pronounced.

"Will he be able to compete on Saturday?" Lisa asked.

"I think so, but only a vet can say for sure," Carole said. "And we'll have Judy check him out as soon as we get back."

"Hmmm. Get back," said Stevie. "I have the funniest feeling that getting back is going to be a mixed blessing."

"You mean, like, Max is going to be glad Polaris is okay and really angry that we took a different trail with our VIP guest whom the State Department of the United States of America asked us to look after?" said Lisa.

"Something like that," Stevie agreed.

"We can tell him we took a different trail to rescue Polaris," Karya suggested. "He'll never know that we didn't start following the horse until we were long gone off the right trail."

Lisa, Stevie, and Carole all looked at their "VIP guest." Nobody spoke for a moment.

"I knew we were going to like her," Lisa said.

"It's because she's just like us," said Stevie.

"It's amazing what a gulf of difference can be bridged by a common love of horses," said Carole.

She offered her hand for a high five, and the president's daughter responded reflexively. Lisa and Stevie joined in.

"High twenty!" Stevie declared.

"Now, let's get back," Lisa suggested reasonably.

Carole took Polaris's bridle and used it to lead him. She and her friends remounted and began what they knew was going to be a slow journey back down the hillside. Going up had been hard; going down was going to be harder.

They took the gentler slope, the one Stevie and Karya had followed up, even though it was a little longer. The horses seemed grateful for their consideration. Still, a good stretch of this trail, like the other one, consisted of slippery switchbacks, all of which were more treacherous going downward than they had been going upward.

As they rode, almost too tired to talk, Karya switched on her walkie-talkie again.

"What are they saying?" Lisa asked, noticing the puzzled look on Karya's face.

"Something about circling the kidnapper and having her in their sights from the helicopter," said Karya. "But I don't understand at all."

"No, it doesn't make sense," Stevie agreed. "Frieda went down the hill—and that's to the west, where there's a highway. You can even see the highway from parts of that meadow, but there's no helicopter there."

"She must have decided the highway wasn't a safe escape route," Lisa said. "She probably went around the hillside and tried to cut through the valley. The woods there come almost to the middle of the town—"

"Actually, really near the strip mall where TD's is," Stevie said. "Speaking of which, there's another tradition I think we may have to introduce you to—"

"Wait a minute—they're saying something else. . . ."

Karya put the walkie-talkie to her ear. The hilly countryside seemed to be interfering with transmission, and she wanted to be sure she heard clearly.

The girls all looked expectantly at her, waiting for the puzzled look on her face to clear up. It didn't. Eventually, though, she turned off the transmitter and clipped it back onto her belt.

"What's up?" Stevie asked. "What's going on?"

"They're circling around someone and are nearly ready to capture the person."

"Well, isn't that what we told them to do?" Stevie asked.

"No, this is someone on horseback," said Karya. "It doesn't make any sense that that woman, Frieda, would be on horseback."

"Oh, maybe she—no," said Stevie, shaking her head, too. "You're right. It doesn't make any sense."

"You mean, they're capturing someone and it isn't Frieda?" Carole asked.

"Sure looks that way," said Lisa.

Carole gulped, glad for a moment that the trail was steep right there and she had to move forward carefully, giving Starlight and Polaris all the guidance she could from Starlight's saddle. Fortunately, that was the final twist and the last steep section of the hill trail. Carole rode forward and paused, waiting for her friends to complete their downward journeys and join her.

The pause gave her a minute to think, and she didn't like what she was thinking. She and her friends had been laughing at the men in black, some dressed in foolish and inappropriate costumes. The girls had made a game of eluding their protective shield, giggling at how badly they rode. But maybe it wasn't so funny after all. Maybe something that involved a dozen bodyguards, a couple of helicopters, special costumes, special horses, thousands of dollars' worth of electronic equipment, and a special request from the State Department— maybe an operation like that was serious. Maybe they shouldn't have been making fun of it. Maybe there *was* danger.

Danger? In the woods around Pine Hollow? Terrorists? Kidnappers? How could that be? How was it possible that their beloved woods, their beloved hills and trails, could be harboring someone who intended evil—an even greater evil than hurting a horse? Was there someone in their woods who intended to hurt their new friend? Kidnap her, hold her for ransom, threaten her and her family?

The very idea horrified Carole, making her feel angry and invaded, and the fact that she and her friends had made a joke of the security men embarrassed her.

She kept these thoughts to herself until the other three riders caught up with her and they reached the clearing by the creek. The girls automatically turned into it and automatically dismounted, leading their horses to the fresh, cool water for a well-deserved drink.

Carole shared her thoughts then, and it turned out that Lisa and Stevie had been thinking the same things.

"We're going to have trouble fibbing to Max, or anyone, about trying to get away from the security guys when it turns out that there really is someone here in the woods who is trying to hurt you."

Lisa reached out and took Karya's hand. "Isn't it scary for you?" she asked.

"Of course it is," Karya said. "But it's always a little bit scary. I think I've gotten used to it, and then something like this happens and it reminds me that I can't get used to it. But I also know that I have a life to live, and my life is more important to me than anyone else. My goal is always to do the things I can do without putting myself or my family at any foolish risk. I knew if we got away from the security men it wouldn't matter, because they'd be able to tell pretty much where we were by the tracking device in the walkie-talkie."

"You mean they never didn't know where we were?" Stevie asked.

"They always knew approximately where we were, as long as I had the thing turned on."

"So then why didn't they come capture Frieda when we asked?" said Lisa.

"I think because they were tracking someone else," Karya said. "And that does frighten me a little bit. I've always thought I would be safer here in the United States than in many other places."

"I think we'd better get back," said Carole. "And I think you'd better leave that thing turned on."

"I suppose," said Karya, clicking on the walkie-talkie.

The girls remounted their horses and began the last leg of their journey, each unsure what they would find when they returned.

12

THEY WERE BARELY out of the clearing by the creek, approaching the point where the trail circled around the last hill before Pine Hollow, before they could tell that something important was definitely going on.

At first they could hear it only faintly, but when they rounded the hill, the sound became loud and then almost unbearable as a helicopter swept through the sky, back and forth over the open area where they often liked to canter their horses on their way to the creek.

Carole could feel herself tense up. She paused, waiting to make sure the other riders were close together on the trail. Starlight danced, startled by the loud sounds overhead. Polaris, true to his fine training and nerves of steel, simply did exactly what Carole told him as she tugged gently on his reins.

"Let's stay close together," Lisa said, echoing Carole's thoughts.

"I think they're right ahead of us," Karya said. She was listening both to the insistent thumping of the helicopter's blades and the static-filled conversations among the security men.

"Should we stay hidden?" Stevie asked.

"I don't think so," said Karya. "I think they should see that we're safe."

That made sense. Moving slowly and cautiously, Carole, Starlight, and Polaris proceeded toward the hullabaloo around the curve of the hill.

Pretty soon they could all hear voices—some calling out in Arabic, some speaking English.

"Don't move!"

"You are completely surrounded."

"You will not escape!" cried out one man in a very threatening tone.

The helicopter neared the ground, its noise now almost nearly intolerable. Carole could see it. She could also see some men dropping down out of it on lengths of rope that extended to the ground. The men were dressed in black coveralls, armed with automatic weapons, wearing helmets with heavy, rigid masks that she guessed must be bulletproof.

Carole proceeded even more slowly, the other riders clustering close behind.

She could see that the object of everyone's attention was in the middle of the field, but it was not yet visible to the young riders behind the trees on the pathway. It was terrifying and fascinating at once. Carole continued to move forward. She had to know the face of the terrorist, the kidnapper, the evil person who was threatening her new friend's well-being.

Carole could see the circle of men in the field—the security agents whom they had seen before, as well as the men who had dropped down from the helicopter—tightening. Once spaced ten feet apart, the men were now only five feet apart, closing in on their prey.

The helicopter pulled up and away. Once again the riders could hear the voices of the security men delivering orders to their prisoner.

"There is no escape for you!" shouted one man as each moved unrelentingly to the center of the field.

And then Carole heard a familiar voice in a familiar tone uttering a familiar phrase.

"Do you know who my father is?"

Carole, Lisa, and Stevie all looked at one another. There was only one person in the world who would utter such a ridiculous question when surrounded by two dozen counterterrorists.

"What's *she* doing here?" Lisa asked, stunned.

Without further ado, the riders urged their horses forward, into the open field. There, standing beside her horse, Danny, surrounded by an entire platoon of security guards, held at gunpoint by two men in ninja black who'd just dropped down out of a helicopter, was none other than Veronica diAngelo.

13

IT TOOK A WHILE to persuade the men to put their guns down, and it didn't help that Veronica refused to raise her arms. She just kept sputtering that these men hadn't heard the last of her. For their part, they kept insisting that she was going to spend the rest of her life in a desert prison. There was, in fact, a major communication gap.

It wasn't easy to explain Veronica to Karya. As everybody who knew Veronica said, she defied explanation. Veronica bristled furiously when Stevie used words like *snob* and *spoiled rich girl*.

"Aha," said Karya, finally getting it. "I think I understand."

"Well, see, her father is the president of the bank in town, and I suspect she thinks that means that you and she have a lot in common," Lisa said.

"Yes, I definitely understand," said Karya. "But you're sure she's harmless?"

"*Harmless* is the last word I would ever use about Veronica," Stevie said. "She's snobby, mean, vindictive, a liar and a cheat. And much as I would love to have her spend the rest of her natural days in a sweltering desert prison—that's what the man said, isn't it?—it would have to be for something she actually did. She's no kidnapper, and she'd never hang around with terrorists, because they just don't come from the right families."

"Yes, I definitely understand now," said Karya.

She rode Barq forward and summoned the captain of the security men. She spoke with him earnestly for a few minutes, making gestures that were unmistakably Veronica, with her eyebrows arched, looking down her nose.

Finally the captain began nodding in understanding. He signaled his men to step back and lower their weapons and waved to the helicopter to leave the area. The men opened a hole in the circle and allowed Veronica, leading Danny, to pass.

Veronica kept her eyes straight ahead. She did not acknowledge the presence of The Saddle Club, though she did offer a teeny-tiny bow of thanks to Karya for intervening on her behalf. Karya waved at her. Slowly and deliberately, Veronica and Danny walked out of the circle and toward the path that would take them back to the stable.

As she left, another horse and rider approached.

"What now?" Stevie asked, trying to identify the rider from a distance. "Agent Double-oh-seven?"

"Nope," said Lisa. "It's Double-oh-Max!"

Max looked utterly baffled by what greeted him in the

clearing, and as Carole thought about what he was seeing, she could understand why. Two dozen heavily armed men were standing in a ragged circle, looking distraught. Three of Max's riders and their VIP guest were on horseback, with Carole leading a fifth horse.

"What the . . . ," Max said, recognizing Polaris.

"It was Frieda!" Stevie said.

"I don't . . ."

"We didn't, either," said Carole.

"But we knew she was up to no good and we trailed her!" said Karya.

"Is that why . . . ?"

"Yep!" said Stevie.

"But how . . . ?"

"Well, it's a long story," Stevie began.

"And I've got a lot of time to hear it," said Max.

"Not yet," Carole said. "First we've got to see if someone can catch Frieda."

"I think I can help with that now that my guards aren't tracking down the infamous Veronica," said Karya.

Again she summoned the captain, who seemed very eager to please her. She spoke in rapid Arabic. He snapped orders into the walkie-talkie. The helicopter quickly returned, hovered over the field with ropes dangling, and seemed to suck up the troopers whom it had so recently lowered into the field. Then off it sped.

"If she's there, they'll catch her," Karya said.

"Well, they certainly have proved this afternoon that they can track down evildoers!" Stevie said.

"What are you talking about?" Max asked.

"Like I said, it's a long story," said Stevie.

"Then let's just get back to Pine Hollow and you can amuse me with details on the way."

"Whatever you want, Max," Stevie said.

The four girls, Max, and the championship horse returned to the stable, followed by a dozen foot soldiers and four guards on horseback. It was quite a parade by any measure.

IT TOOK ANOTHER forty-five minutes to explain the whole situation to Max and to tell him the complete story of Polaris's rescue—well, the *nearly* complete story. Once they could stop being worried about real kidnappers and terrorists in the woods around Pine Hollow, they all agreed, without further conversation, that Max really didn't need to know they'd been playing games with the security men.

The security men, on the other hand, knew exactly what had been going on. Alek, the secretary, was designated by the men in black to have a brief conversation with Karya about following the orders of the men whose job it was to protect her. She had to apologize to them. She didn't mind that, though, because they, in turn, had to apologize to Veronica diAngelo, whose father had called the State Department in less time than it took to give Polaris a decent ration of oats. But The Saddle Club's favorite part was when Veronica was required to apologize to the security men for not obeying them.

"She takes humiliation so well," Stevie observed as Veronica stomped out of the stable and flounced into her mother's Mercedes, slamming the door. Mrs. diAngelo then nearly ran into Judy Barker's truck as Judy, Pine Hollow's vet, arrived to check Polaris's foot to see if there was any residual damage from the stone.

"Fit as can be," Judy announced a few minutes later. "He's going to be fine to compete on Saturday!"

Finally the girls got to put their own horses back in their own stalls, groom them, water them, and feed them.

Barq's stall was next to Prancer's and across from Starlight's and Belle's.

"This has been a wonderful day," said Carole.

"The only problem is that we didn't get to visit enough," said Karya.

"Well, we've definitely got to go to school tomorrow, but we're planning a sleepover at Stevie's on Saturday night. Could you come, or would that mean missing a chance at the embassy dinner for retired—"

"You bet I'll come," Karya said. "And the retired dam workers can have their embassy dinner without me. But aren't you going to go to the horse show and watch these guys perform?" she asked, pointing down the aisle to where Polaris and Blue were gazing out of their stalls.

"Can't get tickets," Stevie said. "The thing's been sold out for months."

"You know," said Karya, reaching for her cell phone, "being the daughter of the president of a small country can be a nuisance a lot of the time, like when you have to do absolutely everything your security guards tell you to do. But it does have *some* benefits." She punched in some numbers and spoke in her rapid-fire Arabic. She smiled, said, "Okay," then hung up.

"Four tickets. Ringside. Is that okay?"

"That's okay!" Stevie told her.

"Yahoo!" Carole agreed.

14

"THAT WAS *wonderful!*" Carole declared.

Lisa, Stevie, and Karya didn't have to ask her what she meant. They all agreed completely.

It was Saturday night. The girls were having their sleep-over at Stevie's. They had had a wonderful time at the horse show, enjoying every single minute of the afternoon. Not only had their seats been ringside, but also they'd been in the VIP area, and the four had been waited on all afternoon by a staff eager to please them. Stevie had been pleased to oblige them by taking a soda every time anyone offered to get her something.

"I don't think I could ever drink another soda," Stevie said now.

"Well, if you eat any more of that popcorn you brought home, you're going to need lots more soda," said Lisa.

"No, I'm just trying to catch up," Stevie told her.

Karya laughed. "Are you three always this silly?"

"Except when we're sillier," said Carole. "And when everything works out as well as this adventure did, we've definitely earned the right to be silly!"

"It's okay with me," said Karya. "So pass me the popcorn and let's talk again about how perfect the horse show was. My favorite part was when Polaris came in third. He's as wonderful in the ring as he is on the Rocky Trail!"

"What competition there was!" Stevie said. "I thought it was a miracle that he got a ribbon at all!"

"It was all those suppling exercises," Lisa declared.

"And that must be why Blue got a yellow in jumping!" said Carole. "Did you see the way she took those fences. Man, I thought she was flying!"

"Like Pegasus," said Karya.

"Exactly," Carole agreed.

"I'll tell you what my very favorite part was, though," said Stevie.

"What?" Lisa asked.

"Seeing the empty seat in the Walkers' box where Mrs. Walker was supposed to be," said Stevie.

"I guess a woman who's been arrested for conspiring to kidnap a horse just doesn't dare to show her face at the show!" said Lisa.

"Well, I felt sorry for Ellen," said Carole. "She knew what her mother had tried to do and she still had the courage to ride in the show."

"And get a ribbon!" said Karya. "That took guts."

"And skill."

"So what's going to happen to Mrs. Walker and Frieda?" Karya asked.

The girls turned to Stevie because her parents were attorneys and they always expected her to have the answer to a legal question.

"Beats me," she said. "I doubt there'll be a trial. When Karya's guards captured Frieda, she was driving a van rented by Mrs. Walker. It's pretty obvious they're guilty as can be."

"You know what I wonder?" said Lisa.

"What?" Carole asked.

"I wonder what Mrs. Walker would have done if she'd known there were all those other horses that were going to do better than Ellen and Blue."

"I don't wonder because I don't want to think about it," said Karya. "She's a dreadful woman!"

There was a knock at the door of Stevie's room.

"Come on in," Stevie said.

The door opened a crack. "Please?" said a quiet male voice. "Ms. Karya?"

"Come in," Karya told the man. It was the bodyguard assigned to stay at the Lakes' that night and look after her welfare.

"Mrs. Lake sent these to you. . . ."

He stepped into the room, carrying a tray with freshly baked chocolate chip cookies, a pitcher of milk, and four glasses.

Stevie made space on her desktop for the tray and then offered a cookie to the guard.

He shook his head politely. "Not while I'm on the job, thank you," he said, smiling at his joke.

"I guess my mom gave you some downstairs, huh?" Stevie asked. He nodded, his eyes shining.

"I am learning all the best things about America here," he said. Then, as quietly as he'd arrived, he backed out of the room and they heard him going down the stairs and back to the kitchen—and the rest of the chocolate chip cookies.

"I'm learning the best things about America, too," said Karya. "I'm so glad you wrote to me. But I still don't understand exactly why you did it. I mean, did you really expect me to, like, show up and muck out stables with you guys just because you wrote me a letter?"

"No," Carole said. "That was the last thing we expected. We were hoping for a postage stamp from the ADR."

Karya looked a little surprised and then started laughing. "Is that really why you wrote?"

Carole nodded sheepishly.

"Well, let's see," said Karya. She rummaged through her backpack. "There's nothing here. But if I were to write you a letter from home—would that be okay?"

"Definitely," Carole said. "Especially if it's okay if I answer it, too."

"Pen pals?"

"Not really," Carole said. "More like horse pals!"

Ever wonder what happened to The Saddle Club when Stevie, Lisa, and Carole went to high school? Now read all about it in Pine Hollow, the new series from Bonnie Bryant.

Each girl is having a lot of new experiences, like going to high school, getting a driver's license, finding a boyfriend, and even getting a job. But one thing remains the same: Stevie, Lisa, and Carole are still best friends, and they still love horses!

Included here is the full text of Pine Hollow #1: *The Long Ride*. Find out what happens to The Saddle Club next!

Full text of *The Long Ride* by Bonnie Bryant
Copyright © 1998 by Bonnie Bryant Hiller
Published by Bantam Books, an imprint of Random House Children's Books,
a division of Random House, Inc., 1540 Broadway, New York, NY 10036
All rights reserved

PROLOGUE

"Do you think we'll get there in time?" Stevie Lake asked, looking around for some sign that the airport was near.

"Since that plane almost landed on top of us, I think we're close," Carole Hanson said.

"Turn right here," said Callie Forester from the backseat.

"And then left up ahead," Carole advised, picking out directions from the signs that flashed past near the airport entrance. "I think Lisa's plane is leaving from that terminal there."

"Which one?"

"The one we just passed," Callie said.

"Oh," said Stevie. She gripped the steering wheel tightly and looked for a way to turn around without causing a major traffic tie-up.

"This would be easier if we were on horseback," said Carole.

"Everything's easier on horseback," Stevie agreed.

"Or if we had a police escort," said Callie.

"Have you done that?" Stevie asked, trying to maneuver the car across three lanes of traffic.

"Yeah," said Callie. "It's kind of fun, but dangerous. It makes you think you're almost as important as other people tell you you are."

Stevie rolled her window down and waved wildly at the confused drivers around her. Clearly, her waving confused them more, but it worked. All traffic stopped. She crossed the three lanes and pulled onto the service road.

It took another ten minutes to get back to the right and

then ten more to find a parking place. Five minutes into the terminal. And then all that was left was to find Lisa.

"Where do you think she is?" Carole asked.

"I know," said Stevie. "Follow me."

"That's what we've been doing all morning," Callie said dryly. "And look how far it's gotten us."

But she followed anyway.

Alex Lake reached across the table in the airport cafeteria and took Lisa Atwood's hand.

"It's going to be a long summer," he said.

Lisa nodded. Saying good-bye was one of her least favorite activities. She didn't want Alex to know how hard it was, though. That would just make it tougher on him. The two of them had known each other for four years—as long as Lisa had been best friends with Alex's twin sister, Stevie. But they'd only started dating six months earlier. Lisa could hardly believe that. It seemed as if she'd been in love with him forever.

"But it is just for the summer," she said. The words sounded dumb even as they came out of her mouth. The summer *was* long. She wouldn't come back to Virginia until right before school started.

"I wish your dad didn't live so far away, and I wish the summer weren't so long."

"It'll go fast," said Lisa.

"For you, maybe. You'll be in California, surfing or something. I'll just be here, mowing lawns."

"I've never surfed in my life—"

126

"Until now," said Alex. It was almost a challenge, and Lisa didn't like it.

"I don't want to fight with you," said Lisa.

"I don't want to fight with you, either," he said, relenting. "I'm sorry. It's just that I want things to be different. Not very different. Just a little different."

"Me too," said Lisa. She squeezed his hand. It was a way to keep from saying anything else, because she was afraid that if she tried to speak she might cry, and she hated it when she cried. It made her face red and puffy, but most of all, it told other people how she was feeling. She'd found it useful to keep her feelings to herself these days. Like Alex, she wanted things to be different, but she wanted them to be very different, not just a little. She sighed. That was slightly better than crying.

"I told you so," said Stevie to Callie and Carole.

Stevie had threaded her way through the airport terminal, straight to the cafeteria near the security checkpoint. And there, sitting next to the door, were her twin brother and her best friend.

"Surprise!" the three girls cried, crowding around the table.

"We just couldn't let you be the only one to say good-bye to Lisa," Carole said, sliding into the booth next to Alex.

"We had to be here, too. You understand that, don't you?" Stevie asked Lisa as she sat down next to her.

"You guys!" said Lisa, her face lighting up with joy. "I'm so glad you're here. I was afraid I wasn't going to see you for months and months!"

She *was* glad they were there. It wouldn't have felt right if she'd had to leave without seeing them one more time. "I thought you had other things to do."

"We just told you that so we could surprise you. We did surprise you, didn't we?"

"You surprised me," Lisa said, beaming.

"Me too," Alex said. "I'm surprised, too. I really thought I could go for an afternoon, just *one* afternoon of my life, without seeing my twin sister."

Stevie grinned. "Well, there's always tomorrow," she said. "And that's something to look forward to, right?"

"Right," he said, grinning back.

Since she was closest to the outside, Callie went and got sodas for herself, Stevie, and Carole. When she rejoined the group, they were talking about everything in the world except the fact that Lisa was going to be gone for the summer and how much they were all going to miss one another.

She passed the drinks around and sat quietly at the end of the table. There wasn't much for her to say. She didn't really feel as if she belonged there. She wasn't anybody's best friend. It wasn't as if they minded her being there, but she'd come along because Stevie had offered to drive her to a tack shop after they left the airport. She was simply along for the ride.

". . . And don't forget to say hello to Skye."

"Skye? Skye who?" asked Alex.

"Don't pay any attention to him," Lisa said. "He's just jealous."

"You mean because Skye is a movie star?"

"And say hi to your father and the new baby. It must be exciting that you'll meet your sister."

"Well, of course, you've already met her, but now she's crawling, right? It's a whole different thing."

An announcement over the PA system brought their chatter to a sudden halt.

"It's my flight," Lisa said slowly. "They're starting to board and I've got to get through security and then to Gate . . . whatever."

"Fourteen," Alex said. "It comes after Gate Twelve. There are no thirteens in airports."

"Let's go."

"Here, I'll carry that."

"And I'll get this one . . ."

As Callie watched, Lisa hugged Carole and Stevie. Then she kissed Alex. Then she hugged her friends again. Then she turned to Alex.

"I think it's time for us to go," Carole said tactfully.

"Write or call every day," Stevie said.

"It's a promise," said Lisa. "Thanks for coming to the airport. You too, Callie."

Callie smiled and gave Lisa a quick hug before all the girls moved away, leaving her alone with Alex. They were going to miss her, but the girls had one another. Alex only had his lawns to mow. He needed the last minutes with Lisa.

"See you at home!" Stevie called over her shoulder, but she didn't think Alex heard. His attention was completely focused on one person.

Carole wiped a tear from her eye once they'd rounded a corner. "I'm going to miss her."

"Me too," said Stevie.

Carole turned to Callie. "It must be hard for you to understand," she said.

"Not really," said Callie. "I can tell you three are really close."

"We are," Carole said. "Best friends for a long time. We're practically inseparable." Even to her the words sounded exclusive and uninviting. If Callie noticed, she didn't say anything.

The three girls walked out of the terminal and found their way to Stevie's car. As she turned on the engine, Stevie was aware of an uncomfortable empty feeling. She really didn't like the idea of Lisa's being gone for the summer, and her own unhappiness was not going to be helped by a brother who was going to spend the entire time moping about his missing girlfriend. There had to be something that would make her feel better.

"Say, Carole, do you want to come along with us to the tack shop?" she asked.

"No, I can't," Carole said. "I promised I'd bring in the horses from the paddock before dark, so you can just drop me off at Pine Hollow. Anyway, aren't you due at work in an hour?"

Stevie glanced at her watch. Carole was right. Everything was taking longer than it was supposed to this afternoon.

"Don't worry," Callie said quickly. "We can go to the tack shop another time."

"You don't mind?" Stevie asked.

"No. I don't. Really," said Callie. "I don't want you to be late for work—either of you. If my parents decide to get a pizza for dinner again, I'm going to want it to arrive on time!"

Stevie laughed, but not because she thought anything was very funny. She wasn't about to forget the last time she'd delivered a pizza to Callie's family. In fact, she wished it hadn't happened, but it had. Now she had to find a way to face up to it.

As she pulled out of the airport parking lot, a plane roared overhead, rising into the brooding sky. *Maybe that's Lisa's plane*, she thought. The noise of its flight seemed to mark the beginning of a long summer.

The first splats of rain hit the windshield as Stevie paid their way out of the parking lot. By the time they were on the highway, it was raining hard. The sky had darkened to a steely gray. Streaks of lightning brightened it, only to be followed by thunder that made the girls jump.

The storm had come out of nowhere. Stevie flicked on the windshield wipers and hoped it would go right back to nowhere.

The sky turned almost black as the storm strengthened. Curtains of rain ripped across the windshield, pounding on the hood and roof of the car. The wipers flicked uselessly at the torrent.

"I hope Fez is okay," said Callie. "He hates thunder, you know."

"I'm not surprised," said Carole, trying to control her voice. It seemed to her that there were a lot of things Fez hated. He was as temperamental as any horse she had ever ridden.

Fez was one of the horses in the paddock. Carole didn't want to upset Callie by telling her that. If she told Callie he'd been turned out, Callie would wonder why he hadn't just been exercised. If she told Callie she'd exercised him, Callie might wonder if he was being overworked. Carole shook her head. What was it about Callie that made Carole so certain that whatever she said, it would be wrong? Why couldn't she say the one thing she really needed to say?

Still, Carole worked at Pine Hollow, and that meant taking care of the horses that were boarding there—and that meant keeping the owners happy.

"I'm sure Fez will be fine. Ben and Max will look after him," Carole said.

"I guess you're right," said Callie. "I know he can be diffi-cult. Of course, you've ridden him, so you know that, too. I mean, that's obvious. But it's spirit, you see. Spirit is the key to an endurance specialist. He's got it, and I think he's got the makings of a champion. We'll work together this summer, and come fall . . . well, you'll see."

Spirit—yes, it was important in a horse. Carole knew that. She just wished she understood why it was that Fez's spirit was so irritating to her. She'd always thought of herself as someone who'd never met a horse she didn't like. Maybe it was the horse's owner . . .

"Uh-oh," said Stevie, putting her foot gently on the brake. "I think I got it going a little too fast there."

"You've got to watch out for that," Callie said. "My father says the police practically lie in wait for teenage drivers. They love to give us tickets. Well, they certainly had fun with me."

"You got a ticket?" Stevie asked.

"No, I just got a warning, but it was almost worse than a ticket. I was going four miles over the speed limit in our hometown. The policeman stopped me, and when he saw who I was, he just gave me a warning. Dad was furious—at me and at the officer, though he didn't say anything to the officer. He was angry at him because he thought someone would find out and say I'd gotten special treatment! I was only going four miles over the speed limit. Really. Even the officer said that. Well, it would have been easier if I'd gotten a ticket. Instead, I got grounded. Dad won't let me drive for three months. Of course, that's nothing compared to what happened to Scott last year."

"What happened to Scott?" Carole asked, suddenly curious about the driving challenges of the Forester children.

"Well, it's kind of a long story," said Callie. "But—"

"Wow! Look at that!" Stevie interrupted. There was an amazing streak of lightning over the road ahead. The dark afternoon brightened for a minute. Thunder followed instantly.

"Maybe we should pull off the road or something?" Carole suggested.

"I don't think so," said Stevie. She squinted through the windshield. "It's not going to last long. It never does when it rains this hard. We get off at the next exit anyway."

She slowed down some more and turned the wipers up a notch. She followed the driver in front of her, keeping a constant eye on the two red blurs of the car's taillights. She'd be okay as long as she could see them. The rain pelted the car so loudly that it was hard to talk. Stevie drove on cautiously.

Then, as suddenly as it had started, the rain stopped. Stevie spotted the sign for their exit, signaled, and pulled off to the right and up the ramp. She took a left onto the overpass and followed the road toward Willow Creek.

The sky was as dark as it had been, and there were signs that there had been some rain there, but nothing nearly as hard as the rain they'd left on the interstate. Stevie sighed with relief and switched the windshield wipers to a slower rate.

"I think I'll drop you off at Pine Hollow first," she said, turning onto the road that bordered the stable's property.

Pine Hollow's white fences followed the contour of the road, breaking the open, grassy hillside into a sequence of paddocks and fields. A few horses stood in the fields, swishing their tails. One bucked playfully and ran up a hill, shaking his head to free his mane in the wind. Stevie smiled. Horses always seemed to her the most welcoming sight in the world.

"Then I'll take Callie home," Stevie continued, "and after that I'll go over to Pizza Manor. I may be a few minutes late for work, but who orders pizza at five o'clock in the afternoon anyway?"

"Now, now," teased Carole. "Is that any way for you to mind your Pizza Manors?"

"Well, at least I have my hat with me," said Stevie. Or did she? She looked into the rearview mirror to see if she could spot it, and when that didn't do any good, she glanced over her shoulder. Callie picked it up and started to hand it to her.

"Here," she said. "We wouldn't want—Wow! I guess the storm isn't over yet!"

The sky had suddenly filled with a brilliant streak of lightning, jagged and pulsating, accompanied by an explosion of thunder.

It startled Stevie. She shrieked and turned her face back to the road. The light was so sudden and so bright that it blinded her for a second. The car swerved. Stevie braked. She clutched at the steering wheel and then realized she couldn't see because the rain was pelting even harder than before. She reached for the wiper control, switching it to its fastest speed.

There was something to her right! She saw something move, but she didn't know what it was.

"Stevie!" Carole cried.

"Look out!" Callie screamed from the backseat.

Stevie swerved to the left on the narrow road, hoping it would be enough. Her answer was a sickening jolt as the car slammed into something solid. The car spun around, smashing against the thing again. When the thing screamed, Stevie knew it was a horse. Then it disappeared from her field of vision. Once again, the car spun. It smashed against the guardrail on the left side of the road and tumbled up and over it as if the rail had never been there.

Down they went, rolling, spinning. Stevie could hear the screams of her friends. She could hear her own voice, echoing in the close confines of the car, answered by the thumps of the car rolling down the hillside into a gully. Suddenly the thumping stopped. The screams were stilled. The engine cut off. The wheels stopped spinning. And all Stevie could hear was the idle *slap, slap, slap* of her windshield wipers.

"Carole?" she whispered. "Are you okay?"

"I think so. What about you?" Carole answered.

"Me too. Callie? Are you okay?" Stevie asked.

There was no answer.

"Callie?" Carole echoed.

The only response was the girl's shallow breathing.

How could this have happened?

135

ONE

"INTERMEDIATE RIDING class will begin in the outdoor ring in five minutes!"

Carole could hear her voice echoing through the corridors of Pine Hollow Stables. It always gave her a kick to use the public-address system. With the flick of her finger, she could make a whole classful of girls and boys nervous. Nobody ever wanted to be late to class because nobody wanted to incur the wrath of a riding instructor.

Carole wasn't an instructor—yet. Though she did help the instructors from time to time, her official job that summer was to be the morning stable manager. She was at Pine Hollow from seven-thirty until noon every weekday, overseeing everything that happened, from ordering grain to assigning horses. Until she'd actually started the job, she'd had little idea of how much went on at Pine Hollow and how responsible she would be for it.

Carole had been a rider at the stable for about seven

years—before she owned her own horse, before her mother had died, long before her father had retired from the Marines. From the first time she'd ridden a horse, when she was four years old, she'd thought the finest job in the world would be getting paid to work with horses. Now, finally, she was doing that.

School was out for the summer, and until she went back as a junior in high school in September, she'd spend at least half of every day at Pine Hollow.

In the past, filling in for the stable manager at Pine Hollow had been a fairly routine task. Max Regnery owned the stable, as his father and grandfather had before him. His mother had been stable manager for years, and she had run the place smoothly, almost invisibly. That had all changed the past spring, however, when Mrs. Reg, as she was universally known, had decided to retire. She'd moved to Florida, leaving the stable in her son's hands, and he was relying on his students to do the work his mother used to do.

Everyone was stunned at how much work Mrs. Reg had magically accomplished. Carole and Denise McCaskill—the girl who was the afternoon manager that summer—were trying to do everything they could to take the huge load off Max's shoulders, but they were finding themselves as overwhelmed as he was.

Two little girls stormed into Carole's office. More accurately, one girl stormed in, chased by another.

"Carole, I want to ride the pinto today," whined Alexandra. "Justine rode him last week, so it's my turn now! You can't give me Nickel again. I had him last week and he misbehaved the whole time!"

"Don't even bother," Justine said to her classmate. "Carole gave me Patch, so I'm going to ride him and that's it. You shouldn't even ask."

"Carole?"

"You had trouble with Nickel last week because you weren't controlling him properly," Carole said calmly to Alexandra. "You won't have trouble with him this week because you will control him properly, but you will have trouble with Max if you don't get to class on time."

Alexandra glared. Justine smirked. Carole ignored them both. She flipped the switch on the PA system.

"Two minutes!" she said sharply. The girls fled from her office.

Carole wondered idly if she'd ever been as annoying as those two. She decided she hadn't been. Then she decided she *hoped* she hadn't been. She knew she'd liked some horses better than others, but as far as she could recall, there had never been a horse she hadn't liked. And there had never been a horse she hadn't been happy to ride.

No, she decided, in spite of the occasional irritating rider, she'd found the perfect job.

Ben, one of the stable hands, came halfway into the office, pausing nearer the door than the desk. Ben was like that. It was as if he didn't really want to commit to a conversation, but there was something he had to say.

"The stall is ready for that new horse," he told Carole. "Almost, I mean."

"Oh, right," Carole said. She opened her drawer and took out the bronze nameplate that had come from the engraver that morning. FEZ, it read. She walked over to give it to Ben.

With anybody else, Carole would have thought it was rude to wait to be handed something. With Ben, though, it was different. He was shy and never seemed to feel as if he belonged. He was as reluctant to go into Carole's office as he was to go into Max's.

The only place Ben seemed comfortable, in fact, was standing next to or sitting on a horse. Carole had never known anyone with as sure a touch as Ben had. He never hesitated with horses the way he did with humans. He could look horses straight in the eye and they'd do what he wanted them to do. People were another story.

Even if Carole had trouble understanding Ben as a person, she had no trouble understanding him as a horse handler. She could watch him work with horses for hours on end. She did, in fact. From her desk, she could see him while he did his chores around the stable, grooming, tending, training, healing, and caring for the horses that lived there. He might stammer trying to utter a complete sentence to a person, but he seemed able to convey a whole world to a horse.

Carole had watched him soothe a frightened horse through an entire vet visit the week before. Anyone else would have had to twitch the horse, squeezing its nose and upper lip with a chain loop that irritated and distracted it so much that it wouldn't notice what the vet was doing. Ben didn't use the twitch, though. He stood by the horse's head, holding it on a short lead. Ben patted its cheek and whispered into its ear. The horse never budged—even when Judy Barker, the vet, took a blood sample. Ben was amazing.

"Must be some special horse," Ben said, looking at the small bronze plaque in his hand. Briefly Carole wondered what had instigated this rush of chatter from him, but then she realized it was the bronze plaque itself and Max's insistence that the stall be completely prepared before the horse's arrival.

"Some kind of VIP?"

"Uh, sort of," Carole said.

"Horse or owner?" Ben asked.

Carole laughed. Ben wouldn't be anywhere near as impressed with an owner's pedigree as he would with a horse's. In this case, however, both were impressive. Carole picked up the folder Max had filled with information about the horse and its rider.

"The horse is an Arabian endurance specialist. He's got a lot of medals and ribbons to his credit. He deserves all the work you've put into the stall, plus the brass nameplate."

"And the owner?"

"Actually, she's not the owner. She's renting Fez for the summer, option to buy and all that. Her name is Callie Forester. She's sixteen years old. She's won a dozen ribbons of her own."

"Never heard of her," Ben said dismissively.

"Not here. She's just moved here from somewhere on the West Coast." Carole ran her finger down the sheet of paper, scanning the notes Max had taken from Callie's parents when they'd made the arrangements. "Oh, I get it," Carole said. "Her father is a congressman. I guess he just got elected last year and Callie was finishing out the school year back home. She's here for the summer. Maybe longer, though it's not clear how long they've leased Fez for."

"Okay," said Ben. He backed out of her office, slinking into the shadows of the stable. That was just like him. He'd heard enough and wanted to flee to the safety of the horses that filled the stalls of Pine Hollow.

Carole knew she was horse-crazy, and she knew it was a trait she'd have all her life. Ben was horse-crazy, too. She liked that about him. Odd as he could be, that single fact about him helped bring them together.

Carole glanced at her watch. This was going to be a busy morning, and she didn't have time to waste thinking about Ben Marlow. One of the things that was going to make it busy was that she had to find someone to cover for her the day after next. She and her best friends, Lisa Atwood and Stevie Lake, had a long-standing date to go for a trail ride.

Stevie, Lisa, and Carole were so close that Carole couldn't remember a time when the other two hadn't been her friends—just the way she couldn't remember a time when she wasn't horse-crazy. Several years earlier they'd formed a club, and it remained a bond between them. It wasn't the formality of the club—not that The Saddle Club had ever been very formal—that kept them together; it was their common love of horses.

The girls were very different from one another and always had been. Carole was acknowledged to be the most serious about horses but the least serious about anything else. Sometimes she thought the only thing that really mattered to her was horses. Sometimes that didn't seem like a bad thing. Now, as she grew older, she was even more convinced that horses would be her life. Just two more years of high school and she could enter a university equine studies program. That was what she wanted more than anything.

While Carole was serious about horses, Stevie sometimes seemed to have trouble being serious about anything. She had outgrown her passion for practical jokes, and her friends were more than a little relieved that she'd given up playing pranks on her brothers. Stevie had three of them: Chad, now in college; her twin brother Alex; and her younger brother, Michael. When the Lakes started playing jokes on each other, things often got out of hand. But everyone had calmed down, or perhaps just grown up, now. Still, Stevie had an irrepressible spirit that tended more toward trouble than practicality.

One constant factor in Stevie's life was her boyfriend, Phil Marsten. They had met at riding camp one summer when they were twelve and in junior high school. They'd fallen in love then and had only gotten closer since. Both Carole and Lisa liked Phil, and he liked them, too.

In fact, the girls were such good friends that it would be difficult for anyone, even a boyfriend, to come between them, but that was put to the test when Stevie's brother Alex and Lisa suddenly fell in love. Carole and Stevie had been there when it happened, and neither had seen it coming. Apparently, neither had Lisa and Alex. The girls had been at dinner at the Lakes' house. In the midst of a raucous conversation about politics and the undesirable high jinks of certain politicians in nearby Washington, D.C., Lisa had asked Alex to hand her the water.

Alex reached for the pitcher and picked it up. He turned to pour water into Lisa's glass, but before he could do it, their eyes met, and it was as if they were seeing one another for the first time. Alex began pouring the water—right onto the table. That in and of itself didn't mean much. What did tell

Stevie and Carole that something important was happening was that Lisa didn't notice . . . until she picked up her empty glass to drink out of it. And at that moment, Lisa's life changed for the good, forever.

Lisa had been having a rough time dealing with her parents' divorce. There had been several years of squabbling and ugly silence in the Atwood home. Then, as Lisa began to think she was accustomed to it, everything got turned upside down again. Her parents told her one morning at breakfast that their marriage was over. Within a month, Mr. Atwood had moved to California. A year after that, when the divorce was final, he'd remarried. Not long after that, Lisa found that she had a baby sister named Lily in addition to a stepmother named Evelyn. She liked Evelyn. She even loved Lily. But so many changes in such a short time were confusing, and nobody knew that better than her best friends.

Lisa, always the coolheaded clear thinker of the trio, had gone through a period when she was as capable of forgetting her coat as Carole or as likely to get into hot water at school as Stevie. All that ended the day she fell in love with Alex. It was as if he were the missing piece—or, as Lisa sometimes thought of him, the missing peace—in her life.

At first Stevie had worried about her best friend's dating her brother, afraid that she'd be forced to choose between them, but that hadn't happened. And now, six months later, Lisa and Alex were still as much in love as before, and Lisa had managed to revert to her normal reliable, calm, logical self. Her friends were glad to have her back.

Other things were also different than they had been when

the three girls had been in junior high school. Back then, they seemed to be able to meet at Pine Hollow every day after school and spend all day on the weekends together, at Pony Club meetings, riding, studying, grooming, and just being around the horses. Now there were huge assignments at school, jobs after school, family obligations, and time spent with boyfriends and even with study groups. Nothing changed the way the girls felt about one another, but life had interfered with their schedule.

Except for the day after next. They'd promised each other one trail ride, just for themselves—no boyfriends, no parents, no interruptions. It was the last chance they'd have to be together before Lisa left for the summer. She was going to California to be with her father, Lily, and Evelyn until September.

Carole hated the fact that Lisa would be gone. Stevie didn't like it any better. Alex was brokenhearted, and Lisa's mother was furious.

And that was the main reason nobody wanted to talk to Lisa about her decision. Her mother had been very badly hurt by the divorce. She had always been a fragile woman, devoted to trivial details, and now her world was shattered. A trivial world shatters easily, Carole had observed. The woman who once obsessed about Lisa's proper upbringing, dancing lessons, painting lessons, piano instruction, and posture had now withdrawn from the whole process, leaving Lisa to her own devices.

Lisa's devices and resources were considerable. She looked after herself and was a straight-A student. She also took on the responsibility of looking after her mother, shopping and cooking for the two of them regularly. No wonder Lisa wanted to go to California for the summer. She needed a rest.

Carole's reverie about her friends was broken by the familiar sound of a pair of crutches thumping along the hallway toward her office.

"Hi, Emily!" she called out.

"Hello, Carole," Emily Williams said. Then the girl peered around the corner into the office, smiling warmly. "Greetings! Anything going on?"

"Lots," Carole told her. "And before you ask, the answer is yes, you can help."

"That's what I get for my generosity of spirit," Emily said, slipping into the chair in front of Carole's desk. She propped her crutches against the chair, crossed her arms in front of her, looked Carole straight in the eye, and said, "Shoot."

"Two things: First of all, can you cover for me in the office day after tomorrow?"

"Of course," Emily said. "As long as I don't have to sort out which of the beginning riders gets Nickel and which gets Patch."

"I'll make a list of horse assignments and leave it for you," Carole said. "I really mostly need you on the phone."

"I'm good at the phone," said Emily.

"You're good at everything," Carole said. "Don't think you can get off easy just because of those." Carole pointed to the crutches.

"I've tried, and it doesn't work," Emily said. Both girls laughed. There were a lot of things Emily had tried to do with the crutches she'd had all her life, but getting sympathy was not one of them. She'd been born with cerebral palsy and wore leg braces, besides walking with crutches. Sometimes if she got really tired, she used a wheelchair. None of that seemed to matter, though, because once Emily had made up her mind to do something, she always managed to do it. And she made up her mind to do just about everything.

Emily had her own horse, a well-trained one she called PC. She rode him every bit as skillfully as the other riders at Pine Hollow rode their horses. She'd won as many ribbons as other fully abled riders, and nobody doubted for a second that she had earned those ribbons. Emily was as devoted to her horse and to riding as Carole and her other friends—more, perhaps. She referred to PC as her great equalizer. When she was in his saddle, there was no thump of crutches. There was no telltale awkwardness in her gait. She could move as quickly as her friends. She could turn, run, and jump just as well as they could. Best of all, they were as happy about it as she was.

"And the other thing?" Emily asked.

"Oh, right. Well, we've got a new boarder arriving this morning. Can you cover the desk while I help with the unloading? According to the notes, he's supposed to be a little tough to handle."

"Sure," said Emily. "But what about Ben?"

"He'll be there, too," Carole said. "I just want to be sure we give this fellow a great Pine Hollow welcome."

"Some kind of VIP?" Emily asked.

"I guess so," said Carole. "The horse is named Fez. The owner is Callie Forester."

"The congressman's daughter?" Emily asked.

"Yeah, how'd you know?"

"I read all about her in one of my horse magazines. Didn't you see the article? I guess not, huh—but anyway, sure, she's won like a zillion ribbons for endurance riding. Fez is a champion in his own right. The junior endurance world has been waiting for these two to pair up. It was a long article, mostly about how difficult it is for her having to move now that her father's been elected."

"It can be tough," said Carole. "Sort of like being an instant princess. Dad met these people at one of those black-tie dinners he goes to—"

"Spare me *Lifestyles of the Rich and Overprivileged*," said Emily.

"I guess," said Carole. "But it can't be easy to be in the public eye the way a congressman's daughter is. And think of all the boring political dinners and conventions and things like that. Must be hard to find time to ride."

"She finds time, trust me," said Emily. "The article was all about how she spends hours a day conditioning herself and her horse. It also said she has a brother who is supposed to be this hotshot kid, president of his high-school debate team, most likely to succeed—like his father. The brother's name is Scott, I think.

"And the horse—well, she only rode him for a few minutes before she knew this was the horse she wanted. Her parents made arrangements to rent him for the summer, and they expect to buy him in September if he lives up to his promise. He's spirited, all right. The woman who wrote the article spent most of her time talking about flared nostrils. In the photographs, his ears were back, flat against his head. I bet he's going to be a handful."

"Well, we'll do our best to make him welcome and comfortable," Carole said.

She thought she sounded like an innkeeper. She had every intention of doing whatever was necessary to make their famous guest and his equally famous rider very comfortable. Usually Carole didn't notice much about riders and horses except how the horses were doing and how the riders rode. For some reason, Fez and Callie were making her nervous, even before she'd met them.

Carole had met congressmen and their daughters before. Pine Hollow was in a suburb of Washington, and there were a lot of people from the government around. It was nothing new. She'd met championship horses before, too. She'd even ridden them. She'd never met a horse she didn't like, and more important, she'd never met a horse she couldn't make like and trust her. What was the big deal here? Maybe it was that, for the first time, she was truly, officially, working at Pine Hollow. She wasn't just one of the riders at the stable, she *was* the stable. The opportunities for error seemed vast. She shook off the thought. Fez would be there shortly. There was no big deal about it. He was a horse, just like any other horse. He'd be fine—and so would she.

"Is that a horse van I hear?" Emily asked, sitting up in her chair so that she could see through the office window.

Carole looked, too. Emily was right. Fez was there. Time to become the welcoming innkeeper, directing her newest guest into the stable.

TWO

"WELCOME TO Pine Hollow," Carole said to the van driver. "My name is Carole Hanson, and—"

"Let's just get this baby unloaded. We're late and it's all because of him. Here are the papers."

The driver shoved a clipboard at Carole and went to the back of the van, where he started opening the latch. Even before the door was open, Carole knew they were in for some trouble. She could hear the horse stomping on the floor. He whinnied. The sound conveyed both irritation and restlessness.

She looked at the papers. Everything seemed to be in order. Fez had come from a farm in West Virginia. He'd been traveling about six hours, and he obviously didn't like it. Some horses took traveling in stride, settled into new homes easily, adjusted to a variety of riders, and did their best for each one. Nothing that Carole had learned so far about Fez made her think he was that kind of horse.

While she finished checking the paperwork, Ben stepped up to give the van driver a hand. It was almost like opening a Christmas present—one that really wanted to get out of the box.

First the outer doors were unlatched and swung open. Then the driver lowered the ramp. Next came the inner door, the stall enclosure inside the van. And there was Fez—or at least Fez's rump. His tail switched agitatedly.

Ben hopped up into the van and clipped a lead rope onto the Arabian's halter.

"You're going to have to mask him," the driver said. "It took that, and more, to get him on. Lord knows what it'll take to get him off."

Carole and Ben each took one side of Fez, guiding him every step of the way, and every step was painful—at least for Carole. With Fez's first step, he managed to give Carole a solid kick in her thigh. She could feel her flesh welting up into a swollen mass and knew it would be a beauty of a bruise.

"Thanks, boy," she said gently. It wasn't what she really wanted to say, but losing her temper with a horse had never done any good. She patted Fez on the neck, hoping to soothe him. He eyed her warily, and then Ben slipped a hood over his head.

The theory was that if a horse couldn't see where he was going, he would follow a lead willingly, since it was probably more reliable than information he was getting with his eyes. Fez apparently wasn't confident about Carole's and Ben's ability to lead him, so he remained almost as balky with the mask as he had been without it.

"Time for a bribe," Carole said. She pulled a carrot out of

her pocket and held it in front of his nose. Fez sniffed and then took it up in his teeth, nipping Carole's hand as he did so. Carole suspected he'd done it on purpose, but she still didn't lose her temper. She had a bruised leg and a sore hand and all they'd managed to do was to get the horse to the top of the ramp.

It took another half hour before the job was done. Step by step, carrot by carrot, sore finger by swollen toe, Carole and Ben finally had Fez on the ground and removed his mask. He thanked them by rearing. Carole wasn't sorry when she could finally ask Ben to take the horse to his stall while she finished up the paperwork. Ben said nothing as he led the balky gelding into the stable. A lot of horses were difficult to get into and out of vans. Few remained cranky when they were on solid ground. Fez appeared to be an exception to that rule. Ben patted him and spoke to him, but Fez's ears remained pinned to his head. Still, he followed Ben.

"Whew, he's a handful," Carole said. "I guess it'll take a few days for him to settle in."

"Don't count on it," said the driver. He took his own copy of the documentation and left Carole wondering what he knew that she didn't.

She could have checked to see if Ben needed a hand, but she headed straight back to the office. Callie was bound to show up in a few minutes, and Carole wanted to be sure her file was complete and all the stable's records were properly prepared. She didn't want to disappoint the congressman's daughter. Each of Pine Hollow's boarders had a notebook in which all the paperwork was kept—everything from transport records to immunizations to feeding schedules to exercise records. There was a lot of information to enter already. She sat down at her desk and took out a new notebook, plus dividers, labels, and forms. She had barely begun to type up the labels before her first interruption.

"Guess what I got!"

It was Stevie, running into the office breathless with excitement. It could only mean one thing.

"You passed?"

"You bet I did!" Stevie said. "I am now a fully licensed driver. Here, look!" she said, holding out the brand-new license. It looked a lot like the one Carole already had.

"It's beautiful!" Carole said, with only a hint of sarcasm. She'd long ago learned that sometimes the easiest way to get along with Stevie was to agree with her—especially when she was being totally irrational. Actually, considering the accomplishment, Carole didn't really think Stevie was being all *that* irrational. A new driver's license was something to be happy about.

"And Alex?" Carole asked. Stevie and Alex were taking their tests on the same day.

"Well, it was a near thing, but he passed, too," Stevie conceded. Carole strongly suspected it hadn't been a near thing at all. Stevie used to spend a lot of time competing with all three of her brothers. Their house still bore the scars of a few water balloons gone astray. Now that they were older, they no longer fought as they had in the past, but it was still sometimes difficult for Stevie to admit in public that her twin was actually related to her. The only thing he'd ever done that she boasted about on his behalf was to fall in love with her friend Lisa.

"He told me he started to turn the wheels the wrong way in the middle of his three-point turn, but he corrected it before they said anything. Can you imagine? Blowing a three-point turn?"

"And you?" Carole asked.

"It went like a breeze," Stevie said. "When they asked me what the rearview mirror was for, I explained that it was for putting on lipstick without lowering the visor. No problem."

Carole almost believed her, but then Stevie had been able to pull her leg as long as they'd known each other.

"And the horn is to let·your friends know you're waiting, right?"

"Exactly," said Stevie. "Now, do you want to go for a ride?"

"Well, sure," Carole said. "I'll be done here in another hour, and I was planning to exercise Starlight then. Why don't you go groom Belle and tack them both up? We can be on the trail right after I'm done. We can't take a long ride, but it should be fun—"

"Actually, I meant in my car. I don't have time to ride Belle today. I saw this ad in the paper—"

"Oh," Carole said, disappointed. It would have been fun to ride with Stevie.

"No, it's really good news," Stevie said, sensing Carole's disappointment. "See, now that Alex and I have our licenses, we can both drive the car Chad left when he went to college. We've worked out a schedule for it, and it means I can get a job. Actually, I just about *have* to get a job, because Mom and Dad are making us pay the insurance and that's a lot of money, which is why Alex is going to be spending the summer breaking his back mowing lawns. Anyway, I heard that

154

Pizza Manor is looking for a delivery person because Alex's friend, Elroy, quit last night and the manager gets in at eleven today and he'll be desperate for a new driver. Who could be more perfect than yours truly?"

"Nobody," Carole agreed. "You are, without a doubt, the ideal person for the job. Go for it."

"Well, the interview isn't for another forty-five minutes, so I thought I'd visit with you."

Carole looked at the pile of work on her desk, including the notebook of Fez's records. Time spent with Stevie was rarely time spent doing a job, much as she would have liked to talk with her friend—even to hear more details about her driving test. But she had to work.

"Look, I can't," she said. "I'm sorry, but the new horse just came in, and I've got to get some paperwork done before the owner arrives. But the good news is that I've asked Emily to cover for me the day after tomorrow so you and Lisa and I can go on our farewell ride before you-know-what happens."

"I sure do know what," Stevie said. "It's the only topic of discussion at my house these days. Well, I mean it's the only thing Alex wants to talk about. I'm sorry Lisa's going away for the summer, but I guess I understand it. It's her father, after all.

"That's great that Emily can cover for you. We should be able to be out of here by ten o'clock or so."

"That's what I thought," said Carole. "And we won't have to worry about your new job meaning you can't go. There aren't too many people who order pizzas for breakfast."

"I think we'll be safe on that score, *if* I get the job."

"Job? What job?" Lisa entered the office.

"I got my license, and now I'm going to apply for a job at Pizza Manor."

"Oh, that's great!" said Lisa. "By any chance, did anybody else in your family get a license today?"

"Gee, who could she be asking about?" Stevie said.

"Both your parents have licenses," Carole said. "And we all know Chad does. So that leaves the dog, right?"

"Only if the dog is named Alex," said Lisa. "Did he pass?"

"Yeah, he did," Stevie assured her. "And that means he can get to all those lawns he's going to mow while you're away. You won't have to worry about him getting into trouble at all. He'll be too tired every night to do anything."

"I wasn't worried about that," Lisa said. "I know you'll look after my interests."

"Actually," Stevie said, "you are the one thing we almost never talk about. He used to confide in me about his girl-friends, but not about you. Oh, sure, he's been mooning around the house, complaining about you going away for the whole summer, but he never says anything really personal. He assumes you talk to me about him."

"Which of course I don't," said Lisa.

"That's the problem with having your brother date your best friend. I'm missing out on all the good dope from two people I used to be able to count on!"

Lisa flopped into the other chair in Carole's office. Carole glanced at Fez's incomplete notebook and the pile of other paperwork that awaited her, but for the moment, her friends' concerns were more important. Fez could wait a few minutes.

"This is the worst!" Carole said. "Stevie and I are going to miss you, and Alex is going to be miserable, and that'll make

Stevie miserable, and you know that when Stevie's miserable, the whole world is miserable."

"Aw, come on," Lisa said, a little bite in her voice. "It's not going to be that long. I didn't ask my parents to get a divorce. I didn't tell Dad to fall in love with someone who lives in California. I didn't choose to have my life split in half."

"Easy, easy," Carole said. "We're just venting. I guess none of us much likes the whole situation, so maybe we'd better stop talking about it."

"Or else we could look on the positive side," Stevie suggested.

"And that is?"

"You're going to spend a whole summer in sunny Southern California. You'll certainly get to see Skye, and that's always lots of fun."

"He's pretty busy," Lisa said.

"Starring in another movie?" asked Carole. Skye Ransom was an actor the girls had known for a long time. They'd met him by accident—his accident—when he'd fallen off a horse. They'd helped him out, and they'd been friends ever since.

"No, it's not a movie," said Stevie. "It's a television series. A contemporary series set on a horse ranch. He's been cast as the young romantic lead. All the girls who come to the ranch fall in love with him."

"That's more like fact than fiction," Lisa remarked. Then she realized that her boyfriend's sister might not find that very funny. "Not that he's my type, mind you. Personally, I prefer the lawn mower type to the handsome young star type."

"I'll be sure to tell Alex you said that," Stevie promised.

"No, don't," said Lisa. "I don't think he likes to hear any-thing about Skye Ransom. He can't help being insecure, but, honestly, he has nothing to be insecure about. Skye's just a friend."

"Even with all the razzle-dazzle of Hollywood?" Carole asked.

"Especially with all that," Lisa said. "It's a nice place to visit, you know?"

"But you wouldn't want to live there?"

"Never," Lisa said. "Absolutely never."

"Well, that's good enough for me," Carole said. She pulled a pile of papers in front of her.

"I think that's a hint," Lisa said. She stood up. Stevie stood up as well, then glanced at her watch.

"Oh, look! It's time for me to go to Pizza Manor. Do you want to come along for a ride?" she asked Lisa.

"Sure," Lisa agreed.

"You can't apply for the job," Stevie said, suddenly a little concerned that super-organized Lisa might beat her to the job she was counting on, just to avoid being away from Alex.

"Don't worry. I'm hungry. I'll have some veggie pizza while you wow the manager with your driving skills, your reliability, and your sparkling personality."

"Deal," Stevie said.

The two of them said good-bye to Carole and headed out.

Carole opened up the notebook, and on the top of the first page, she wrote *Fez*.

THREE

"STEVIE, RELAX. You don't have to hold the wheel so tightly," said Lisa.

"I do kind of clutch it, don't I?" Stevie acknowledged. She tried to relax her hands. Her knuckles changed from milky white to a healthy flesh color.

"Are you nervous when you drive?" Lisa asked uneasily.

"No, not really," said Stevie. "But you know, it's kind of new, with my driver's license and all. I don't want to make any mistakes."

"You won't," Lisa said. "All you have to do is to keep a few things in mind. Keep your hands steady, your foot limber, and your eyes moving, and concentrate on where you're going."

"Sounds just like riding a horse," Stevie said.

"I guess so, and, like riding a horse, it's a matter of being able to focus on fifteen or twenty things at once, like that double-parked—*Stevie!*"

Stevie swerved to the left, avoiding the double-parked car

by a good tenth of an inch. Lisa felt her heart slowly settle back into her chest.

"No problem," Stevie assured her.

"Right," Lisa agreed. She decided not to distract Stevie by giving her any more instructions until they reached Pizza Manor. It hadn't been all that long ago that Lisa had gotten her own driver's license. She was a year older than Stevie, a year ahead of her in school, and a year more experienced as a driver. Her own first day had been spent driving her friends to and from every place in town where they'd wanted to go. It had been wonderful fun, even if they had never gone above fifteen miles per hour. Now, a year later, she was an able and confident driver. Soon enough Stevie would be, too.

Stevie managed to complete the trip without any more near misses or even not-so-near ones. She looked at her watch. She was right on time for her interview. Being on time had never been one of her strong points. Perhaps getting her driver's license and being on time for an appointment on the same day meant she was turning over a new leaf. She took a nice deep breath. Everything was going to be wonderful. She would get the job. She was sure of it. She and Lisa walked in together.

Pizza Manor was a small restaurant in the shopping center near Pine Hollow. The shopping center had few things to recommend it. Besides Pizza Manor, which was a relatively new addition, there were a handful of other stores that seemed to change regularly: a shoe store that became a record store; a gift shop that turned into a liquor store and then into a dry cleaner's. The two things there that never seemed to change were the supermarket and TD's. TD's stood for Tastee Delight. It was an ice cream shop that Stevie, Lisa, and Carole had been going to as long as they'd been friends. They still liked crowding into their favorite booth every now and then for something sweet and gooey.

"Welcome to Pizza Manor. May I help you?" said the smiling girl behind the counter.

The girl was Polly Giacomin. She rode at Pine Hollow with Stevie and Lisa. It felt funny to have her offer to wait on them.

"Hi, Polly," Lisa said. "I'll have a slice of veggie pizza and a small diet soda."

"M'kay. . . . Stevie?"

"I'll have an interview."

Polly smiled. She knew Stevie.

"So you passed the test?"

Stevie nodded.

"The manager's in the back. I'll let him know you're here. He's been tearing out his hair all day because Elroy quit last night. He's afraid he's going to have to make the deliveries himself. Just smile nicely, show him your license, and you'll get the job."

She drew a soda and slipped a slice of pizza onto a red-and-white-checked paper plate, then handed them to Lisa. "Hang on a second," she said to Stevie.

Lisa took her lunch to a nearby table and sat down to eat and wait.

Stevie didn't move, afraid that she couldn't. The day had been something else. In spite of what she'd said to her friends, her driving test hadn't gone *that* smoothly. She loved driving.

161

She'd loved it from the first moment her father had let her sit behind the wheel the day she'd gotten her learner's permit. She loved the powerful feel of the car, knowing that she and she alone was in charge. It was similar to but not exactly the same as riding, since the car was only a machine and not a living, responsive animal. But what a machine it was—big, noisy, shiny, expensive. It could take her anywhere. She didn't have to feed it or groom it. She only had to give it gas—and pay the insurance.

She'd almost blown it, too. Or maybe she hadn't. The man who gave her the driving test had sat stony-faced during the entire ordeal, not speaking except to issue instructions. She had no idea what she'd done wrong or right. She only knew that in the end, it had worked. Had he noticed that she didn't really look over her shoulder when she pulled out of the parking place? Had he been aware that she was a little bit over the center line when she was making a left turn? Maybe he had, or maybe he hadn't. She'd passed. That was the important thing.

And now here she was, ready for another test—this time to get a job. Who was she kidding? She barely knew how to drive. She didn't know the first thing about the restaurant business except that she was a pretty good eater. She was usually late for things, but she'd made it that day. She was wearing an old pair of jeans and a wrinkled shirt, and she hadn't combed her hair, and she probably smelled of horses because she'd stopped by Pine Hollow, *and* she'd never had a real job before.

Suddenly a man was standing in front of her on the other side of the counter. He was stocky and had a mustache. He had combed his thinning hair from one ear to the other to make stripes of hair across the top of his head.

"You here about the delivery job?" he asked.

"Me?" Stevie asked, glancing over her shoulder.

"Yeah, you."

"Oh, right, yes," said Stevie, offering her hand. He shook it.

"Polly said there was a boy here, too. Steve something."

"That's me. Except I'm not a boy. I'm Stevie Lake—it's short for Stephanie, but don't tell anybody that."

"My daughter's named Stephanie," he said.

I've blown it, Stevie thought. *I've made him think I'm crazy and I've insulted his daughter. He's not going to hire me. In fact, nobody will ever hire me. I can't really drive and—*

"You have a license?"

"Yes."

"May I see it, please?"

"Oh, sure," Stevie said, fishing it out of her purse. She handed it to him.

"Kind of rushing things, aren't you?" he said.

What had she done wrong now?

"Sorry?"

"I don't think I've ever seen a license as fresh and new as this," he said. "It's like holding a newborn baby. Did you come straight here, or did you stop to show your friends?"

"Um, my friends," Stevie said, pointing to Lisa, who was calmly eating her pizza, totally unaware of the fact that Stevie was making an idiot of herself just out of earshot. Then Stevie looked at the man. It took her another two seconds to realize he was teasing her.

"I would have come straight here, sir, but I thought it would impress you more if you could see how much business I would bring in for you."

"That's just one customer," the man said.

"Right, but she's *very* hungry."

"Okay. Come on back to my office. You've got to fill out an application and tell me a little bit about yourself. So far, all I know is that the Commonwealth of Virginia thinks you're an adequate driver, and you've got a smart mouth on you. Anything else?"

"No sir, that's me in a nutshell," Stevie assured him.

She followed him, wondering what she was getting herself into.

FOUR

CAROLE HEARD a knock at her office door. At least she'd been able to finish putting the papers in Fez's notebook before the next interruption. She looked up.

A very handsome guy leaned in the doorway, looking back at her. She smiled automatically in response to the smile he gave her.

"Is Callie here?" he asked.

"Forester? Uh, no," Carole said. "She hasn't been here yet. But her horse is here. Would you like to see him?"

"No thank you," the boy said, smiling wryly. "I hear enough about him to satisfy any curiosity I have."

That was all the hint Carole needed. Only a nonriding brother could respond that way to his sister's horse.

"You must be Scott," Carole said. "I'm Carole Hanson, morning stable manager for the summer."

He took her hand and shook it. "Well, I'm glad I didn't

come in the afternoon or the fall. Otherwise I would have missed the opportunity to meet you."

"Instead, you've only missed your sister. I don't know when she's going to be here. Would you like me to give her a message?"

"No, I'm waiting for her. I'm supposed to pick her up after she's checked on Fez. My father is dropping her off on his way into town, but he can't wait for her, so I've got chauffeur duty—which is an honor I accept in return for being able to use the car."

"Oh, it's station-wagon bingo, huh?" Carole teased.

Scott laughed and took a chair across the desk from her. "Don't you know it. You must have brothers and sisters, too."

"No, I'm an only," Carole told him. "And there's no argument over the car in my house. My father gets it when he wants it. See, he's a retired Marine."

"Can't be any harder to argue with than a man who makes his living as a politician."

"I think you've got me there," Carole said. "But when he says 'Ten-*shun!*' . . . Well, enough about that." She stood up from her desk. "I was about to go look in on Fez, so if you want to come with me, you're welcome, or you can stay here."

Scott stood up. "Oh, sure," he said. "I'll come along. I guess I might as well have a face to put with this superhorse after all."

He followed Carole down the wide aisle that separated the horses' stalls. Fez's stall was on the other side of the stable. Carole took the opportunity to introduce Scott to a lot of horses as they went, including her own, Starlight, and

Stevie's horse, Belle. If Scott didn't like horses—and he certainly hadn't given Carole the impression that he did—he was pretty good at feigning interest. He patted them warmly and asked good questions. He asked Carole why it was so important to his sister that her horse was an Arab.

"I mean, your horse—um, Starlight?" he said. Carole nodded. "You said he's part Thoroughbred. I thought they were the best. Why wouldn't she want a Thoroughbred, then? I mean, if there's one thing you can count on about Callie, it's that she wants the best when it comes to horses."

"Me too," Carole said. "But *best* is a relative term. I wanted a horse I could ride for pleasure and competition. Starlight is fine in a ring and a great jumper, but he's no match for most Arabs on an endurance ride. Thoroughbreds were developed for their speed. Where they're 'best' is at the racetrack. Arabs were bred for desert life. They're surefooted and powerful, and they can go for long periods without water. They have stamina and a lot of heart. That's why they tend to stand out in endurance competitions. Now, quarter horses, for instance, are faster than Thoroughbreds—for short distances. They're like sprinters."

"I think I'm getting this," Scott said. "An Arab is like a marathon runner; you want a Thoroughbred in the four-forty, but a quarter horse in the hundred-meter dash."

"You're a quick study," Carole said.

"And you're a good teacher," Scott countered.

Carole blushed. She actually blushed. And she felt more than a little dumb about it. She hoped he didn't notice. Scott was friendly and really cute. He was easy to talk to, he was interested in what she had to say—or at least very good at pretending he was—and he seemed like a good listener, too. It made her all the more pleased that Callie was going to be riding with them. If Scott was so nice, then Callie was bound to be, too. That was something to look forward to.

Ben was still working with Fez when they got to his stall. The horse seemed only marginally happier to be there than he had when he'd arrived, and Carole suspected that all of the improvement was due to Ben's presence. He was holding Fez gently but firmly by a lead line and currying his neck when they approached. Horses liked to be groomed. The coat on Fez's neck was already shiny and clean. Clearly, it didn't need one more second of attention, but Fez needed a lot more attention to calm him down. Ben understood that and was doing what was necessary.

"Scott, I'd like you to meet Ben Marlow . . ."

"Pleased to meet you," Scott said, offering Ben his hand.

Ben regarded it quickly and then nodded instead. He had his hands full with Fez and wasn't about to let go. Carole thought it wouldn't have hurt for him to say as much. Scott pulled back his hand.

"I guess this must be the fabled Fez," Scott said.

Ben nodded again.

"Um, he's been fussy since he got here," Carole said. "Ben's trying to give him the old Pine Hollow welcome and help him settle in. I think he doesn't like traveling much."

Scott leaned up against one of the pillars, propping his elbow over his head and leaning easily. Carole remembered how he'd taken to the chair in her office, immediately making himself at home. She was struck by the fact that Scott managed to make himself comfortable wherever he was, and as a result she was comfortable, too—as long as he didn't compliment her too much.

"Is that one of those qualities of various breeds you were talking about?" Scott asked.

"Oh, I don't think so," Carole said. "Every horse has its own personality, regardless of breed. Some horses love to be vanned and walk up and down the ramp without any trouble. There are a couple of horses here who try to get on every van that comes into the yard. Others hate it, and every time they go anyplace, it's a struggle. Your friend Fez here falls into that category."

Carole became aware that the two of them were talking around Ben—almost as if he weren't there. Since he was, however, she thought it would be polite to bring him into the conversation.

"Ben, why don't you tell Scott what we had to go through to get this guy off the van?"

"Oh, it wasn't too bad," Ben said. "Just had to persuade him. He's okay now."

That was it. That was all Ben intended to say. He could be infuriating, Carole thought. What was the matter with sharing the tale with Scott? Some people would have enjoyed hearing about the mask and the bribes. Scott was one of them, Carole was sure.

"We kind of took the carrot-and-stick approach," Carole said. "Literally. Except we didn't dangle the carrot off a stick. I held the carrots close enough for him to be able to sniff them—which he had to do because he had a mask over his eyes."

"You blindfolded him? You mean he's so dumb he couldn't figure out where he was going?"

Carole had never actually thought of it in those terms. "We hope so," she said. That made Scott laugh. His laugh was so infectious that it made her laugh, too. It didn't, however, make Ben laugh. He simply kept up his work, grooming Fez.

Fez's ears perked up suddenly, and then Carole heard a car door slam. It didn't surprise her that Fez had heard it open when the humans hadn't. Horses had very keen hearing.

"Excuse me, but I bet that's Callie," Scott said. "I'll go check and bring her back here, okay?"

"Oh, sure," Carole said. Scott was gone instantly. That meant Callie would probably be there in a few minutes. Carole glanced around. Was the stall ready for Callie's inspection? Ben had been so busy with his grooming that he hadn't noticed that Fez had eaten some of the hay in the tick. What if Callie thought they hadn't given him enough food? And the water? There was work to be done.

Callie stepped back from her father's car. "I'll see you tonight," she said through the open car window.

"Bye, honey," the congressman answered. "Remember to be home on time. Your mother has promised to make everybody's favorite dinner."

"Oh, right, that pizza place that delivers—"

"Full pepperoni, half mushroom," he said.

"Hope they're as good as the place back home."

"They are," he said. "You'll see."

Callie waved, and her father pulled out of the drive.

She paused to look around. The place didn't look like much, but then stables usually didn't win awards for architecture. There was a single large house, probably where the owner lived. Max something. Regnery—she remembered. He'd had a couple of pretty good riders come through his school. Dorothy DeSoto, who had been big about ten years earlier, had trained here. He had a good reputation. Not that he was known for endurance riding, but he was good with horses and riders. That was all that mattered to Callie. She had her own trainer. Or at least she used to have her own trainer. Back home.

It was the second time in as many minutes that the phrase had gone through her head. Home was a long way away, on the other side of the country. But her father's work was here now most of the year. Some congressmen left their families "back home." For her father, that wouldn't do. He wanted them to be together. So Scott and Callie had finished out the school year at their high school "back home" and had come to join their parents. They'd go to school here next year. She'd finish high school in Virginia, apply to college from Virginia, call Virginia home. No, she couldn't do that. Home was back there, on the West Coast, where she came from, where she belonged.

She wasn't ever going to belong here. She wasn't ever going to like people, make friends, understand that soft Southern accent so many people had. Her friends were going to be on the other end of a long-distance call or on e-mail. She'd ride this horse. She'd earn ribbons, maybe even a few blues.

But staying in a house in Virginia wasn't the same thing as living there. As far as Callie was concerned, "back home" was still home.

The screen door of the stable swung open and slammed shut.

It was Scott. She'd seen the car, so she knew he was there. Typical of him to have found his way into the barn. He'd probably already made friends with everyone. Scott was a natural-born friend to everyone. It was a skill he had clearly picked up from their father. He was funny, warm, kind, attentive, amusing, and comfortable with everyone. The worst part was that he actually meant it, too—at least when it came to everyone else. When he came to his sister, he wasn't always Mr. Smooth.

"Where have you been?" he demanded.

"I was waiting for Dad," Callie said. "I couldn't leave without him."

"Well, I may leave here without you," he said. "I've got an appointment with the coach of the debate team in exactly fifteen minutes, and I have to get you to the dentist first. You've got to get in there, check out your horse, who looks just fine if you want my opinion, and then we've got to get out of here in five minutes so I can take you to your appointment."

"Five minutes? Scott, I can't do that! This is the first time I've seen the horse in months. I can't just wave to him. You don't know the first thing about—"

"What I know is that I don't have a lot of time. Make it snappy."

"I'll do my best." She sighed. Scott wasn't improving her mood.

"Inside, turn right down the aisle. He's in the last stall on the right. There's a girl named Carole and a boy named Ben looking after him, but I think the horse is in a really bad mood. I guess they had to go to a lot of trouble to get him off the van—not that he got hurt or anything. I'll be waiting in the car."

"Thanks," she said.

She stepped into the stable and paused for a moment. She heard Scott turn on the motor. It irritated her. She knew it was his way of reminding her, as if she hadn't gotten the message, that he really was in a hurry. She knew he was rushed, just as she knew that he hadn't been thrilled with his assignment to pick her up and drive her around. He wasn't a lot happier about moving to Willow Creek than she was, and the only thing that made it easier for him was the excellent reputation of the Willow Creek High School debate team, a reputation he fully expected to help improve.

It took a few seconds for her eyes to adjust to the darkness after the bright summer sun outside. The stable was clean, with just the right amount of disarray. The pitchfork was precisely (and safely) tucked in a corner, but three lead ropes hung loosely around a peg, available on a second's notice. Just as they should be.

She peered into the tack room. Tack rooms always looked messy to the untrained eye. Callie's eye wasn't untrained. She could see that everything in there had a place where it belonged. The pungent smells of leather, horses, and saddle soap combined comfortably.

She'd never been to Pine Hollow before, but she knew the place. It had all the best qualities of every fine stable she'd ever walked in. This would be okay, even if it wasn't back home.

There was a long row of stalls on each side of the aisle before the right turn Scott had alerted her to. Every stall held a horse. Every stall was clean, all the horses were groomed, each of the hay ticks had a good supply of hay, and all the water buckets were filled. Pine Hollow had an excellent reputation for horse care, and Callie wasn't surprised to find everything in order. She was pleased to have the reputation confirmed, even if she could only make the judgment based on a quick peek. Once again, she found herself more than a little annoyed with her brother and his rush to deliver her to the dentist an hour before she needed to be there so he could spend extra time with the debate coach. Why was it that his appointment with the debate coach was more important than her appointment with her horse?

She hurried on along the aisle and turned right.

"Oh, hi. Where's Scott? You must be Callie."

Callie looked up to see an African American girl about her own age. The girl wore her black hair in several braids that hung down to her shoulders. She was dressed in riding jeans, stable boots, and a T-shirt. Her hair was full of straw, and there was a large splash of water down the front of her shirt. She brushed ineffectively at the straw and water.

"Right, I'm Callie," Callie confirmed testily. "And you are?"

"Oh, well, I'm Carole. Um, Carole Hanson," the girl said. "I'm in charge of the office in the mornings this summer, so I guess we'll be seeing a lot of one another, and you'll have to be sure to let me know if there are things I can do for you because we want you to be happy with Pine Hollow. It's a wonderful stable. I've been riding here since I was—oh, I guess about ten or something, and you're just going to love it here, Carrie—um, Callie."

Carole couldn't believe what she was saying, but there didn't seem to be any way to stop herself. Her mouth kept going when it was more than apparent that her brain had stopped working eight or ten sentences before. And even while those thoughts were crowding into her mind, she was still talking, by now onto the subject of feeding schedules. "And everyone pitches in. We all help around here. Of course, I do because I work here, but even when I was just a rider with her own horse here—you passed right by Starlight's—"

"Where's Fez?" Callie asked.

That stopped Carole. How could she be so dumb? Callie didn't need anyone to give her a sales pitch on Pine Hollow. Of course the only thing she cared about was her horse.

"Um, right here," Carole said. She took a few steps back and revealed the Arab to his new owner. "We even had his nameplate installed."

"Right," Callie said brusquely. She stepped up to the horse and took a critical look at him. "He seems to have come through the trip okay. Did he give you much trouble getting off the van?"

Carole was about to answer when she realized the question hadn't been directed to her. Callie was speaking to Ben.

"Yup," he said. He didn't elaborate. Carole envied his restraint.

Callie reached up and patted the horse. His first instinct

175

was to pull back, but he had second thoughts about that and let her touch him. She clicked her tongue and scratched him on the cheek. He responded with as much affection as Carole had seen from him since he'd arrived.

"You're good," Carole said, genuinely admiring Callie's skill.

"I love horses, it's that simple," Callie said.

That smarted. Callie had managed to imply that Carole didn't love horses, and nothing could be farther from the truth. But Callie was a customer, a paying boarder, a congressman's daughter, a champion rider. And Carole was in charge of making her feel welcome at Pine Hollow.

"It shows," Carole told Callie. What she didn't say was that other things showed, too.

FIVE

CAROLE PASTED a smile on her face. "I'd like to show you the office and let you see how we keep our records," she said.

"On computer, I presume," said Callie. "I don't really need to see it. I'm sure it's just fine. That's the way Henry did everything at the stable back home. It's all standard. I'm sure you're up to date."

Carole swallowed. In fact, Max had long considered shifting Pine Hollow's records to computer, but he believed that the books had the advantage of being very portable and entirely secure from the dangers of power outages. Perhaps Callie would be interested to know about that.

"Actually, we keep notebooks for each horse. That way, if there's a problem with the power, or whatever—well, you know."

"Right, whatever," Callie said, dismissing Carole and her explanation. She seemed annoyed and harried. Carole lost every bit of self-confidence she'd ever had and became convinced that Callie's annoyance was completely her fault. Normally, when the subject was horses, Carole was relaxed and at ease. Today she felt like a bundle of nerves.

Callie swallowed hard. This wasn't easy on her. Everything, including the horse she was expected to ride, was new. New wasn't something that Callie liked or did well with. She liked things that were familiar. For the umpteenth time, she found herself wishing she were as flexible as Scott. Scott was always instantly at home wherever he was—except now, of course. Right now he was out in the car, drumming his fingers on the steering wheel, waiting for Callie and wishing he could already be at the high school talking with the debate coach.

Well, Callie still had a few minutes, and she intended to use them to find out all she could about Pine Hollow and her new horse's care.

"What about the exercise schedule for boarders?" Callie asked. At her last stable, Henry had set aside Monday and Wednesday mornings and Friday late afternoons exclusively for horse owners. There were no classes at those times, so the owners could use all the facilities without competing with classes and occasional riders. It had worked well for Greensprings Stable, and she wondered if Pine Hollow had anything like it.

The question confused Carole. Boarders were expected to exercise their own horses, and they could do it whenever they wanted. It helped if they let the office know when they were coming, but they were certainly entitled to come over anytime at all. But maybe that wasn't what Callie meant. She was, after all, a champion rider *and* the daughter of a congressman, so she was probably used to getting VIP treatment. There was no way Pine Hollow was going to come in second to any other stable.

"We'll see to it that Fez gets all the exercise he needs," said Carole.

"You turn the horses out on some sort of schedule?"

"Well, that, of course," Carole said. "But every horse has individual needs, and we'll see that they're met. A champ like Fez needs to be ridden to stay in top form."

"At least four times a week," said Callie.

"Just what I thought," said Carole. "We'll see to it as part of his board here."

"You'll do the exercising?" Callie asked.

"Well, me or whoever is available," Carole said. "Nothing but the best for our clients—and their owners."

"Oh, that's interesting," said Callie. "Back home, I always had to exercise my horse myself, and four times a week is a lot, especially when school's open. But if you can do the exercising for me—well, that takes off a lot of pressure. It'll mean that when I do ride him, I can focus on skills and not just on seeing to it that he's getting enough exercise to stay supple and strong. That's great news."

Perhaps it was great news for Callie, but Carole didn't think it was such good news for herself. She'd blundered into making an outrageously generous offer, and Callie had taken her up on it. If she'd heard herself right, she'd just told Callie she would ride Fez for at least an hour four times a week. Carole caught Ben looking at her darkly.

"Ben?" she said, hoping for some kind of rescue.

She got no rescue from him. He just nodded.

179

"Fez is a spirited horse," Callie began.

"I know that," said Carole.

"He's going to need a good workout every time he's ridden."

"Yes, I know."

"I always take my horse through a set of exercises, really a program, designed to work on various skills and to maintain all his body strength, because when we compete, we'll need it all—both his strength and mine. Fez'll need to be worked hard, but not exhausted. You can't wear him out; you need to strengthen him."

"I know," said Carole.

"A horse that's worked too hard before a competition doesn't have anything to give when it counts."

"Of course," said Carole.

"So it's very important that you follow a rigorous schedule. That's what I've always done in the past. I knew exactly what my last horse needed. In the case of Fez, well, it's a whole new horse with new needs. I can't take the time now to give you a program—but maybe you have some ideas."

"Sure," said Carole. By now she was feeling totally lost. She'd committed her afternoons to Fez. Why not add her evenings, too? She could develop an exercise program for this horse, couldn't she?

Callie edged toward the door. Carole was more than a little relieved to see that she was leaving. She was afraid if Callie stayed another minute, she'd make another offer Callie couldn't refuse. Perhaps their new house needed some rugs, in which case Carole was sure to offer to lie down and let the whole family walk on her!

"Look, I'll call in a couple of days and we can talk about the program you've got planned. I'll need to check it."

"Definitely," Carole said.

"Bye." Callie gave Carole and Ben an ever so slight wave of her hand and hurried out of the stable.

Carole was stunned. She still could hardly believe what had happened, what she'd said, what she'd promised. She turned to Ben for comfort. For a long moment they didn't say anything to one another. Then Ben spoke.

"Sounds like you're going to be busy this summer, Carole."

He was right about that. She'd just made a deal to exercise another owner's horse. This wasn't a service Pine Hollow normally provided, and even if it did, it wasn't something Carole was being paid to do. That meant that she was going to be doing it on her own time, and for no money. Worse still, every afternoon she spent riding Fez was an afternoon she couldn't be riding Starlight.

SIX

"LISA! I got it!" Stevie whispered gleefully as she emerged from the manager's office. "I got a job! I'm going to make money. I'll be rich, rich, rich!"

"You mean you'll be able to pay for your insurance, insurance, insurance," Lisa teased.

"Well, that, and maybe a little bit more. People give tips, you know."

"For good service," Lisa said.

"You're being the voice of reason, and I'm not at all sure I like that."

"I'll try to do better," Lisa said. She stood up and threw her trash in the can. The two of them headed for the door. "When do you start?"

"Tonight—five o'clock sharp," Stevie said. She reached for the door.

The manager hurried out of his office. "Oh, Stephanie, I

forgot to give you this," he said. He handed her a package. "It's your uniform."

"Uniform?"

"Well, really, just a hat and a T-shirt. You can wear your own jeans or skirt—whatever you want. But when you're knocking on strangers' doors, you must have something to identify yourself as the delivery person from Pizza Manor."

"Sure," Stevie said. She opened the package. The T-shirt was simple enough. It had the store's logo, a cartoon character dressed as a medieval knight. That was why it was called Pizza Manor. The hat, however, was not so simple. It was like the one the little cartoon character wore. It was made of felt, with a brim that was rolled up along the edges but pointed in front—like something Robin Hood might have worn on a bad hair day. Worst of all, feathers sprouted from the headband.

"Isn't it cute?" the manager asked.

"Very," Stevie said, hoping she was keeping her voice even. She didn't want him to sense her rising panic.

"See you later!" he said cheerfully. He retreated to his office before Stevie could reply. She turned to Polly Giacomin, who was still standing patiently behind the counter.

"Nobody told me about this!" Stevie exploded.

"Didn't you wonder why he was so worried about having to make the deliveries himself tonight?" she teased.

Lisa began giggling. "Put it on," she said. Stevie donned the hat and slipped the elastic band under her chin. She grimaced.

Lisa adjusted the hat to a jaunty angle. "It's you!" she declared. Polly grinned.

"It's a good thing there aren't any mirrors in this place," Stevie said. "I have a feeling I'm better off not knowing how I look. Now, Polly, tell me—are there any other nasty surprises in store for me?"

"No," Polly said. "We make good pizza, so people are usually happy to have it. And they do give good tips, so all of our delivery people in the past have been pleased with that—Oh, there is one thing."

"Uh-oh," said Stevie.

"Not that bad, but I just ought to warn you. Mr. Andrews is a really nice guy, but he's totally gung ho about this place—like it's his life. He's always worried that one of us is going to do something to upset a customer. That's when he tells us to 'Mind your Pizza Manors.'"

"I'm not sure I need insurance this badly," Stevie said.

"Oh, yes you do," Lisa said.

"You're just afraid Alex will have to pay all of it," Stevie accused her.

"No. I'm just afraid you're going to want to borrow money from me and Carole," Lisa said. "Well, we're both broke, so you are going to have to wear a dumb hat and earn it. Or let Alex have the car all the time, which might be okay, too. Come on. I have to get home. Say good-bye to Polly, um, politely," she said.

Stevie turned to Polly, slid the silly hat off her head with her right hand, brandished it gallantly, then placed it over her heart while she bowed, her left foot in front of her right one. "Milady," she said.

"And you haven't even taken the training course yet!" Polly said.

Lisa hurried Stevie out of the shop before she could ask Polly what she meant. Stevie did need the job, and Lisa didn't want her to quit before she even started. Moreover, she was now crunched for time. They had to get going. She settled into the passenger seat of Stevie's car.

"Where to?" Stevie asked. "Your place or mine?"

"Mine," Lisa told her. "I've got to do some organizing for my trip, and life is easier if I do that kind of thing when Mom isn't around. Although it's been more than a year since Dad got remarried, Mom still resents it and the fact that he moved across the country. She calls Dad's new wife 'that woman,' and she won't even mention the baby. I guess I can understand. It wouldn't make me happy if I were her, but it sure has made him happy."

"It doesn't make me or Carole or Alex happy, either," Stevie said, just to remind Lisa that her mother wasn't the only one who would miss her that summer.

"It changes everything. I know that," Lisa said. "Change can be great, but sometimes it's just too much. When my parents split up and Dad moved to California, I felt like I was being cut in half—half of me loved Mom and the other half loved Dad, and the half that loved Mom hated Dad and the half that loved Dad hated Mom. It's tough having all that love and hate all mixed up inside. I mean . . . I still wish it hadn't happened, but the fact is that there was so much tension in our house all the time that life is a lot easier with them apart from one another. The real trouble is that Mom is miserable and Dad is deliriously happy. When I spend time with Mom, I try to make her feel better, and when I spend time with Dad, I'm relieved that I don't have to cope with that, and then I feel guilty that I'm relieved. Isn't that great? No matter what I do, it hurts. I feel like I'm caught in the middle. I know that how I'm feeling isn't particularly rational. I mean, none of this is my fault. But it still hurts. But as time goes by, I feel it a little bit less and hurt a little bit less. I think it's the same for Mom and Dad, too. Mom is getting better, slowly. Dad is admitting that what he did was hurtful—even if it wasn't wrong for him. And we're all going on with our lives."

Stevie was glad she was behind the wheel and could pretend she was concentrating on the road in front of her. This was the first time in more than two years that Lisa had talked so much about her parents and how their divorce had affected her. Both Stevie and Carole had known that all these things were going on in Lisa's mind and heart because they were best friends, but Lisa had never shown much inclination to talk about them. Now she was talking, and Stevie's sole job was to listen.

"So now I'm going off to my dad's. It'll be more relaxed than here—if you don't count looking after Lily. She's the cutest thing. I never thought I'd have a baby sister, and I certainly never thought it would happen when I was in high school—in a way, that's an awful thought—but it's happened and she's adorable and I love her and I'm glad to spend time with her and I'm glad to be with my dad when he's so obviously happy to have me and Evelyn and Lily there with him. It's like there's enough air out there to breathe, and there isn't here, certainly not at my house, anyway. Do you think the air in California is really different?"

"I've never been there," Stevie said. "I guess the weather's better."

"I don't think that's it," said Lisa.

"Probably not," Stevie agreed. She pulled into Lisa's driveway and stopped the car smoothly. She didn't know what to say. Everything seemed inadequate. Lisa smiled understandingly.

"Tell Alex I'm home, will you?" she asked.

"I think he knows already," Stevie said. She pointed to her own home, a few houses down the block. Alex had emerged from the front door and was heading toward Lisa's house. "Radar," Stevie said in explanation.

"Thanks," said Lisa. "For the lift and for letting me talk."

"You're welcome," Stevie said, meaning it.

"And congratulations on getting your job. Don't worry about the hat. It looks so silly on your head that nobody will take it seriously at all."

"You really know how to make a girl feel good, don't you?"

"That's what friends are for," Lisa said before she closed the car door and headed into her house.

Stevie waved at her twin as she passed him on her way back to their house. He was so focused on getting to Lisa's that Stevie didn't think he really saw her at all. That was okay. She was glad that her best friend had someone who loved her that much—even if it was only Stevie's brother.

"Hi, Lis'," Alex said, giving her a quick kiss on the cheek and taking her hand. "Got a minute?"

"Always," Lisa said, squeezing his hand back. "I wanted to

see you today anyway. I've got a bunch of stuff to do, and you can help."

"Like choose what shirts you're going to take to California?"

"No, actually, what CDs I should take. That's more up your alley than fashion, right?"

"Definitely," he agreed. She led him into the den, where she kept her music collection.

As they walked in, Lisa's mother came out, saying she was on her way to the grocery store. "Not that I'm going to need to keep much food in the house once you're gone for the summer, Lisa," she said. The sigh was apparent, even though inaudible.

"That makes it unanimous, then," Alex said when the door closed behind Mrs. Atwood. "Nobody wants you to go away this summer."

"That doesn't change the fact that I'm going, Alex, and it doesn't make it easier when you talk like that."

"I know, I know. I just can't help myself sometimes."

"Look, we'll talk on the phone. I'll send you e-mail from my dad's computer. I'll be in your hair so much you'll start wishing I were farther away!"

"I don't think that'll happen," he said. Gently he pulled her to him and wrapped her in his strong arms. He gave her the kiss he'd wanted to give her when he first saw her: warm, lingering, and deep. She circled her arms around his neck and kissed him back. It made her feel good—very good—but it also reminded her how hard it was going to be to be away from him for the whole summer.

They came up for air. "I'm going to miss you," he said.

"Me too. But being apart isn't going to change how we feel about one another. Besides, Alex, saying good-bye is really hard. I'm dreading it, and it doesn't help when you start doing it now. I'm not leaving yet. Let's save the good-byes until the last minute, okay?"

Alex looked at her, savoring her sweet smile and lovely face. "I hadn't thought of it that way, but, as usual, you are totally sensible and absolutely right. No good-byes. Just hellos. I do a good hello kiss, too. Want to try it?"

"Silly!" she said, pushing him away. "You're as incorrigible as your sister! Who—by the way—got herself a job today."

"Ah, my sister the pizza girl, huh? I've heard that Mr. Andrews is something else. The two of them should get along just fine."

"As long as she 'minds her Pizza Manors,' " Lisa said.

"You're kidding!"

Lisa told him all about Stevie's interview, including the hat. It was a useful way to change the mood because the image of Stevie in the feathered hat was so hilarious.

"And I guess she won't be the only one with a new look this summer."

"You have to wear a uniform while you mow lawns?" Lisa asked.

"No, of course not," he said. "But I will be spending the summer in the great outdoors, getting a tan that will be the envy of everyone but lifeguards."

"You be sure to wear sunscreen," said Lisa.

"Don't you want me to be a bronze god?"

"Better to be pasty white than to have skin cancer."

"Maybe a little tan?"

"Maybe," she said, relenting. "Just a little. If you get too handsome, the girls will all be after you, and I don't want that!"

"I'll beat them off with a stick," Alex promised.

"That's what I like to hear," Lisa said. "Now, here are my CDs. Which ones do you think I can't live without for the summer?"

Alex studied the CD holder and started pulling out boxes. He made three piles. "These are mine that you borrowed," he said, pointing to the first pile. "And these are yours that you should take with you."

"What's the third pile?" she asked.

"Yours that you want to lend to me for the summer," he explained with a smile.

She was about to protest when the phone rang. She walked into the living room and picked it up.

"Hey, Lisa! You're there. It's Skye. I'm on a quick break, so I don't have long to talk, but I heard you're coming out here—that's great! Listen, will I get to see you?"

"I don't have a lot of plans, like, for instance, I'm not in any television shows or anything. My schedule is pretty much open. You're the one with all the work."

"Well, not so much I can't visit with friends sometimes. And there's something else."

"What's that?" Lisa asked.

"Um . . . ," he said. "I guess it'll be better to talk about it when you get here. When'll you arrive? Want me to send a car?"

"No thanks, Skye. My dad'll meet me."

Alex peered through the doorway, looking curious. "Who are you talking to?" he whispered.

"Skye Ransom," she mouthed back.

The concern on Alex's face was immediate and obvious. She shook her head as if to dismiss his worry. She slipped her hand over the mouthpiece. "Just a friend," she added in a whisper.

Alex nodded broadly in a general display of disbelief.

"Look, you're going to be so busy it's going to be awfully hard for us to get together," Lisa said, as much for Alex's benefit as Skye's.

"Never too busy to see a friend," Skye told her.

"I'll call your service when I get to my dad's house and we can talk."

"Good idea," Skye said. "But why don't you call me at home? You've got the number, right?"

"Right," she said. "And you have my father's number in case we get crossed up."

"Of course," he said. "From the last time you were here. That was so much fun, wasn't it?"

"Yes," she said, remembering the great time they'd had when she had come to California for her father's wedding. Lisa was uncomfortable with the idea that Alex might misinterpret what Skye was saying to her, so she was revealing as little as possible about the other end of the conversation. But she was also uncomfortably aware that Alex knew perfectly well what she was doing.

"I bet you have to get back to the set now, right?"

"Well, in a minute," Skye said.

191

"Okay, then I'll talk to you when I get out there."

"It's a date," he said, and hung up.

Lisa cradled the phone.

"Are you making plans with Skye?" Alex asked.

"Not likely," Lisa said. "He's so busy with his career that he hardly has any time for a life. But, Alex, even if I do see him, remember, or try to remember, that he's a friend. He's been a friend for a long time. He's never been any more than a friend, or any less. You're number one on my list, and that's not going to change."

"But you're so beautiful," Alex said. "And he's not blind."

Lisa blushed. "I suppose that means you want another kiss," she teased.

"No, it means I *really* want to borrow the Zero Gravity CD for the summer."

"But that's my favorite!" she protested.

"All the better to remember you by while you're gone," he said.

Lisa smiled and gave in. Love was complicated.

SEVEN

STEVIE CHECKED over her shoulder. In the backseat of the car was a large insulated container. Each container could hold two pizzas. On the front seat, next to her hat, was the list of addresses, in order, where she was to deliver the pizzas. It wasn't actually a very long list. There was just one address left.

Delivering pizzas was just about as routine as Stevie had thought it would be. She delivered the pizza, she took the money, she thanked the customer for the tip, she took off her hat and gave her courtly bow, she waited for the inevitable giggle, and then she left. Sometimes the door closed before she bowed, sometimes not. She didn't have much time to think about that. People expected pizzas to be delivered quickly, whether they were being reasonable or not. Pizzas that were late were also cold, which meant the customer wouldn't be happy, meant they wouldn't tip, meant there wasn't anything funny or not that she could do with her silly hat that would change that. She had a job to do.

She backed the car down the Applethwaites' driveway. There was a bump, and then the left rear of the car dropped an unnerving number of inches. Stevie opened her door and looked behind her. The Applethwaites had a little flower garden bordering their concrete driveway. It now had about eight inches less of impatiens than it had had a minute earlier. She closed her door, pulled the car forward, adjusted the wheel, and backed out without inflicting further damage on the pink and white flowers. She had a brief conversation with her conscience about the damage she'd caused. She had two more pizzas to deliver right away. The Applethwaites had only tipped her a quarter, and a quick examination of the flower bed confirmed that she was hardly the first person to make that mistake. She didn't feel wonderful about her decision, but she decided to go away without saying anything.

At the next house, she banged into a garbage can and knocked it over as she came into the driveway. It was a rubber one, so it didn't make a lot of noise, and it was tightly closed, so nothing happened. Stevie righted the thing before she even rang the bell, wondering all the while why the Singers had put their garbage can right in the middle of their driveway. It belonged by the curb.

The Singers were very grateful for their pizza—two dollars more grateful than the Applethwaites. Stevie was glad she'd put the garbage can back and hoped they would want to order pizza a lot when she was on duty. She made a note to be on the lookout for their garbage can next time.

This wasn't complicated, but it was hard work—harder than she'd thought it would be, anyway. She was always rushed, and she wanted to appear unrushed. Mr. Andrews said people liked fast service, not hurried service.

Stevie returned to the shop for her next set of pizzas. This time there was only one waiting for her. She checked the slip and the order. She'd already learned that sometimes they got mixed up, and if she delivered anchovies to a sausage household, nobody would be happy. This one was right. It was a large pepperoni with mushrooms on half, and it was going to someone named Forester.

Stevie checked the address. It wasn't too far from her house. She knew the place, but she didn't remember anyone named Forester there. She was getting a vague image of the kids in the family as she drove to the house. It was a big one, nicely kept, but she was sure the family wasn't Forester.

The outside of the house was well lit. There was a two-car garage, but a vehicle was parked sideways in a turnaround part of the driveway. Beside the garage, there was a large stack of cardboard boxes. Moving cartons. Obviously, the family Stevie remembered had moved out. And now the Foresters lived there. Well, whoever they were, Stevie hoped they were big tippers.

She got out of the car, put on her silly hat, took the Foresters' pizza—still toasty warm—out of the container, and rang the doorbell.

As soon as the door began to open, Stevie spoke.

"Pizza Manor at your service, milord," she said, just as she'd been instructed.

"You've got to be kidding," said the boy who held the door.

Stevie found herself gazing into the very blue eyes of one of the best-looking guys she'd ever seen.

"I wish I were kidding," she said. "But right there in my employees manual, it says I have to say that stuff. Wait till you see what I do as I leave!"

"Well, don't hurry the process on my account," the boy said. "I'm enjoying your company."

Stevie was quite aware of the carton she was holding. The heat from the pizza had penetrated the cardboard and was doing the same to the palm of her hand. She was less than comfortable.

"Perhaps milord would like his pizza?" she asked, trying not to sound pained. " 'Twould be fully of pepperonius and a moiety of fungal deliciosity. Surely such victuals are sufficient to please the palates of the gourmettiest consumer in all the realm."

"Who can resist that?" the boy asked, and took the pizza from Stevie's hands. She blew on her palm to cool it.

"Oh, I'm sorry," the boy said. "I didn't realize the pizza would be that hot when it arrived." He turned and spoke to someone else in the hallway. "Callie, can you bring an ice cube and a piece of paper towel for our delivery person?"

"Sure," said a girl's voice.

"You've just moved in?" Stevie asked.

"Yup," said the boy. "My name's Scott Forester, and this is my sister, Callie."

Callie handed Stevie the ice cube and paper towel. Stevie thanked her and introduced herself, explaining that she lived just a few blocks away. By the time Scott had the money for Stevie—with a nice tip—they'd established that they were neighbors and that Willow Creek was a nice place to live.

Scott took the pizza into the kitchen. Callie stood and chatted with Stevie for a few minutes.

"I like your earrings," Callie said. Stevie's hand flew up to her ear—she couldn't remember which pair she'd put on that morning. She shouldn't have had to check. It was her horseshoes. What other earrings would she have chosen on the day she was going to apply for both her driver's license and a job?

"Are you a rider?" Callie asked.

"As much as possible," said Stevie. "And you?"

"Definitely. I ride endurance. But we've just moved here, so I haven't tried out your trails and competition."

"Do you have a horse?"

"We're leasing a horse for the summer, with an option to buy. In fact, he just got here today. I'm boarding him at Pine Hollow. Do you know the place?"

"Every inch of it," Stevie said. "And I can tell you, you've just made the best decision of your life."

"Well, I'm glad to hear that," said Callie. "It seemed a little—"

"That's where I keep Belle—she's my horse—and my friends ride there, too. We're probably going to be seeing a lot of each other. I promise you that the next time you see me, I won't be wearing this silly hat or shirt—that is, unless you order another pizza tonight. But I spend all the time I can at Pine Hollow. Max is great. So are Red and Ben. They're the stable hands, but you probably haven't met them yet."

"Brooding kind of guy."

"That's Ben," Stevie said. "He's wonderful with horses. And my two best friends ride there, too. You're going to love them. We tried endurance riding once. But just the once. We learned a lot, but I bet you could teach us a lot more."

"Well, if you're interested—"

"I am," Stevie assured her. "Say, my friends and I are planning a trail ride in a couple of days. Would you like to come along? We'd be glad to show you the woods around here. We know just about all the trails and the nice places to stop, and where we can canter, and some fallen logs to jump—you know, that kind of thing."

"Well, are you sure it would be okay with your friends?" Callie asked.

"Absolutely," Stevie said. "We love to show off the place to newcomers."

"Well, then, I'll be there."

"Day after tomorrow," Stevie said. "We'll take off about ten, so we'll get to Pine Hollow about nine."

"See you then, if not before," Callie said. "And, uh, thanks."

"You're welcome," Stevie said. And then, just the perfect way she was supposed to, she held her hat to her chest and bowed.

"Enjoy thy pizza," she said. Callie laughed and closed the door.

Stevie felt wonderful. She'd met two nice people, one of them a rider who already had a horse at Pine Hollow. What a great day this was turning out to be—if you didn't count some mushed impatiens, and Stevie didn't.

Stevie slid behind the wheel of her car and plopped her silly hat on the seat. That was when she noticed that her beeper was going off. Mr. Andrews had given it to her so that he could let her know when she had to hurry back to the shop. She'd been so happy about chatting with the Foresters that she'd almost forgotten she actually had a job to do. She'd taken a long time to deliver just one pizza.

She fastened her seat belt, turned the key, and shifted into reverse. She checked the mirror and began backing down the driveway carefully. There was a flower bed on the left side and the parked car on her right.

"What is it about impatiens?" Stevie asked her rearview mirror. "Why does everybody in this town have a border of impatiens next to their driveway? Is this a test?"

She checked over her left shoulder and then looked back into the mirror. The flower bed was safe this time. Cautiously she proceeded.

There was an unfamiliar feeling that Stevie didn't like at all, and she met some resistance when she put her foot on the gas pedal ever so lightly. She looked over her right shoulder. The car that was parked sideways in the turnaround area was right there. Stevie gulped, shifted into drive, and pulled ahead about a foot. She hurried out of the car, dreading what she might find.

She was right to worry. She'd broken her taillight and dented the area all around it. It was bad, really bad. She could barely bring herself to look at the other car, but she forced herself.

The other car was a Jeep. That meant it was expensive, but it also meant it was tough. Where Stevie's car had really visible damage, it wasn't so clear that the Foresters' car did. There was a scratch. And there was a slight dent—or maybe that's how the car was made. Stevie scooted over to the other side to see if it went that way, too. But it was dark outside, and the lights from the house cast dark shadows on that side of the car. She couldn't see. She really didn't know.

It wasn't like the impatiens at the Applethwaites' house. Stevie knew she'd done that and didn't really care because they'd been so stingy and because so many other people had obviously done exactly the same thing she had to the flowers.

There was a scratch on the Foresters' car, but Stevie couldn't believe she had done that. She'd been driving so slowly, how could she possibly have done any kind of damage? And *if* there was damage, there wasn't much of it. A little scratch like that could have happened anytime. Yesterday, last week, a year ago. How would anybody ever know?

Stevie heard the beeper go off again. She had to hurry or Mr. Andrews would be totally annoyed with her.

She was pretty sure she hadn't damaged the Foresters' car. The damage to her car had almost certainly been caused by the big protective bumper on the van. Definitely, Stevie decided.

She got back into her car and backed down the driveway very carefully. She decided that from then on, she would park at the curb and carry the pizzas up to the houses.

EIGHT

"COME ON, boy," Carole said to Fez the next morning. "You're about to get your first taste of riding Pine Hollow style." She gripped the horse's reins firmly and led him out of his stall toward the schooling ring, where she was going to begin fulfilling her inexplicable promise to the congressman's daughter.

Carole had ridden many horses over the years—easy ones, tough ones, old plugs, champion hunter jumpers, and priceless racehorses. Every one of them was a new experience for her, and every new experience was a good one in its own way. She wondered how this horse was going to fit into that.

Fez followed Carole dutifully out of his stall and down the stable aisle. He was getting his first real look at his new home, and Carole didn't rush him. He had every right to be curious. He eyed all the other horses as he passed them. He showed little interest, but Carole was sure he was taking it in.

She mounted and then walked him over to the good-luck

horseshoe, one of Pine Hollow's oldest traditions. Three generations before, the founder of Pine Hollow, Max Regnery, Sr., had nailed this horseshoe over the entry to the main outdoor ring. He instituted a rule for all his students that they had to touch the horseshoe before riding—every time, without fail. He told them the horseshoe had special good luck, and if they followed the rule, they wouldn't get hurt. It seemed to work. In fact, no one at Pine Hollow had ever gotten seriously injured while riding.

The little kids who rode at the stable believed deeply in the magic of the horseshoe. Carole suspected something else was at work. Touching the horseshoe was a way of reminding oneself that riding could be a dangerous sport. People could, and did, get hurt when riding, but a lot of riding accidents were the result of carelessness. Riders who remembered the dangers tended to be sensible and cautious. The horseshoe was strong preventive medicine.

Fez flinched and nearly bolted before Carole had a chance to make contact with the horseshoe.

"No way!" she said. "I know you're a handful, and there's no way I'm taking a chance. I'm going to touch that horseshoe before we take one more step."

Fez pulled at the reins and pranced nervously, but he did what he was told, and Carole managed a successful swipe at the horseshoe before she and Fez entered the schooling ring.

It was early in the morning, and she had the place to herself. The only way she could get in a brief stretch of exercise for Fez that day was to do it before work. She'd been hoping to have a chance to ride Starlight, but that would have to wait until the trail ride the next day.

Carole's plan was to give Fez an easy workout for his first full day at Pine Hollow. She wanted it to be easy for both of them, since she had a full morning ahead of her, including a whole class of young riders who needed pony assignments and a meeting with the grain salesman to go over a mysterious and complicated bill. They began at a walk, and after a few times around the ring, she gave Fez a signal to trot. He was slow to respond. A well-trained champion horse like Fez should be eager to move to a more rapid gait, but he didn't seem eager to do anything she asked of him. It took three kicks and a flick of her crop to get his attention.

It was a frustrating business. Carole wondered if her annoyance with herself was affecting the way she was riding Fez and the way he was reacting to her, but she dismissed the idea. She knew how to ride. She also knew better than to take out her frustrations on a horse.

As the ride went on, she found that she had enough frustration to take out on a hundred horses. Champion though he might be, Fez was no joy to ride. She felt as if he were giving her a fight about everything. No wonder he was an endurance champion—any rider would have to have a lot of endurance to put up with this!

Carole took a deep breath and held her temper. How could she be mad at Fez? He must be terribly confused. He'd just had a long trip, which he clearly hadn't liked. He was in a new stable, surrounded by totally new horses, handled by totally new people, probably eating a new mixture of grains, exercising in an unfamiliar schooling ring. Everything had to be frightening to him. There was no reason why his rider should be frightening, too.

Carole leaned forward and gave him an affectionate pat on his neck. "Good boy," she said. "I know you're trying, and I'll try, too. We'll do just fine together. You don't have to worry, because I'd never do anything to hurt you. I'll be gentle as can be and take good care of you."

In thanks, Fez bucked.

Fifteen frustrating minutes later, Carole began thinking about how much fun it was going to be to assign ponies for the beginner class. That was when Stevie arrived. As far as Carole was concerned, Stevie was the proverbial knight on the white horse—only in this case, it was a good thing she arrived without a horse, because Carole was more than willing to provide one.

"Can you give me a hand here?" Carole asked.

"Sure," Stevie said. Carole wondered briefly if she should leave Stevie in blissful ignorance and abandon her to Fez. Somehow that didn't seem fair.

She rode over to where Stevie stood by the fence and dismounted. Fez relaxed instantly, and Carole was amused to see that he was clearly as relieved to have her out of his saddle as she was to be out.

"I've done something dumb and I really need some help," Carole confessed. "This is Fez. He's new at the stable and he's like a VIP. The owner was here yesterday. She was difficult, fussy, and moody, and she kept telling me how wonderful her last stable was. Well, you know how I am. I can't stand the idea that anybody thinks any other stable is better than Pine Hollow, and she gave the strong impression that her horse was exercised by the staff as part of his board there, so naturally—"

"Carole, you didn't!"

"Well, I guess I did," Carole said. "I told her I'd exercise him four days a week."

"Right, like Max is going to pay you for that?"

"Not a chance," Carole said. "I know. It's on me. I'm going to have to deal with it, and soon. But until I do, I made a promise. Now, I've got a whole bunch of stuff to do in the office before the beginners arrive. Can you give this guy the rest of his workout?"

"I'm always happy to ride," Stevie said.

"This may be an exception," said Carole. "He's a real handful—as bad as his owner. The workout is simple, though. He's just got to get some kinks out. Loosen him up until he's relaxed, maybe another half hour."

"Oh, sure," Stevie said. "You let me take care of this boy. All he needs is a little of Stevie's special tender loving care. He'll be putty in my hands in no time."

"Thanks," Carole said, handing her the reins. "But don't forget to touch the horseshoe."

Before Stevie could ask for any more information, Carole had headed for the office.

It only took a few minutes for Stevie to see what Carole was talking about. This horse was a handful. There were some horses it would be wonderful to exercise, but this guy—what was his name?—was going to take more than a little getting used to.

Walk, trot, canter. He did them all, but he balked and fussed. She didn't like to use her crop on an unfamiliar horse, but when she did, he didn't pay any more attention to her. She decided to use a gentle hand while she and the horse got used to one another. It meant generally letting him have his way, but it also meant they weren't fighting all the time, and at the very least it meant that he got the exercise he needed, even if he didn't get the discipline routine training required. Tomorrow would be another day.

When she'd finished putting him through his paces—or, more accurately, letting him put himself through whatever paces he wanted to go through—she dismounted and walked him around the ring to cool him down. They'd need to be out of the ring before the beginner class started.

The second time around the ring, she noticed that she was being watched. It was Callie, the girl she'd met last night. Stevie walked over to her.

"Welcome to Pine Hollow!" she said.

"Well, thank you," said Callie. "You're riding early this morning."

"I'm doing someone a favor," Stevie said as she dismounted. "This horse belongs to some difficult VIP who has just started here, and my friend was trying to soothe some ruffled feathers, so she offered to exercise him for the owner—"

Something was wrong, and Stevie knew it before she could stop the words from tumbling out of her mouth.

"I guess that would make me the difficult VIP with the ruffled feathers," Callie said.

"Oh, no, I'm sure there's a mistake here," Stevie said, but she knew the mistake was hers. "I probably totally misunderstood. Anyway, I've been riding this horse and he's a handful, so I guess what my friend meant was that the horse is difficult.

I just wasn't listening too carefully because the horse is so, um, well, he's a beauty, but he *is* hard to handle. Didn't you say he was a new horse for you?" There had to be some way to deflect the conversation into a safer zone.

"We're renting him with an option to buy. Fez has been winning endurance ribbons all over the place. I'm sure he's feisty. I know he gave that girl—Carole?—trouble yesterday when he got off the van. But I rode him before we signed his papers and he's good—that is, if you know how to handle him."

"I guess I have some learning to do," Stevie said, still trying to recover from one of the most embarrassing situations she'd ever created. "But I'm about done with his exercise. I think he's loosened up, and he won't be so difficult tomorrow."

"I'm sure you're right," Callie said. "I have to go now—unless you need me to do something with Fez?"

"No, no, I'll take care of him," Stevie said. "I'd like the chance to get to know this champ a little better. Grooming is a good way to make friends. Um, how was the pizza?"

"The—? Oh, right, the pizza. Last night. It was fine. Thanks. Well, see you sometime."

"Tomorrow," Stevie said. "Remember the trail ride?"

"You sure? This isn't just something nice to do for a hard-to-handle VIP?"

"No, I'm sure. And it'll be good for Fez here," Stevie said. "He'll love to spend some time in the woods. It'll feel like home to him."

"Right," said Callie. "Tomorrow. Bye."

"Bye," said Stevie. She leaned against the fence and

watched Callie walk back to the car that was waiting for her. Stevie thought she had never in her life been so glad to have a conversation end. She'd liked Callie from the moment she'd met her the night before, and she thought Callie liked her. This was someone she could be friends with, and any friend of Stevie's was bound to be a friend of Carole's and Lisa's. Well, that was a great way to begin a friendship! She'd insulted Callie and betrayed Carole's confidence.

Fez broke into her unhappy thoughts by nipping at her shoulder.

"I guess I deserve that," Stevie told the horse. "That and more. Think you could kick me a few times? Throw me when we go over a fence? Whatever you do, it wouldn't hurt as much as what I've done to myself, that's for sure."

Fez just stared at her silently. "All right, then I'll groom you. If I work hard enough, maybe it'll make me forget what I just said to skewer my best friend. Shall we give it a try?"

For the first time that day, Fez behaved perfectly. He followed Stevie's slightest signal to return to the stable and stood absolutely still while she groomed him.

The work wasn't enough to distract her, though. All she could think of was how much she'd been looking forward to going on the trail ride with Carole and Lisa. This would be their last trail ride together for months, until Lisa got back from California.

And now she had two little things she had to share with Carole. First she had to confess that she'd told Callie that Carole thought she was difficult, and then she had to tell Carole that she'd had the foresight to invite the aforementioned difficult rider along on their trail ride!

No, Stevie told herself. It wasn't even nine o'clock in the morning and she'd already made enough terrible mistakes for a week, much less a day. Confessing to Carole was almost certainly going to lead to at least one more mistake. That could wait.

NINE

CAROLE WAS on the phone when Stevie stuck her head into the office the next morning at quarter of nine. Stevie had arrived early so that she'd have a chance to talk to Carole and let her know she'd invited Callie along.

Stevie waved to get Carole's attention.

"No, of course we're having the class, Mrs. Van Buren," Carole said into the phone. "It's just that Max will be teaching it instead of—um, yes, he's a good instructor—Well, he owns the place. He's taught for years. He was practically born on a—Mrs. Van Buren—"

Carole's eyes rolled up to the ceiling. Obviously she was having a difficult phone conversation with somebody who (a) wasn't listening and (b) wouldn't have understood what she was hearing even if she had been listening. Carole circled her ear with her finger to indicate her feelings about Mrs. Van Buren's sanity. Stevie nodded.

Finally Carole convinced Mrs. Van Buren that Max would be a worthy instructor for her first lesson. She cradled the phone. "The whole world has gone crazy," she told Stevie.

"Well, since we're on the subject," Stevie said, recognizing a chance to segue when she heard one. "There's something—"

Four little girls shoved past Stevie and planted themselves in front of Carole's desk.

"Erin said you said she could ride Patch today," one of them began.

"But you told me Max said the one who did the best in the relay races could have Patch this week, but Erin didn't do best, even though her team won. Sophie was the best and she doesn't want Patch, she wants to ride Penny, so Caitlin should get Patch, but she told Max I kicked Peso too hard, but that's not true, so she shouldn't be able to ride Patch—"

"Stop, stop, stop!" Carole said, putting her hands over her ears. "The pony assignments are posted in the tack room. No changes will be made. Period. Nobody's riding Patch because he's got a swollen ankle and I know you didn't kick Peso and there's only fifteen minutes until class starts so what are you doing here?"

The little girls fled.

"Uh, speaking of difficult, well, I mean, fussy riders—" Stevie began.

The phone rang. Carole answered it and then listened intently. "No, Mr. Burns. I am sure that what we ordered was oats and not pellets. We have pellets left, so we wouldn't—" She covered the mouthpiece and looked at Stevie. "I spent half an hour with this man yesterday and today he wants to go over it all again— Uh, yes, Mr. Burns. I have a copy of the purchase order. I gave it to you yesterday. . . . Yes, sure, I'll fax you another copy, but in the meantime, Mr. Burns—Mr. Burns?" She hung up the phone. "That man is impossible!" she said.

"Well, yes, some people are," said Stevie. "Look, there's something I need to talk to you about."

"Thank heavens we'll have time to talk on the trail ride. This place is a zoo; I can't wait for the peace and quiet of the woods. Could you tack up Starlight for me?"

"Of course," Stevie said. "But before then, Carole, you should know—"

The phone rang again. "Yes, Mr. Burns. Well, I'm glad you found it. . . . No, Mr. Burns, that's not this order, you're looking at the purchase order from last month." Carole put her hand over the mouthpiece and spoke with Stevie while Mr. Burns droned on. "I'll see you in the stable as soon as I can get away from here. Okay?"

"Okay," Stevie agreed. It wasn't okay, but she knew she couldn't do anything about it right then.

Lisa was giving Prancer a quick brushing when Stevie returned with Belle's tack. The two of them worked side by side, chatting about the commotion around them while they tacked up their horses.

"Morning, Stevie," Callie Forester said.

"Oh, hi, Callie. I want you to meet Lisa Atwood, one of my best friends. Lisa, I didn't have a chance to tell you yet, but I invited Callie to come along on our trail ride. She's new to Willow Creek as well as to Pine Hollow, so I thought this would be a good chance to show off the place." She quickly explained how she'd met Callie when she'd delivered pizza to her house.

Lisa smiled warmly at Callie, but the glance she gave Stevie was quizzical. Stevie knew she deserved it. This was supposed to be a trail ride for three old friends, not for newcomers, even nice newcomers.

"Welcome to Pine Hollow, Callie," Lisa said. "Is that pretty Arab down the hallway yours?"

"Yep, that's right. And this will be the first chance I've had to ride him here. I'm really looking forward to it."

"Callie does endurance riding," Stevie said. "I mean, she's really good. She's won all sorts of junior competitions."

"Not here," Callie said. "Back home."

"Where's home?" Lisa asked.

"Out on the West Coast. We just moved here. Well, my dad's been here since January. He's a congressman, and he just got elected. So we'll be here at least two years—just long enough to get me and my brother through high school. He'll be a senior, and I'm going into my junior year. It was really tough moving."

"I can relate to that," said Lisa. "Not that I've moved, exactly, but my parents got a divorce and my dad's remarried and he's living in California—"

"Where?"

"Near Los Angeles. And I'm going there for the summer—"

"It's so hard!" said Callie. "Maybe even harder for you

213

because it's not permanent. It's just for a couple of months, and without going to school, it's almost impossible to get to know people."

"Thanks for reminding me," Lisa said sardonically.

"I'm sorry. I just meant I understand."

Lisa smiled. "I know that's what you meant. Did you live near Los Angeles?"

"No, we were up north, in a little town. I could do a lot of riding there."

"That's one thing your little town and Willow Creek have in common. You can do a lot of riding here. The school is close enough that you can actually come over every day after school if you want. Before, too."

"You can count on me being here," said Callie. "Even though the stable said they'd exercise Fez for me, I'd like to do it myself most of the time."

"Max'll ride him for you?" Lisa asked. That didn't sound like Max at all. In the first place, he didn't have time, and in the second place, he thought it was really important for the owners to ride their horses. Otherwise, why did they have them?

"No, it wasn't Max. It was that girl—I keep forgetting her name. She said she'd take care of it, so how could I refuse? Oh, that's her," she said, nodding at Carole, who was walking toward them.

"Hi, Carole," Lisa greeted her friend. "Did you meet Callie yet? Yeah, I guess you did. Anyway, she's coming along on our trail ride. Stevie met her the other night when she was delivering pizza to her house. Small world, huh? And, wait until you see her horse. Oh. You probably did see her horse, didn't you?"

"Callie and I have met," Carole said.

"Right after Fez arrived," Callie added.

Lisa knew an undercurrent when she was standing in the middle of one. What she didn't know was where this one had come from. Carole was upset about something, and it seemed as if it had to do with Callie, but maybe it was something that had happened in the office. "Stevie said things were wild in the office. The phone wouldn't stop ringing and the kids kept barging in. You must be glad to have an excuse to escape for a while. Is Emily here?"

"Yes, she's here," Carole said. She glanced back and forth between Stevie and Callie, recalling how Stevie seemed to have been in a rush to tell her something when everything was going crazy in the office. Of course, now she realized it was about Callie. Carole hadn't known they'd already met. And she certainly hadn't known that Callie was coming along on their special farewell ride. What could Stevie have been thinking?

Then she figured it out. Stevie had invited Callie to ride with them so that Carole wouldn't have to exercise Fez that afternoon. She was probably just trying to do the right thing, so it was hard for Carole to be angry with her, but that didn't mean Carole wanted to spend a couple of hours riding with Callie. Maybe Carole hadn't made it clear to Stevie that the human VIP was as difficult as the horse one. But that didn't make it okay, and it didn't make Carole want to be a part of it.

"Listen, something's come up."

"With that Mr. Burns?" asked Stevie.

"That and about fourteen other things. You know how

215

crazy it can get on summer mornings. It was probably a mistake to think I could go riding in the first place, but I definitely can't go with you guys now. I've got to stay here. Starlight needs a little workout, for sure, but I'm going to have to do it in the ring so that people can hassle me about pony assignments, grain orders, and manure disposal while I ride. You all go on ahead."

"But Carole—" Lisa protested.

"Don't worry. We'll have some time together later. You'll be back about noon, and I'll meet you guys at the usual place."

Without offering further explanation or waiting for protests, Carole spun around to leave her friends alone. She was angry. Very angry. And hurt. Their final trail ride of the summer was being interrupted by Callie Forester. If the girl loved "back home" so much, Carole wished she'd just go there—go anyplace, in fact, other than Pine Hollow.

What was done was done. Carole couldn't change it. She just didn't want to upset her friends, and she wasn't going to let Callie see her cry.

Stevie felt terrible. She knew she'd made a mistake. In fact, it seemed as if she was doing nothing but making mistakes these days. She'd hurt Carole's feelings and that bothered her, but it bothered her even more that she had messed up this trail ride. It was supposed to be fun. It was supposed to be great. When she'd invited Callie along, she'd been sure that both Lisa and Carole would like Callie as much as she did. How could she have known that wouldn't be so? And what had Callie done to make Carole think she was difficult? She seemed perfectly nice to Stevie.

Time would tell. And time was passing.

"Boy, it's too bad Carole can't come along," said Lisa.

"Yes," Callie agreed. "I wanted a chance to get to know her better. It was sort of rushed before."

Stevie wondered what that meant.

"Come on, let's get going," Lisa said. "If we stand still for a minute longer, Max will try to con us into helping tack up the ponies for the beginners."

"Okay," Stevie said, mounting Belle. "We're off, and Lisa and I promise to give you the grand tour of Pine Hollow. First stop, the good-luck horseshoe."

Stevie led the way out of the stable, through the paddocks, and into the woods behind Pine Hollow. Although it wasn't yet ten o'clock, the summer sun was already hot. The sweet scent of fresh field grass combined with the ever wonderful smells of horses and leather. It was a combination that never failed to make her feel better. The sun sparkled through the leaves, dappling the bridle trail. Beneath her, Stevie felt the wonderful warm power of her beloved Belle. She could feel her own worry and distress practically melt in the warm June day.

Behind her, Lisa and Callie were chatting easily.

". . . Well, the worst part of the election was when the whole family got interviewed by this local television station. Do you know how hard it is to smile for two hours? And out of that, they only ran about three minutes of the interview. Just two and a half seconds of that was about me."

"Were you smiling?"

"You bet I was!" Callie said, laughing. "I wasn't going to ruin Dad's future with a single grimace."

"It must be awful being on display all the time."

"Well, it really isn't all the time. In a way, too, it was harder out there where there's only one congressman in the district and it's Dad. Here, near Washington, there are loads of them. It seems like nobody gives it a second thought."

"People aren't impressed here until you get to be a senator," said Lisa, smiling.

"Unless you're indicted," Stevie said. "I mean, if you can rustle up a good scandal, everybody will be wowed!"

"I think we'll try to avoid that," said Callie. "My dad's not the love nest type."

"So, you've got a great set of parents and a funny, flirty brother—wait'll you meet Scott, Lisa. It's a perfect life," said Stevie.

"Not totally," said Callie. "I mean, I don't have a car to drive because I'm still grounded for something I did back home. If I want to go anywhere I'm at the mercy of my flirty brother, who, as you may have noticed, is interested in chatting with almost anybody but me. Most of the time I'm stuck with a bicycle, and I feel like I'm too old for a bike. I envy you your car."

"It's just part-time," said Stevie. "I share it with my twin brother. Sharing has not always been our strongest quality, but we do okay on that because we agreed to a schedule. So far, it's worked out. But that may not mean much. We just got our licenses this week."

Callie laughed.

"You'll do fine on the sharing," Lisa said. "I'll see to it."

"Maybe," said Stevie. "Anyway, I love driving, and anytime I actually have the car, I'd be glad to drive you anywhere. No excuse is too slight for a good long ride—whether it's in a car or on horseback."

"Check," said Callie. "And I'm glad I've got a witness to what you just said, because I will definitely take you up on that."

"No problem," Stevie assured her. "And I already know where you live. And what you like on your pizza."

"See what happens when you're in the public eye?" Callie said to Lisa. "People keep dossiers on you. *Lifestyles of the Impoverished and Not Very Famous*. Now, where's this famous creek you kept talking about? My feet are getting hot and sweaty. They could use a good cool dunk."

"Right this way, milady," Stevie said.

Callie laughed and followed Stevie, happy and relaxed for the first time since she'd arrived in Willow Creek. She liked these girls. Fez was behaving better than he had the last time she'd ridden him, and she suspected it was because he was comfortable being sandwiched between Stevie's Belle and Prancer, the horse Lisa was riding.

Callie just wished everybody at Pine Hollow was as nice as Lisa and Stevie.

TEN

CAROLE SLID the final updated notebook onto the shelf above her desk and stretched. She'd finished the work she'd needed to get done, and she could relax because it was noon. Denise would be at the office in a few minutes to relieve her for the day. That meant Carole could go home—or she could wait for her friends and go over to TD's for something to eat. It wouldn't be as good as a trail ride would have been, but at least it would be just the three of them. She promised herself for the umpteenth time that she wouldn't say anything to Stevie about inviting Callie along. Stevie had her reasons and that was that.

As soon as Denise arrived, Carole walked out to the schooling ring. From there, she'd be able to see her friends when they returned from their ride.

Everything at Pine Hollow seemed wonderfully normal on this hot summer day. Max was finishing up a jump class with the beginning riders. The next class was warming up their horses by walking them around the ring, waiting for Max to come teach them equitation. Nearby, Ben waited to help riders untack their horses and groom them. The riders would do all the work—or at least most of it—because that was the way it was done at Pine Hollow, but Ben would be sure it was done correctly.

"A penny for your thoughts," said a familiar voice.

Carole turned to see Emily Williams grooming her horse, PC, in the stall closest to the door.

"They're not worth that much," Carole assured her.

"I'm not so sure about that," Emily countered. "It takes more than a penny's worth of thinking to figure out why it was that you skipped the trail ride with your friends today. It wasn't because you don't trust me to look after the office."

"No, of course it wasn't," Carole said. "It's just that something came up."

"Okay," Emily said agreeably. "I don't have to know everything, but that doesn't keep me from *wanting* to know everything."

"Right," Carole said. She really didn't want to tell Emily everything that had happened. None of it felt right, and that wasn't something she wanted to share, even with a good friend. "Can I give you a hand with PC?" she offered.

"No thanks. I thought I'd take advantage of the extra free time I have to give him a first-class grooming. What I didn't know was how badly he needed it. His idea of the perfect way to celebrate the beginning of summer is to roll in the mud in the little paddock. So it's been beauty day for Prince Charming."

Carole peered at her friend. She was wearing a Pine Hollow T-shirt over her riding clothes to keep them clean. Emily supported herself with one crutch while she groomed her horse with one hand. Everything she did took her twice as much effort as it would anybody else, and she still managed to do three times as good a job.

"Pass me the rag, will you?" Emily asked. Carole stepped into the stable and handed her the towel. As Emily rubbed, PC's coat began to shine.

"I'd better go get my sunglasses," Carole said. "All that glare . . ."

"Flattery will get you nowhere," Emily said. "You're going to have to groom your own horse."

"I already did that. Now I'm just waiting for Lisa and Stevie to get back." Carole turned to look outside. Across the field, she could see some riders emerging from the woods. "And I think my wait's over. Listen, thanks for being willing to cover for me this morning, Emily, even if it turned out I didn't need you."

"Anytime, Carole," Emily said.

Carole walked to the door of the stable and climbed onto the paddock fence so that she could welcome the trail riders back. The three of them rode abreast, Callie in the middle. Callie was doing well with that handful of a horse she had. Carole didn't like to admit it, but Callie was doing much better with Fez than she had. She wished she could flatter herself by saying that Fez was easier for Callie to ride because Carole had exercised him so successfully, but she suspected there wasn't any truth to that.

Carole had to wait until the riders were within a hundred

yards of the stable before any of them saw her perched on the fence.

It was Lisa, finally, who spotted her. "Hi, Carole. We missed you!"

"Terribly!" said Stevie.

"Did you show Callie everything?" Carole asked.

"Absolutely," Stevie said. "Now she and Fez know all our secrets."

Carole smiled on the outside. She knew Stevie was just joking, but it didn't feel like a joke.

Carole opened the paddock gate, and the girls rode to the stable entrance before dismounting. Carole had brought a small supply of carrots for the horses. Just riding on a trail was generally considered as much of a treat for the horses as the riders, but no excuse was too slight to give Belle and Prancer rewards for good behavior. Carole handed some treats to Callie to give to Fez as well.

"Speaking of treats," Stevie began, "did you say something about TD's?"

"I did," Carole said. "And as soon as I've groomed Fez, we can go over there."

"You don't have to groom him, Carole. I'll take care of it," said Callie. "You've already had one plan canceled this morning. You should have time for a nice long visit with Lisa and Stevie without worrying about me or my horse."

"Okay, thanks," Carole said, looking at Callie curiously. What she'd said sounded perfectly normal and straightforward, but Carole wondered if perhaps Callie just didn't trust her to groom the horse. No, that didn't seem likely. After all, she was trusting her to ride him.

Carole set her concerns aside and focused on helping Lisa and Stevie finish their chores so that they could get down to the serious matter of spending precious time together. It didn't take long. Less than an hour later, they were sliding into their usual booth at the ice cream parlor.

This had been a tradition among the friends for a long time—as long as they'd known one another. It was always TD's, it was always the same booth, it was almost always the same waitress. Every once in a while, they'd find someone else in "their" booth. They all swore the food didn't taste as good if they ate it at another table.

Stevie picked up a menu. "This should be something special," she said. "We won't be doing it again for a long time."

"Don't remind me," Lisa said. "I've already lectured your brother about not beginning to say good-bye before we absolutely have to."

"Okay, okay," Stevie agreed. "So I'll pretend I'm not sorry you're going away. But I'm still going to have something special. What I mean by that is something that isn't pizza."

Stevie ordered a sundae of hot fudge on pistachio ice cream. With peanut butter sauce. "Oh, and can you put some granola on it, too?"

Carole and Lisa never ceased to be amazed at what Stevie chose to call a treat. They each asked for frozen yogurt.

When the waitress left their table, Lisa continued where Stevie had left off. "Let's pretend I'm not going away at all," she said.

"I'm with Lisa," said Carole. "Let's ignore the obvious and change the subject. So, how did the ride go with Callie? That was so nice of you to look after her and get her to ride her *own* horse."

"No problem," said Lisa, ignoring Carole's rather pointed comment. "She's awfully nice. We had a good time, except for missing you.

"She was telling us this funny story about one night during her father's election campaign when she had a big research paper due but she had to be at this dinner instead of doing history homework. The paper was about a factory in their state that had been shut down because of toxic dumping. She hadn't had time to do enough research—and then it turns out that at the dinner, she was sitting next to the man who'd been governor when the factory had been closed. He'd signed the papers to do it! Her teacher couldn't believe how much primary source material she'd gotten."

Lisa and Stevie laughed as they retold the story, describing how Callie had written quotes from the former governor on the evening's printed program, on her napkin, even on the palm of her hand, while her father was trying to get votes.

Lisa noticed that Carole wasn't laughing. "Well, I guess you had to be there. Anyway, Callie has done a lot of stuff, and she tells great stories. You're really going to like her when you get to know her better."

"I'm sure you're right," Carole said. Their desserts arrived before she had to say any more.

Callie was glad to have some quiet time with her horse. She'd enjoyed the ride with Lisa and Stevie. They were nice, and they might even be friends one day. What mattered more than friends, though, was looking after Fez. He was a handful. He was more of a handful that day than he had been when she'd taken him for his test ride. He'd been at Pine Hollow for three days and should have settled in a little bit. As talented as he was, it was going to be a nuisance to have a horse who hated traveling and took a long time to get used to a new stable. Competition horses traveled a lot and stayed in unfamiliar lodgings all the time. She was going to have to find a way around that. Maybe he'd like a stablemate, a dog or a goat perhaps. Maybe she could find some kind of toy for him that he could take wherever he went. Sometimes horses became particularly fond of something in their own stable, a bucket or a hay net. Whatever it was, it would be a sort of security blanket for him. There had to be an answer, because if this was his best behavior, she wasn't going to keep him any longer than the summer lease.

"Whoa there, boy," she said, patting Fez's neck. He liked that and stood still for a moment. He stood still while she picked his hooves, but he got fussy as she was combing him. His ears flicked back and forth and then lay flat against his head. His eyes opened wide.

She put away the comb and took out a brush. He seemed to like that better. She worked carefully and methodically, trying to see if there were any particular places Fez didn't like to have brushed. He tolerated it.

As she worked, she noticed that there was another girl about her age grooming a horse in the stall across from Fez's. She was wearing a T-shirt that said Pine Hollow. It was the same kind of shirt that Ben had been wearing the day before. In spite of all the talk about how everybody at Pine Hollow took care of their own horses, it seemed that there was at least one stable hand doing an owner's work.

Callie finished using her brush and tossed it into the grooming bucket. It made a louder sound than she'd expected, startling her. Even more, though, it startled Fez. He tossed his head up. His ears went back, and his eyes opened wide until the whites showed. He began prancing nervously, and that was when Callie realized that she might have made a terrible tactical error by failing to cross-tie her horse before she groomed him, though it hadn't seemed necessary as long as he was in his stall.

Callie tried to shift around so that her back was to the door of the stall and not the back wall, where she could be pinned easily, but Fez was blocking her way. He whinnied and fussed. He wasn't threatening her, specifically, but he was upset, and it was a really bad idea to be in a stall with a loose horse that was upset.

Then she remembered the girl across the hall.

"Can you help me?" she asked.

"No, I can't," Emily answered. "Do you want me to call Ben?"

The response stunned Callie. How could anyone refuse to help someone who so obviously needed it?

Then, as suddenly as he'd spooked, Fez calmed down and Callie didn't need help from anyone. She took the set of cross-ties out of her bucket, clipped them onto the walls of his stall and to his halter, and finished grooming him.

"Did you get your horse under control?" the girl across the hallway asked.

"Yes, no thanks to you," Callie shot back.

"But I couldn't—"

"I understand that you *wouldn't*," Callie said, cutting her off angrily. She'd really been in danger. It was inexcusable that someone would refuse to give her a hand. "I don't think I have anything further to say to *you*."

But she had a few things to say to someone else. As soon as she could have an appointment with Max Regnery, he was going to get a piece of her mind about a certain stable hand who was too good to help a rider who was in trouble.

"All right, so there's one thing I have to say about this summer," Lisa began. "And that is that I've heard from Skye. He called me. I can't wait to see him. It's always exciting. He even said there was something he wanted to talk to me about when I get to Los Angeles."

"He wants you to meet his movie star buddies," said Stevie, licking the last bit of fudge off her spoon.

"In which case, I'll give you a list of the ones you *must* give my phone number to," Carole said as she finished her dish of frozen yogurt.

"I don't think so, but count on me to be looking out for your interests if that's what Skye has in mind."

Stevie looked at Carole. "She's never going to come back! She'll go out there, where they have good weather year-round, where she knows the most famous and desirable of all the young stars—"

"Don't be silly," said Lisa. "Not come back? How could you even think that I would ever consider leaving all this behind?" She gestured around her, indicating both TD's and the town of Willow Creek, which lay beyond the windows.

228

Stevie and Carole glanced around. What they saw was an ice cream parlor that hadn't changed much since the late 1960s. It had probably been humble then, and time hadn't improved it any. Willow Creek was a nice enough town, but there were no movie stars, very few celebrities (unless you counted Mr. Jenson, who had won more than forty-three thousand dollars when he was on vacation in Las Vegas), and zero glamour.

"Look on the bright side," Stevie said. "At least we'll have a good excuse to go to California!"

"Stop it!" Lisa said. "I have no intention of moving out there. I promise you I'll be back in time for school. I'll be ready to come back. The hardest part about this whole summer is going to be leaving. And I don't mean just the saying good-bye part, either. Even getting to the airport is going to be tough. My mother says she can't do it. I think she means she won't because she hates the whole idea. Thankfully, Alex said he'd take me."

"But I've got the car tomorrow," Stevie protested. "I'll need it for work in the evening, and I promised to take Callie over to the tack shop at the mall in the afternoon."

"I know. Relax, Alex told me you'd have the car," Lisa said. "He's going to borrow someone else's. I wasn't expecting you to offer. Besides, Alex really wants to be there."

"I'm sure," said Stevie. "He wants to give you the kind of send-off that'll guarantee you'll be back."

"Guarantees aren't necessary," Lisa said. "I'll be back. Count on it."

Stevie and Carole were both already doing that.

ELEVEN

"YIKES!" STEVIE said, looking at her watch and then at Carole. "I promised you a ride home and I still have to shower before I go to work. We'd better get going. Can I give you a lift anywhere, Lisa?" She glanced at the check and put her share of it on the table. Carole followed suit.

"No thanks," Lisa said. "I have to go back to Pine Hollow. I left a library book in my cubby, and I'd better return it today or I might not have a chance." She took out her wallet and added her share.

The three girls stood up.

"We'll talk to you before you go," Stevie said.

Lisa nodded. "Definitely," she agreed. She gave them each a quick hug and headed for the door.

Stevie and Carole walked the short distance to Stevie's house.

"Where's the car?" Carole asked.

"In the garage," Stevie said. Carole was a little surprised.

Normally both Stevie and Alex left the car in the driveway, ready to go in a second. "Wait here, I'll bring it out," Stevie said.

Stevie had backed the car into the garage so that it could be stored with the broken taillight and dented end in the place least likely to be detected by her brother or her parents. She knew she was going to have to confess at some point. She just wasn't at that point yet, and the longer she could put it off, the better. She could tell Carole, of course—but why? If nobody knew, nobody would be nagging her to confess.

In a few minutes Carole was buckled into the passenger seat and the two of them were on their way to her house.

"So, what are we going to do about our farewell for Lisa?" Carole asked.

"We'll go to the airport, of course," Stevie said.

Carole smiled. It was exactly what she had in mind, too. "Alex won't be able to give her all the send-off she deserves," she said. "He's definitely going to need some help from us."

"Definitely. We can do balloons and stuff if you want."

"No, just us," said Carole. "A strong reminder, along with Alex, of everything she's leaving behind."

"That's a deal, and then I can take Callie to the tack shop on the way back from the airport before I go to work."

"Callie?"

"Well, yes, I promised I'd take her to the tack shop at the mall."

"Aren't you going to a lot of trouble for someone you just met?" Carole asked.

"It's really no trouble. I like driving, remember?"

Carole didn't think driving was the issue. She needed to

231

remind Stevie of the sacrifices they all seemed to be making for Callie Forester. "I was sorry to miss the ride this morning, and I meant to thank you for helping out with Pine Hollow's newest difficult tenant," she said, referring to Callie.

"It was no problem," Stevie said. "I mean, he acted up a few times on the trail, but Callie controlled him just fine. She said she thought it helped having him between Belle and Prancer, too. He'll settle down in a few days, I'm sure."

Carole thought that was probably true; she just wondered when his owner would settle down. For whatever reason, Stevie didn't seem concerned about that. Carole thought it best to drop the subject.

The book was right where Lisa knew it would be. She picked it up, tucked it into her backpack, and was about to leave for the library when she realized she hadn't given Prancer a proper farewell for the summer. She wasn't *just* leaving her human friends for two months.

Prancer's stall was on the far end of the U-shaped hallway that housed all the horse stalls at Pine Hollow. The nice thing about that was that she passed all the horses in the place on her way. She greeted them by name, waving, patting, and talking to them sweetly. Most of the horses were in their stalls. The place was quiet.

"Hi there, PC," she said, giving Emily's curious horse a welcome scratch on his neck. He nuzzled her neck with his damp nose.

"Oh, forget it," she said, giggling at the tickle. "I don't have any goodies with me. Besides, I'm absolutely certain I saw Emily giving you an apple this morning."

He relented and returned his attention to his hay tick.

"Hi, Fez," she said, greeting the horse across the hall. "Are you worn out from our— Oh, Callie, you're in there. I didn't see you."

Callie stood up. "Yeah, I was working on his coat. It's amazing how much mud gets on the coat—to say nothing of his fetlock, which I brushed for five minutes before I got the ball of mud off."

"I know," Lisa said. "Horses are very absorbent. Do you want some help?"

"No thanks. I'm actually finished cleaning up my dirt sponge," Callie said. She brushed her hands off on her apron, stowed the last of her equipment in the bucket, and unlatched Fez's cross-ties. "I really do appreciate your offer of help, though. It seems to me that the riders here are always offering to help out—much better than the staff. And that reminds me that there's something I need to talk to Max about."

"What's that?" Lisa asked. The remark really surprised her. She'd always found everyone at Pine Hollow very helpful. "I mean, what happened?"

"Well, it was partly my fault, I know," Callie began. "I got in here to groom Fez and didn't put him on cross-ties. He got upset and threatening. I asked the stable hand to help me and she refused."

"We don't have any girl stable hands now," Lisa said. "It must have been a rider." She couldn't imagine who would refuse to help.

"Well, she was wearing one of the stable T-shirts," Callie said. "And she was grooming that horse over there—the one you were talking to."

233

"PC?"

"That's his name?"

"Right, this one here," Lisa said. "This is PC, and he belongs to Emily Williams. It must have been Emily— Oh, no. What did she say? I mean, exactly."

Callie described what happened. "I asked her to help me. She said, 'No, I can't,' and then she said she'd call for Ben if I wanted—like I needed help calling for help."

"She was right," said Lisa. "She couldn't help you."

"All I needed was for someone to run over here and hand me the cross-ties. Even a child could do that."

"As long as the child wasn't on crutches," Lisa said.

"What?"

"There's no way you would know, I guess, but Emily has cerebral palsy. She can walk, but only with crutches, and it's slow. When she said she couldn't help you, she meant it. You were going to do a lot better with Ben's help than hers."

Callie put her hand to her mouth. "I didn't know," she said quietly.

"Why would you? Look, don't worry about it. Emily doesn't like special treatment. She always says she's not a disabled person, she's a person with a disability. It's not the first thing she wants anybody to know, and as a result a lot of people get to know her before they notice. That's okay, too."

"As long as they don't insult her the way I did," said Callie. "I . . . I threatened to report her to Max. I thought she was an employee—"

"Well, we're all kind of like employees here, so you weren't so far off the mark on that one."

"Well, I was making noises like I thought she shouldn't be

an employee any longer. I must have come off like a total jerk. I'm so embarrassed!"

She stepped out of Fez's stall and closed and latched the door behind her. "Do you think she's still here?" she asked Lisa. "I've got to find her and apologize."

"I didn't see her, but let's look."

The two of them hurried to the office. Denise was behind the desk, trying to straighten out a rider's bill for the month.

"Is Emily still here?" Lisa asked.

"Nope," Denise said. "She left about half an hour ago. She used the phone to call her mother and asked her to come right away. She seemed pretty upset about something. Do you know what it was about?"

"I'm afraid I have an idea," Callie said. "I need to talk to her. Can you give me her phone number?"

"I'm not really supposed to give out phone numbers," said Denise.

"It's important," said Lisa.

The look on Lisa's face must have convinced Denise to get out the stable address book. She jotted down the number and address on a scrap of paper and handed it to Callie.

"Hope it turns out okay," said Denise.

"Me too," said Callie. "Thanks, and bye." She was out of the office before Lisa had a chance to offer to walk with her. Callie wanted to get home and to the phone as quickly as possible.

TWELVE

IT WAS getting harder and harder to pretend that nothing was going to be different that summer. Lisa and Alex had a date—their last date before she left. They'd seen a movie, though Lisa doubted she could have told anyone the name of it or anything about it. She and Alex held hands tightly all the way through the film, and she was far more aware of his presence, the tender pressure on her palm, his gentle caresses on her fingers, than she was of anything happening on the screen in front of her.

He walked her back to her house.

"This is going to be hard," Alex said finally.

"I know," said Lisa. "I guess it's time to acknowledge it, too. We'll talk, we'll send e-mail. You're probably going to be spending more time communicating with me over the summer than you do now."

"Probably," he said. "But it won't be as much fun." He

stopped her in a shadow, and they kissed. "I'll be thinking of you a lot."

"When?" Lisa asked.

"Often," he said, a little surprised by the question.

"Why don't we make a date to think of one another—say every night at nine or something like that?"

"That's midnight here."

"So, you'll still be up. You'll probably be in your room then. You can look out the window at the moon. The very same moon will be looking down on me in California, and I'll be looking up at it at the same time."

"It won't even be dark some nights—"

"So I'll look where the moon probably is," Lisa said. "I'll know. If you're looking at the same time, I'll know. I'll be able to feel it, and that's how I'll know where the moon is."

"How could I have ever been in love with anyone before I met you?" Alex asked. And then he kissed her again.

Lisa took that as a yes.

The house was dark and the phone was ringing when Lisa unlocked the door. Her mother was at what she called Group. It was supposed to be a therapy session, but the group was comprised of women whose husbands had left them. Behind her mother's back, Lisa referred to it as Gripe Therapy.

She picked up the phone in the still-dark kitchen.

"Hi, honey!" a cheerful voice said. It was her father. He knew when Lisa's mother was likely to be out of the house and often called then.

"Hi, Dad," she said, flipping on the light.

"It's just one day now and I can't wait to see you."

"Me too," she said, meaning it. Sad as she was to be leaving Virginia for the summer, she loved her father and was looking forward to having time with him.

"I wanted you to know that I'll be at the airport to meet your plane. Evelyn has all the ingredients to make the vegetarian chili you liked so much, so don't worry about eating any lousy airplane food. We'll feed you when you get here."

"Will Lily still be awake?" she asked.

"Lily is *always* awake," said her father. "Why didn't someone remind me how little sleep babies get at night? The only time she sleeps really well is in the daytime. Whatever it means, it seems to be good for her because she's thriving. Wait until you see her."

"I can't wait. I got the pictures from Evelyn and I can't believe how much she's grown."

"She's a real beauty—almost as lovely as her big sister."

"Thanks, Dad," said Lisa.

"And speaking of her big sister, you got a piece of mail here today."

"What is it?"

"I'm not exactly sure, but it's from WorldWide Studios and the initials on the envelope are *SR*."

"Skye? He said he'd talk to me when I got out there."

"Well, apparently he decided to write first. You can see what he wrote tomorrow."

"As if I could wait that long. Go ahead. Open it and read it."

"Your private mail?"

"What do I have to do to convince the world I'm not in

love with Skye and he won't be writing anything all that private?" she asked.

"I guess the best way is to let me read the letter," her father said. She could hear him opening the envelope. There was a pause. "Okay, here it is. 'Dear Lisa, I'm so glad—' yadda-yadda. 'Lots of things to show you—' blah-blah. 'One thing I—' Got it. 'One thing I want to ask you about, though, is if you know anyone who might be interested in working on our show's set this summer. The show is about horses, as you know, and we have a whole stable full of them. One of the assistant stable hands has left and we need to replace her. The job requirements are knowing something about horses and being willing to look after them. It's not glamorous, of course. A lot of it is going to involve mucking out stalls and carrying buckets of water. Do you, by any wild chance, know of anyone, over sixteen years old, who might, possibly, fit that description, who could be persuaded to take a summer job on a television film set?' "

"Wow! Oh, Daddy, can I? Please?"

"You mean you think he might have you in mind for this job?"

"Dad!"

"Well, I guess he probably does," her father conceded. "Sounds perfect. We'll talk with him when you get out here. We have to consider things like hours and transportation, but it might be a good idea."

That sounded enough like a yes that Lisa didn't think she'd have to ask again. Now she really had some news for Carole and Stevie!

"Dad, I'll see you tomorrow. Thanks for calling. Love to Evelyn, and give Lily a little hug, okay?"

"Deal," he said. "I love you, honey."

"I love you, too, Dad."

She hung up the phone just long enough to get a dial tone. Stevie's line was busy. She was probably talking to Phil, and there was no telling how long that would be. Lisa tried Carole next.

Carole was every bit as excited as Lisa about her news. "A whole summer working with horses and Skye Ransom!" Carole said. "Sounds like every girl's dream come true."

"I don't think I'll be spending that much time with Skye," Lisa said sensibly. "He'll be on the set most of the time, or in his trailer, or rehearsing. But I will see him, and, best of all, I'll be with horses. It's almost perfect."

Carole was still grinning when she hung up the phone. That sounded like great news for Lisa. Carole sighed. If only the news around Pine Hollow were better. Lisa would be gone. Stevie wanted to be friends with Callie. And Carole's world felt a little more mixed up than she wanted it to be.

Stevie glared at the phone. It had been glaring back at her ever since she'd walked into the house after work. Its glare was almost as bad as the broken taillight's. She hadn't had any run-ins that night—no crushed impatiens, no mangled garbage cans, and no more dented fenders.

But it was the dented fender that was causing her trouble. Every time she'd looked at her own taillight, she remembered the scratch on the Foresters' car. Her mind was doing flip-flops. One second she was sure she'd done it. The next second it could have been anyone at any time. Then she knew she'd done the damage to her own car that night. How could the Foresters' car not have gotten damaged? But the damage to her car was so obvious—there was no way that bad dent would have made just the tiny scratch she'd seen on the Foresters' car.

She picked up the phone. She had to talk to Callie and Scott—or, worse, their parents. She had to know. No, that wasn't entirely true. She was actually doing pretty well not knowing. Nobody had asked her about it. Nobody had called Pizza Manor and complained. They would have noticed. Wouldn't they?

She hung up the phone. But if she didn't ask, she'd never know. She picked up the phone. In another second she'd cradled it again. Finally she picked it up and dialed. She got a busy signal. That was really good news. She hung up again.

Callie held the phone tightly in her hand and punched in the now-familiar number. This time, she punched in *all* the numbers and listened to the phone ring.

"Hello?" It was an adult, probably Emily's mother.

"Is Emily there, please?" Callie asked.

"Who's calling?"

"This is Callie Forester."

There was a long pause. Emily's mother held her hand over the mouthpiece so that Callie couldn't hear what was being said. Finally the woman came back on.

"Uh, Callie, Emily is busy now and can't come to the phone."

"It'll just take a minute. I promise," said Callie.

"Not now," the woman said.

"May I call later?" asked Callie.

"I don't think she'll be able to talk," the woman said. "Tomorrow, maybe."

"I guess it's getting kind of late," Callie said. "Tell her I'll call again."

"Sure," said Emily's mother. And then she hung up.

Callie couldn't remember a time when she'd done something as thoughtless as what she'd done to Emily, and it bothered her a lot that she wasn't getting a chance to apologize. Not that she really deserved it. She'd been rude. Apologizing wasn't going to change that. It probably wouldn't make Emily feel any better, but it might make Callie feel better. She couldn't wait until the next day. She needed to do something that night.

She turned to her desk and took out a sheet of stationery. If she wasn't able to talk to Emily, she could at least write to her.

Everything she wrote felt clumsy and inadequate, but by her fifth sheet of paper, she had something that expressed her shame and sincerity. It would do until they had a chance to talk.

Callie asked her mother if she could "borrow" some of the flowers from their backyard for a friend who wasn't feeling well. It wasn't exactly a lie. Her mother agreed. The impatiens were thriving. She should take some of those. Callie made a pretty arrangement, wrapped the stems in a moist paper towel, and bound it all together with aluminum foil. She put a ribbon around it and clipped her note to the ribbon.

Emily's house wasn't far from hers—perhaps a fifteen-minute walk or five minutes by bicycle. She told her parents she'd be back soon. Her mother said she hoped her friend would feel better. Her father had something else on his mind.

"Callie, can I ask you something?" he said.

"Sure."

"Do you know anything about a scratch on the rear end of the van?"

"Rear?"

"Well, on the side, at the rear. I noticed it this morning. I meant to ask you earlier."

"Um, no, Dad. I don't know anything about that," she said. "I'll see you guys later!" She slipped out the door before her father could ask any more questions. Her father was as persistent as a committee chairman at a televised hearing when he started asking questions. She didn't need that right then. She had problems of her own to deal with without covering for anyone else.

THIRTEEN

CAROLE DIDN'T work at Pine Hollow on Saturdays—at least she didn't get paid for any work she did at Pine Hollow on Saturdays. That made her all the more eager to be there Saturday mornings because it meant she could do the work she wanted to do: primarily looking after, and riding, her own horse.

This Saturday was going to be a little different. She had to make good on her promise to exercise Fez. Once that was done, she could look after Starlight, and then that afternoon, she and Stevie were going to surprise Lisa by meeting her at the airport. The girls had said good-bye to one another about four times on the phone the night before, amid excited conversations about Lisa's potential job on Skye's show in California. Lisa didn't know she was going to see her friends one more time. This would be a good surprise.

Carole opened the door and checked in at the office. Emily handled the office on Saturday mornings, and she was busily assigning horses for the early-morning class. The plain, battered desk had a small vase of flowers on it.

"What's the occasion?" Carole asked, pointing to the flowers.

"They were a gift," Emily said.

"From an admirer?"

"Hardly. More like an apologizer."

"So? Give," said Carole.

"Kind of strange, but a little nice," Emily said. "It was Callie. Yesterday she asked me for help, which I couldn't give her because running is not my best event, but I did offer to call Ben for her. That ticked her off and she got huffy and threatened to report me to Max or some such. I didn't pay much attention. I guess somebody told her about me and she was embarrassed—embarrassed enough to get my phone number, but when she called, I was getting therapy, and then I went out to the movies with my parents. When we got home, Callie had left these flowers on our doorstep, along with the nicest note."

"Really?"

"Really," said Emily. "Of course, that made me feel bad because I should have explained in the first place."

"You don't have to explain anything," Carole said.

"No, normally I don't. My crutches do it for me. But she couldn't see my crutches. I owed her an explanation. You know I never expect anybody's sympathy—I don't need it—but I do need some understanding, and the only way people can understand is if they have information. Callie didn't have the necessary information. That made her feel like a jerk."

"Is that what she wrote?"

"Just that she felt she'd behaved like a jerk and she hoped I'd give her a second chance."

"And?"

"Well, sure," said Emily. "She tried to do the right thing. And the flowers are pretty."

"I guess," Carole said. "They sure dress up that messy old desk."

"So, are you going to take Starlight out now?"

"No, I'm going to work with Fez first."

"Operation Impress the Congressman's Daughter?"

"No, more like Operation Big Mouth," Carole said.

"Someday soon, you'll find a way to tell Callie that Pine Hollow really doesn't exercise boarders for free."

"If this horse were any fun to ride, I'd keep on doing it forever," said Carole. "But he's not. He's a pain."

"You mean you've finally met a horse you don't like?"

" 'Don't like' may be a little strong. Let me just say that I haven't had much fun riding him. So far we've spent all our time together trying to decide who's in charge. He's winning."

"You'll find a way. You always do," Emily said.

Carole carried that thought to Fez's stall.

Fez was as feisty as ever when Carole passed him on the way to the tack room. Even tacking up this horse was a chore.

"Morning, Ben," she said. Ben was sitting in a corner of the tack room adjusting the leathers on the saddles that the youngest riders would use that morning.

"Morning, Carole," he said. "You working with Starlight?"

246

"Not yet. Fez comes first," she said. "Can you give me a hand with his tack?"

"Sure," Ben said. He set aside the leathers he'd been working on and helped Carole carry Fez's saddle to his stall. They both knew it wasn't carrying the saddle that Carole needed help with. It was putting the saddle on the irritable horse.

Carole approached Fez cautiously and clipped a lead rope on him for Ben to hold while she put on the saddle. Fez never stopped moving while Carole dodged his prancing.

"This darn horse," she hissed. "He's as bad as his owner!"

"She's not so bad," Ben said quietly. "Better than her brother."

That surprised Carole a little.

"What's the matter with her brother?"

"Talks a lot," said Ben.

Carole laughed to herself. Ben wasn't much of a talker. No wonder he resented Scott, who talked as easily as some people breathed. Carole buckled the girth on the saddle and tightened it. Fez didn't play games by holding his breath while she tightened the girth. That was the first really nice thing she could say about the horse.

Ben held Fez's head steady with the lead rope while Carole coaxed him into his bridle, and then he was ready for his ride—with little more than twice the effort any other horse in the stable required for tacking up.

Carole led him out to the indoor ring. She thought it might be wise to work inside where there would be fewer distractions than outside. Also, the younger riders would be using the outdoor schooling ring, and if there was a chance

Fez might run away, Carole didn't want it to happen where anyone could be hurt.

Max was there, sitting on a bench, jotting out his lesson plan.

"What're you up to?" he asked. "I thought you'd be riding Starlight now."

"Well, I sort of told Callie I'd give this guy a workout," Carole said. Fez backed off and tugged at the reins, nearly pulling them out of Carole's hands. She gripped more tightly.

"He's a handful. He'll do well learning a few things from you," said Max.

Carole was flattered that Max thought she could teach this fellow anything, but not at all confident he was right.

"Make sure you touch the good-luck horseshoe before you climb aboard," he said.

Maybe he wasn't so sure Carole could do anything with him. Sighing, she took Fez over to the mounting block, climbed into the saddle, walked him past the horseshoe—which she tagged quickly—and returned to the ring.

Carole began by walking Fez in circles, clockwise and then counterclockwise, to warm him up a bit. He did all right at that, so she asked him to trot. He cantered. She slowed him down to a walk again and began the process over. It was the same thing they'd gone through two days before. She wasn't any more successful, and it wasn't any more fun.

Carole wished Max weren't sitting there. She knew how busy he was, and she hated to disturb him, especially when she was riding so badly. His eyes were mostly on his paperwork, but Carole knew he wasn't missing anything. All his riders were amazed by how many mistakes he could see in a whole classful of riders all at once. The record was eight simultaneous errors, though there were those who suspected that his stream of corrections—"Heels down, hands steady, eyes ahead, legs straight, seat back, shoulders up, chin in— oh, and tuck in your shirttails!"—was more automatic than actual. They were all common errors among new riders, even the shirttails.

The third time Fez bolted to a canter when asked for a trot, Max stopped pretending to work on his lesson plan. He set his papers down and turned his full attention to Carole's struggle with Fez.

Carole tried to ignore Max and to convince the horse to listen to her.

Finally Max interrupted her efforts. "Carole, you're going about this all wrong," he said.

She drew to a halt. "I know, Max. I should keep my hands steady, but he keeps yanking at them. It's almost impossible."

"No, I don't mean that. It's not your form, it's your approach. You're letting him be the boss. From the moment you walked in here with him, it was apparent who was in charge—and it wasn't you."

Carole felt herself flush with anger. She knew better than to express it, though. What she was angry about was simply the truth.

"So?" she said, containing her irritation.

"So, think about it. This is a strong, fiery horse. It's in his nature to challenge authority. If the authority doesn't challenge him back, he's going to assume he's in charge, and, clearly, that's what's happened. You've lost control, and you're never going to get it back."

"Never?" Carole asked weakly.

"Not now, not this way," said Max. "You're being too nice to him."

"I can't hurt a horse, Max!" Carole protested.

"I'm not suggesting that you do," he said. "But I do suggest that you put him away now."

"He needs the exercise," Carole said. "And I don't want to give up on him. I'm better than that."

"Yes, you are," said Max. "So here's what you're going to do. You are going to start all over again, from the very beginning. You have to be in charge, and he has to know it. I don't know why it is that you thought this particular horse wanted a velvet-glove treatment, but you were wrong. He needs a strong hand, a firm voice, a powerful leader. You've been elected. Go do the job." Max sat back down on the bench, crossed his arms in front of him, and waited to see what Carole would do.

Carole had a world of choices in front of her. She could try striking the horse, but she never thought that was the right way. She could try yelling at him. She rejected that because he hadn't shown any indication that he was deaf, so there would be no point. She could yank back at his reins and abuse him in the same way he was trying to get the jump on her, but she didn't like it when he did it to her, so she doubted he'd like it if she returned the favor. Or she could, as Max suggested, start all over again.

She dismounted and led Fez back to his stall. She removed his tack, gave him a quick brushing, some fresh water, and a bite of hay. Then she left him alone.

Ten minutes later she reappeared at his stall, carrying his saddle and his bridle. As she approached the stall, instead of looking fearful—the way she felt—she glared directly into Fez's eyes. He backed up. She wasn't actually threatening him in any way that humans understood. She was merely challenging him in a way horses understood. Fez stood still and glared back.

Without showing any hesitation, Carole clipped a lead rope on him, cross-tied him, and put his saddle back on. She talked to him because it was almost impossible for her not to talk to a horse while she worked on him, but it was in a matter-of-fact tone, not a soothing tone or a fearful one. Her theory was that if she was able to fool him into thinking she wasn't afraid of him and didn't expect him to misbehave, he might not intimidate her and act up.

He stood quite still while she tacked him up. When she took hold of his reins and led him back to the ring, she looked straight ahead. Looking back at him would have appeared questioning. She wasn't in a mood to question anything. She was being positive. He was, for the first time, being relatively obedient. He was still no Starlight or Belle. He wasn't in the least bit docile, but he was obedient. That was all Carole needed from him.

They reached the ring. Carole signaled him to stand still while she mounted, and he did. He tried to take one step while she swung her right leg over his back, and she tugged firmly on the reins. He stopped fiddling.

She walked him over to the good-luck horseshoe, touched it, and began walking him in circles around the ring. He did what he was told. He shook his head a bit, but he stopped that when she tugged, not yanked, firmly on the reins. She signaled him to trot. He trotted.

He was like a different horse. He had all his power and fire, but he was much more obedient than he had been earlier, at least as well behaved as he had been when Callie rode him.

Max, in his usual reserved manner, just said, "Nice work, Carole."

Half an hour later, still pleased by her success with Fez, she returned the horse to his stall, untacked him, and gave him a quick grooming.

As she worked on him, she wondered at the transformation. It wasn't that this horse hadn't been trained. He had. But she had been allowing him to get away with bad behavior, allowing him to ignore his training. That made it her responsibility to remind him what was okay and what wasn't. She'd done it. She now had a horse that, while not as enjoyable for her to ride as Starlight, was a horse she could manage. Now maybe she wouldn't hate herself so much for the foolish promise she'd made to Callie.

Carole shrugged. If she could transform Fez's personality, maybe she could do the same with Callie. No, that wasn't right. She had to take some responsibility for Fez's problems. She'd let him get away with murder because she'd been treating him like eggshells. She hadn't done that with Callie. Or had she?

She'd definitely gotten off on the wrong foot with Callie, just as she'd gotten off on the wrong hoof with her horse. Maybe she should do something to change that.

Well, if Callie was big enough to make an effort to square

her mistake with Emily, Carole thought she should be big enough to square her own mistake with Callie.

In the meantime, she thought she owed Fez a little more reward than she'd given him so far. She decided to turn him out in the paddock. He'd been cooped up in the van and then in his stall long enough. He could use a chance to run free for the afternoon. She got Max's permission to let him stay out until she returned from the airport. Carole walked Fez through the gate, took the lead rope from his halter, and gave him a gentle slap on his flanks to tell him it was okay to run free. He didn't have to be told twice.

Carole glanced at her watch. It was noon. Lisa's plane took off at four. The hard work Carole had done with Fez had used all of her riding time. Now she had to get home, shower, and change her clothes for the trip to the airport.

Her heart ached. Lisa's departure was going to change everything. Just four hours to go.

FOURTEEN

FOUR HOURS later, everything in the world had changed.

Stevie listened dully to the rhythmic *slap*, *slap*, *slap* of the windshield wipers for a few seconds before she realized what the sound was, where she was, and how she'd gotten there.

"Carole?" she whispered. "Are you okay?"

"I think so. What about you?"

"Me too. Callie? Are you okay?" Stevie asked.

There was no answer.

"Callie?" Carole echoed.

The only response was the girl's shallow breathing.

"What happened?" Carole asked, trying to remember the last few minutes. It was all a blur.

"We hit something—a horse, I think. We spun, rolled, and landed. I think we're at the bottom of the hill by Janson's farm across from Pine Hollow."

Carole looked in the backseat. Callie lay still, her eyes closed.

"Callie? Callie? Wake up!" There was no answer. "She's breathing, but she's unconscious," Carole said.

"Can you move all right?" Stevie asked Carole.

"I think so," Carole said. She did a quick inventory. She could feel a throbbing in her wrist, which must have hit the dashboard when they rolled over. She was aware, too, of a dull ache in her arm. She wiggled her toes and her fingers. Everything worked. "Yeah, I'm okay," Carole said. "What about you?"

"I've got an awful ache in my belly where the steering wheel hit me, but everything moves. I'm hurt, but okay."

"Well, we can get out, but we'd better not move Callie. We've got to go for help."

Stevie peered through the windshield, which was still being methodically cleaned by the wipers. She could see lights at the top of the hill.

"No, I think help has come for us," she said.

Carole and Stevie opened their doors. Carole stood up. Rain pelted down on her. In spite of her aches, it made her feel incredibly, wonderfully alive.

She and Stevie looked at the top of the hill, where more flashing lights were gathering. Several people were looking down at them. The girls waved.

"Are you okay?"

"We are, but there's another girl in the car and she's unconscious!" Stevie called back.

"Don't move her!" an emergency medical technician yelled.

255

Stevie and Carole waited for help to arrive. It didn't take long. Within minutes several EMTs skittered down the hill, carrying a stretcher and medical bags. As soon as they were sure Stevie and Carole could walk, one of them helped the two girls up the hill, while the others turned their attention to Callie.

Carole started to shiver. It seemed strange to be shivering in the warm rain. "It's shock," the ambulance driver said. He gave her a blanket and settled her in the back of the ambulance. He made her lie down and gave her an oxygen mask, though she didn't think she needed it.

As she lay there, Carole began to drift off into a pleasant, painless sleep. Stevie sat beside her, holding her hand.

"Stevie! What happened to Carole? Are you okay?"

It was Max, climbing into the shelter of the ambulance. He'd run all the way from the stable when he heard the sirens.

Carole opened her eyes and nodded to Max. "I'm okay," she said. "Just shook up."

"Me too," Stevie said. "But Callie's hurt. She was unconscious in the car. We didn't try to move her."

"Good," Max said. "The EMTs are down there now. But how did it happen?"

Stevie explained. "The rain just came out of nowhere, pelting down so hard I could barely see, and then something came at the car. I tried to get out of the way, but I slammed into it. Was it a horse, Max? Did I hurt a horse?"

"It was," Max said. "The police called Judy. She's with him now."

"Who was it?" Stevie asked, her voice rising hysterically.

Carole didn't need to hear the answer. She knew exactly which horse it was. She knew which horse had been in that paddock, and she knew which horse would be seriously spooked by thunder, which horse had the strength and endurance to jump or smash down one of Pine Hollow's high fences and flee.

"Fez," she said quietly.

"Right," Max confirmed. He put his arm around Stevie comfortingly.

"Is he okay?" Stevie asked.

"He was hurt badly," Max said. "Judy will save him if she can. Look, you two are going to go to the hospital. I'll go back to Pine Hollow and call your parents. They'll meet you over there. I'll come over later. Okay?"

"Okay," Stevie agreed. "Max, I didn't mean to do it. I didn't mean to hit Fez."

"I know that," Max said. "Everybody does. Don't worry about him. Worry about making sure you're all right."

Stevie and Carole nodded glumly. Max left them.

An EMT climbed into the back of the ambulance as a second ambulance drew up behind theirs. The rain that had started so suddenly was tapering off. Through the crowd, Stevie and Carole could see a gurney being rolled up to the other ambulance. Callie was strapped flat onto it. Her eyes were closed, and she had an IV bag suspended above her head. The EMTs who were pushing the gurney looked grim.

"Callie?" Stevie called out. "Is she okay?"

The EMT pulled the doors of the ambulance closed. "They're doing what they can," he said. "Now, let's get you two to the ER."

All her life, Stevie had thought it would be fun to ride in an ambulance, lights flashing, siren wailing. What she'd never fully absorbed before that, however, was that a ride in an ambulance meant something was wrong, really wrong. The thought made her shiver. She pulled a blanket tightly around her.

The siren wailed, the lights flashed. Ahead of them traffic pulled aside to give them the right of way. They drove right up to the hospital door and walked off the ambulance into the emergency room. There were nurses there, offering them wheelchairs, and they were taken to an examining room.

Nobody would tell them anything about Callie.

"It was my fault. I was driving," Stevie said.

"You couldn't help it," Carole consoled her. "You did what you could. The horse ran right at us. I saw it happen."

"There must be something I could have done," Stevie said. She didn't even want to say what was in her heart. Anybody could have an accident. They happened. It wasn't the accident that upset her. It was the consequences of that accident. Callie and Fez, but mostly Callie.

"I never told her I was sorry," Carole said. "I wanted to. I wanted to tell her about how I rode Fez today, but, but . . ." She choked on her own thoughts. Tears streaked down her cheeks.

"Carole! Are you okay?" It was her father. He hurried into the examining area and ran over to her. "And you, Stevie? Are you okay?"

The two girls nodded. "We're both okay, Dad," Carole said. "I mean, we got some bumps. The EMT thinks Stevie might have broken a rib, but we're basically okay. What about Callie? Did they say anything?"

"Not yet," he said. "They're examining her. She's still unconscious."

Stevie's parents arrived then. Once again she and Carole promised that they were okay. Once again they asked for news of Callie. There was none.

Outside the curtain that surrounded them, they heard the congressman arrive. "Where's my daughter?" he demanded, his voice filled with uncertainty.

"This way, Congressman, Mrs. Forester," a doctor said.

The next few hours were a confusion of questions, X rays, questions, pain pills, and even more questions. Stevie did have a broken rib from the steering wheel. Carole's injuries were limited to scrapes and bruises. Everybody who talked to the girls told them how lucky they were and how smart they were to wear their seat belts. Neither of them felt lucky or smart.

The police asked them questions about what had happened. Stevie and Carole each described the events over and over again. Each time was more painful than the last. Stevie could still hear the awful silence in the car when Callie didn't answer.

Outside, they could see the flurry of activity around the trauma room where the doctors were working on Callie.

Finally, when the doctor said they could go, Stevie stood up weakly and walked over to the plastic-covered couch where Congressman Forester and his wife were sitting with Scott, talking in hushed tones.

"Is Callie going to be okay?" Stevie asked.

"We hope so," said Mrs. Forester. "She's in a coma. The doctors say she hit her head and got a bad concussion. There was some bleeding. They have to operate. They keep saying we're going to have to wait."

Stevie gasped involuntarily. It was so utterly frightening.

"I'm sorry," she said. "I don't know what or how, but if I could have—"

The Foresters just looked at Stevie. The usually garrulous Scott was out of chatter. And so, for once, was Stevie. She didn't know what to say anymore. There were no words to make it better. The best any of the Foresters could do was the nod of acknowledgment that Mrs. Forester gave.

"Come on, Stevie. I think it's time to go home," Mr. Lake said, putting his arm around his daughter. She took strength from his warmth and walked meekly to the car.

It was still raining when they left the hospital. Stevie sat in the backseat of the car, listening to the windshield wipers all the way home.

FIFTEEN

WHAT FOLLOWED were the longest two weeks of Stevie's and Carole's lives. Every time Stevie breathed, moved, spoke, or laughed, her broken rib reminded her of what had happened. Medicine could help with the pain she had in her body, but it couldn't do anything to repair the agony she felt in her heart. Even the comfort of her daily conversations with Carole and Lisa couldn't ease her pangs of guilt.

Fez was getting the best care veterinary medicine could offer. Most horses hurt that badly would have been put down because the cost of healing would be so great and the chances of a successful recovery so slim. The accident had left Fez with cuts and scrapes, which would leave him scarred, and a broken leg, which might have rendered him totally incapacitated. Judy Barker didn't have to spell it out. Everybody knew that a horse bore half its weight on its powerful, muscular rear legs and half its weight on its slim and fragile front legs. Horses asked a particularly heavy task of their forelegs, and weaknesses there were particularly troublesome. The accident had broken Fez's foreleg.

Judy had kept Fez at her clinic so that she could watch him closely. He was suspended in a sling. It wasn't for Fez's leg but for his body, holding him up in a standing position so that his legs just touched the floor. He could reach his grain, water, and hay, but he couldn't walk around at all.

It wasn't easy on Fez. In spite of everything Carole had learned about controlling him, the horse was as enthusiastic about being immobilized in his sling as he had been about being in a van. He flailed and fretted all day long, and every attempt to loose himself from the sling brought a scream of pain caused by his broken leg. Judy gave him as much pain medicine as she dared, hoping to spare him a fate that was worse still.

Stevie and Carole took turns visiting him, anticipating his needs, calming and soothing the fretting horse. By the end of a week, he had learned to trust them just enough that he didn't kick and fuss constantly—merely most of the time.

And while they worked to help Fez, Callie lay in a hospital bed. She had two operations to relieve pressure on her brain, and she remained in a coma. While Stevie and Carole spent every minute they could looking after Fez, neither one of them could stand the idea of seeing Callie. Not yet.

A week after the accident, the police formally dismissed all potential charges against Stevie. Another driver had been on the road, behind Stevie's car. He'd seen everything that happened and said there was no way Stevie could have avoided the horse, which had run straight into her car.

Still it wasn't enough. Even though the law exonerated her, Stevie wasn't ready to exonerate herself.

"It almost doesn't matter what they say," she told Carole. "What matters is Callie."

"At least you were nice to her," said Carole. "I never gave her a chance. I was going to tell her I was sorry, but I couldn't think of a way to say anything when we went to the airport, and now I don't know if I'll ever have a chance."

There was nothing more to say. Fortunately, there was a lot to do. Fez was a demanding patient, and they were determined to do everything they could for him, since they couldn't do anything for his owner.

After two weeks Callie woke up. She opened her eyes for the first time at three o'clock in the morning. Scott was by her bedside, sleeping in a chair, when he heard her speak.

"Hello? Who's there?" she asked.

Scott sat bolt upright, hardly believing what he'd just heard.

"Callie? Are you all right?"

"I guess so," she said. "Where am I? What's going on? What happened?"

Scott was so relieved to hear his sister speak that he almost didn't notice his own tears.

"Oh, it's a long story," he said. "You've been out of it for about two weeks. Do you remember anything?"

"I don't think so," Callie said. "I just remember windshield wipers. I thought they'd never stop. Oh, my god, Stevie and Carole. Are they okay?"

"They're fine," Scott said. "Minor injuries. Now, just relax.

I'm going to call Mom and Dad. Then I'll tell you everything. Like I said, it's a long story."

"In that case, get me something to eat before you talk. I'm starving!"

Over the course of the next few hours, Callie learned everything that had happened since the accident. Scott told her how Stevie and Carole were looking after Fez and that they called every day to say how he was doing. Callie's parents came over to the hospital to see her and just hug her. Callie ate some Jell-O, which the hospital provided, and some pizza, which her father brought from home.

And then the doctors arrived. They tested, questioned, poked, prodded, tapped, tickled, and beamed.

"Good . . . Hmmm . . . Interesting . . . Very good . . . Amazing," they said.

In the end they were very pleased with how well Callie was doing.

"When can we bring her home?" her parents asked when they spoke with the doctors in the hall after they'd completed their examination.

The doctors looked at one another. Dr. Amandson shook his head.

"Not for a while," he told them. "You see, she's partially paralyzed on her left side."

"We thought you said she was doing well."

"She is. Extremely well. With the kinds of injuries she sustained, we were expecting much worse. She's doing extraordinarily well, in fact. She is alert. She can talk, think, reason, and use all five senses. The only residual damage to the extreme trauma her brain suffered is that her left side doesn't work very well."

"But paralyzed? What does this mean?" Mrs. Forester asked.

"She's going to need physical therapy—lots of it," said Dr. Amandson. "What's happened, basically, is that some of her brain was damaged—the part that controls movement on the left side of her body. That part of her brain may heal itself in time, or it may not. The brain is a marvelous invention, especially the brain of a young, healthy girl like your daughter. If the damaged part doesn't heal, another part of the brain can be encouraged to learn whatever got lost in the accident. With hard work, concentration, and endurance, Callie will be up and walking soon. Eventually she may be as good as new. The therapist will be here in the morning to help plan a program for her. Now, tell me, do you have any questions?"

"Not right now," said Mr. Forester.

"Yes, one—or maybe a few," said Mrs. Forester.

"Yes?"

"Is Callie out of danger?"

"I don't know," Dr. Amandson told her. "We'll have to watch her closely, for a long time, until we're sure."

"Is there any way this physical therapy could be dangerous to her?"

"No, not really," said the doctor. "As long as it's carefully monitored."

"What kinds of things will they do?"

"The therapist will develop a program that will begin very slowly, building up muscles and working on balance and coordination skills. We've found that the progressive healing of patients in physical therapy is a lot like the way babies learn motor skills, crawling, walking, and so on. They try to create a program that is interesting as well as useful. I don't know Callie other than as a comatose patient. Is there some activity that she enjoys more than others that we might try to incorporate in her therapy? Swimming perhaps?"

"Well, she does like to swim," said Mrs. Forester.

"Horseback riding," Mr. Forester said. "It's the thing she loves the most in the world."

The doctor smiled. "Have you ever heard of therapeutic riding?" he asked.

"No," said Mrs. Forester. "But I have the feeling we're going to hear a lot about it—and soon."

A few weeks after that, Emily found Carole and Stevie in Fez's stall.

"Ouch!" said Carole, shaking her hand. Fez had nipped at her fingers when she gave him a carrot. "Didn't you ever hear the saying Don't bite the hand that feeds you?"

"Being sick has not improved his disposition," Stevie said.

"It rarely does," Emily told them. "And, speaking of being sick, guess who called me. I hate it when people say things like that, so I'll tell you. Callie Forester. She was calling me from the physical therapy room at the hospital. Her therapist thinks horseback riding would be good. They wanted her to go to Free Rein—the therapeutic riding center where I learned to ride—but she said that if she was going to ride again, it was going to be at Pine Hollow. She wants me to be her instructor."

"Perfect," said Carole. "Absolutely perfect. You'll be perfect for her."

"Maybe I will be, but PC definitely will be. He'll be glad to have another rider from time to time." Emily had utter faith in her horse, and everybody who had ever seen him perform knew she had reason to feel that way.

"When will she be at Pine Hollow?" Stevie asked.

"Right, how soon?" Carole echoed.

"We made a date for next Wednesday morning. You'll both be here, won't you?"

"Absolutely," said Stevie.

"Of course," Carole told her. "We wouldn't miss that for anything."

"Good, because she'll be here with her therapist and her parents. I think Scott's coming, too. It's going to be a real family outing for them. There's a lot of work to be done before then, too."

"Yes," Carole said. She knew what Emily meant, but she had work of her own to do before she saw Callie. She had to figure out how to apologize for the past and make the future better.

"Both her parents?" Stevie asked. "They'll be here?"

"That's what she said."

Stevie felt a shiver. The whole family would be there. She hadn't seen them since the hospital. Now she'd see them all. Scott, whom Stevie liked because he was charming and funny, probably wouldn't be funny anymore. Stevie had been driving in the accident that hurt his sister. Congressman and Mrs. Forester wouldn't want to see Stevie because Stevie's car had nearly killed their daughter when it struck their horse.

267

And Callie?

Could Stevie look at any of them? What would she say? How could she say she was sorry in a way that meant anything when she'd hurt them all so badly? Could she ever face them?

She didn't know.

SIXTEEN

THE FIRST person to arrive on Wednesday was Scott. Carole, Stevie, and Emily were tacking up PC for Callie when Scott came up the driveway, riding a bicycle.

He looked around uncertainly and then, recognizing Carole, walked over to the girls. Stevie was glad she was standing on the far side of the horse. Maybe she'd never have to speak to anyone.

"Hi," Carole said. "I guess it's Callie's big day."

"I don't know. This seems pretty crazy to me." Scott shook his head.

"You'll see." Carole introduced him to Emily, who leaned forward with a crutch under her left arm to shake hands with her right.

"I know, I know," she said, anticipating his concern. "You're trying to figure out if this is a case of the blind leading the blind . . ."

Scott blanched. Clearly Emily had been right on the mark.

"I wasn't going to put it that way," he protested, shifting his eyes away from her crutch and back to her face.

"Of course not," said Emily.

"Well, I guess my sister knows what she's doing."

"We'll see, won't we?" Emily asked. "Anyway, I was as uncertain as you are, but I've talked with Callie's therapist, and we have a pretty good program lined up for your sister. Besides, it's not me who is going to be doing the instructing. It's good old PC here. He knows absolutely everything. He's the best teacher in the world." She gave him a firm pat on the neck to punctuate her statement. The well-behaved horse didn't budge.

"You named your horse after a computer?" Scott asked, smiling for the first time.

"No, it stands for Physical Courage," said Emily.

Carole laughed. Stevie smiled tentatively. PC's "real" name was an ongoing joke. Whenever somebody asked Emily what PC stood for, she had a different, and apt, answer.

"Is something wrong with your car?" Carole asked, noticing the bike for the first time. Stevie cringed, shifting herself even farther behind the horse. She had noticed the bicycle immediately and didn't want to hear the answer. It wasn't going to help to talk about cars.

"Uh, no—Well, yes—Sort of," Scott stammered.

It was the accident. Stevie was sure. It had to be. Because of her carelessness, the congressman and his wife must have decided that all young drivers were unsafe. Or maybe it had frightened Scott so much that he couldn't drive anymore.

"I've been grounded," Scott said.

Stevie had to know. "Is it because of me?" she asked.

270

"No," he said, looking at her for the first time. He seemed to be about to say something but changed his mind. Instead, he turned his attention to Carole and continued. "Not at all. It's because of me. I was driving the Jeep a couple of weeks ago before we moved here and I backed into a stone wall on our neighbor's property. I just made a small dent, but Dad found it last week and blew up at me. It wasn't so much that I'd done the damage, he said, but that I'd tried to hide it. Being a congressman makes him especially touchy on the subject of cover-ups. Anyway, I'm on two-wheel transport for a month."

"S-Scratch? Dent?" Stevie stammered.

"Yeah," said Scott.

"Left rear?" she asked.

"You must have seen it in the body shop, I guess," said Scott. "It really wasn't much of a dent. It won't even reach our deductible, but it definitely annoyed my father. He's tough."

That dent. It seemed like such a small thing compared to everything else that had happened, but it made Stevie feel a little better to know that she hadn't made the dent in the Foresters' Jeep. That didn't change the fact that she'd tried to hide it, but that was too complicated now. She patted PC vigorously to mask her relief.

Carole looked over at Stevie. Stevie never was any good at hiding her feelings. She knew something had just happened to her friend, but she had no idea what. She'd find out later. For now, she had her own weight to lift.

The Foresters' car pulled into Pine Hollow's driveway. Carole could see Callie's parents in the front seat. Callie and another person—presumably her physical therapist—were in the back. It was time for Carole to talk to Callie, to do it right, to start all over again.

She walked over to the car when it stopped and waited for the door to open. With the help of the therapist and a pair of crutches, Callie got out. She was unsteady, unsure, and insecure in every way.

Carole took a deep breath, smiled at the girl, and stepped forward. She was determined to make this a new beginning, just as she'd done that day with Fez when she'd untacked him and started over.

"Callie, I want us to have a fresh start," she said.

Callie nodded.

Carole offered her hand. "Welcome to Pine Hollow," she said. "You're going to love it here, I know."

Callie looked at it uncertainly for a second, then tucked her left crutch firmly under her arm for balance and reached forward with her right hand, much as Emily had done a few minutes earlier with Scott.

"I'm sure it'll be great," said Callie, shaking Carole's hand. She smiled back.

Callie's parents also got out of the car. Max came out of the stable and greeted them warmly. The therapist helped Callie over to where PC was waiting for her. Max introduced Emily and PC to the Forester family.

Callie looked awkwardly at Emily. "I never really—and now—"

"It's okay, Callie," Emily said, cutting off the apology she knew was coming her way. "You already took care of that. What's past is past."

"I only wish . . . ," said Callie. She helped herself forward so that she could pat PC. "This is the boy who's going to teach me to walk again?" she asked.

"He's going to do his best," said Emily. "And his best has always been pretty good. Stevie, can you bring him around to the mounting block?"

Stevie had been working so hard to be invisible that she was almost surprised that Emily had noticed her presence. And now everybody looked at her.

She didn't say anything. She just walked the horse to where Callie would be able to mount. As soon as Callie was in the saddle, Emily and the therapist took charge. Stevie, Carole, and the Foresters stood back.

Stevie found herself next to Callie's parents. *Apologize.* She had to do it. She had to say something. She'd been driving. *I'm sorry. So sorry.* The words stuck in her mouth.

She glanced at Congressman Forester next to her. She opened her mouth to speak. And then she closed it. He was watching his daughter on horseback, walking sedately around the schooling ring. Tears filled his eyes. He reached over to Stevie and put his hand on her shoulder as much to silence her as to accept her unspoken apology. He didn't want to talk about it, either.

There would be another time when they could talk, and now Stevie knew that she could say what she had to say—that he would listen and maybe even understand.

The work was done for Stevie and Carole. This was a time when Max, Emily, the therapist, and the Foresters were all the help Callie needed. Carole and Stevie withdrew and retreated to a shady spot on a hill overlooking the ring where they could watch. It was at times like this that they missed Lisa most. They each wished she could be with them to share their healing, to be a friend. Lisa had a way of seeing the calm center of a confusing world. Her presence touched her friends now from the other side of the country.

"Think she's going to be okay?" Stevie asked, nodding toward Callie.

"Yeah," Carole said. "She'll be fine."

"Not today. I mean ever. Will she get all better?"

"Everything will get all better one day," said Carole. "Probably. You, me, Fez, Callie—we're already better. A little better, anyway."

"I guess," said Stevie. "And I guess we shouldn't ask for more."

"Not yet," said Carole. "There's still a lot of healing to be done. We've got a long way to go."

"But we've started, right?"

"Yes, we've started," Carole agreed.

ABOUT THE AUTHOR

BONNIE BRYANT is the author of nearly a hundred books about horses, including The Saddle Club series, Saddle Club Super Editions, and the Pony Tails series. She has also written novels and movie novelizations under her married name, B. B. Hiller.

Ms. Bryant began writing The Saddle Club in 1986. Although she had done some riding before that, she intensified her studies then and found herself learning right along with her characters Stevie, Carole, and Lisa. She claims that they are all much better riders than she is.

Ms. Bryant was born and raised in New York City. She still lives there, in Greenwich Village, with her two sons.